LOVE YOU NEVER

JENNIFER SUCEVIC

Love You Never

Copyright© 2023 by Jennifer Sucevic

All rights reserved. No part of this book may be reproduced in any form or by any electronic or mechanical means, including information storage and retrieval systems, without written permission from the author, except for the use of brief quotations in a book review.

This is a work of fiction. Names, characters, businesses, palaces, events, locales, and incidents are either the products of the author's imagination or used in a fictitious manner. Any resemblance to actual persons, living or dead, or actual events is purely coincidental.

Cover Design by Mary Ruth Baloy at MR Creations

Editing by Evelyn Summers at Pinpoint Editing

Proofreading by Autumn Sexton at Wordsmith Publicity

Subscribe to my newsletter and get a free book!

Jennifer Sucevic Newsletter

CHAPTER ONE

CARINA

"What the fuck are you doing here, Fischer?" a deep voice barks from behind us.

There's no need to turn.

I know exactly who I'll find.

It's like I have a sixth sense where Ford Hamilton is concerned. And I absolutely hate it. If there were a way to douse the flames that spark to life whenever he's in the vicinity, I'd do it in a heartbeat.

Maybe what's needed is some voodoo. Or an exorcism. Something that will eradicate him from my thoughts once and for all.

An aggravated sigh escapes from me. I knew that inviting Justin to this party was a mistake. It was more of an accident. We ran into each other at the Union a couple days ago and he asked if I wanted to get together. When I mentioned the party, he offered to pick me up and voilà—here we are.

Justin's jaw stiffens as he straightens to his full height, which is still a handful of inches shorter than my ex-stepbrother. It would be impossible not to compare the two guys when they're squaring off. Justin is a baseball player and has a leaner build. Ford plays hockey. He's chiseled and muscular. The way his biceps bulge…

It takes effort to suppress the little shiver that attempts to dance down my spine.

Don't even go there, Carina. That's exactly how you get yourself in trouble.

Every.

Single.

Time.

"I was invited."

Ford glares at the other guy as he folds his arms across his chest. The movement makes his body look even broader. It's enough to make my mouth turn cottony.

"Who the hell by?"

A well-known fact I should have taken into consideration is that hockey and baseball players mix about as well as oil and water. None of the athletic teams at Western really get along. Inevitably, everything devolves into a pissing match.

Trust me, it gets old fast.

It crossed my mind as I walked through the door five minutes ago with Justin in tow that this probably wasn't the smartest idea. But by then, it was much too late to do anything about it. I'd hoped to avoid Ford for the night, but clearly that plan has backfired.

By the pissed-off expression darkening his face, I'd say it's backfired spectacularly.

Clearly trying to get under Ford's skin, Justin snakes an arm around me before flashing a smug smile. "Carina did."

Ford's lips peel back into a snarl before he pierces me with a steely look. If I weren't made of such stern stuff, I'd be shaking in my Jimmy Choos. Voice turning frigid, he says, "This isn't her party. Maybe you should do us all a favor and take off."

Justin turns his head just enough to brush his lips across the side of my face. It's like he's trying to poke the bear. "Nah. Don't think I will."

The party is jampacked with people as the heavy beat of music reverberates off the walls of the house. With every second that ticks by, tension ratchets up until it turns suffocating.

My muscles tighten, anticipating that a fight will erupt any moment. That's pretty much standard operating procedure at a hockey party. Hell, it would be odd if it didn't happen.

Ford's eyes darken as his expression turns thunderous. Just when it seems like he'll totally lose his shit and throw the first punch, his gaze slices to mine and he grits out, "Can I talk to you outside?"

Heat stings my cheeks as people swivel their heads in our direction, trying to figure out what's going on. Even though fights break out regularly, no one wants to miss having a front-row seat.

I scowl, silently willing him to let this go. "Is that really necessary?"

"Yeah, it is." His gaze stays locked on mine as he jerks his head toward the back door. "Let's go."

It takes effort to force my attention from him to my date for the evening. "Give me a minute and I'll be right back." Then I flick another glance at my ex-stepbrother. "Apparently, Ford has decided to be an inhospitable dick tonight."

"He's a dick every night," Justin shoots back with a smirk.

Before I can agree, Ford's fingers shackle my wrist. That's all it takes for a sizzle of awareness to zip across my flesh and the delicate hair at the nape of my neck to rise. His eyes fasten onto mine, sifting through them for a heartbeat before shifting to the baseball player. He shoots him one last hostile glare before dragging me away. Ford moves through the crowd as if he's Moses parting the Red Sea. People scatter out of his way, not wanting to get run over in the process. It takes less than a minute to reach the backdoor before he's shoving me into the cool night air.

His nearness has my heart thrashing painfully against my ribcage.

Ever since we met the summer before freshman year of high school, his touch has affected me.

I freaking hate it.

Hate that he's the only one capable of tying my insides up into painful little knots.

There was a time when I couldn't get close enough.

Now the opposite is true.

I want as much distance as possible between us, which is no easy feat considering that we live next door to one another. Sometimes it feels like I can't go anywhere on this campus without running into Ford.

Another point of contention?

The guy is too damn hot for his own good. His messy, coffee-colored hair is shaggy on top while being buzzed on the sides. His eyes are a honeyed gold color that sucks unsuspecting girls in, ensnaring them like a Venus fly trap.

Full disclosure, I've experienced it firsthand.

I'm not proud.

One miscalculated stumble and you're tumbling down the rabbit hole, never to be heard from again.

His T-shirts cling to a sculpted chest like a second skin. When he returns from the athletic center, joggers hanging low on lean hips, showing off the chiseled V that disappears beneath the cottony material, girls lose their ever-loving minds.

What I'm trying to say is that the guy is catnip for the ladies on campus.

Although, I'm using that term loosely.

What they are is a bunch of hockey-loving hos.

Western has its fair share of puck bunnies.

Then again, all the male athletic teams have their groupies and fan clubs.

Hockey just so happens to have the most. Everyone wants to date or bang a hockey player.

What is it about a guy who knows how to use his stick that makes the girls on campus go a little stupid—all right, a lot—in the head?

Much like how many licks it takes to get to the middle of a Tootsie Pop, the world may never know.

Unable to take the intensity of his touch, I jerk my hand away. My fingers massage the skin of my wrist that now feels as if it's been scalded. It wouldn't surprise me in the least to find the imprint of his hand tattooed there for eternity.

With a scowl, I retreat a few steps, trying to put a safe amount of distance between us. One where his woodsy scent can't slyly wrap around me and do funny things to my insides.

"What the hell is your problem?" Before he has a chance to respond, I fire off a second question. "Have you lost your damn mind?"

Instead of answering, he asks one of his own. "What the hell are you doing with that baseball playing douchebag?"

"That's none of your business."

His expression sharpens, becoming even more formidable. "Don't fool yourself, sweetheart. You *are* my business. And that will never change."

That's all it takes for a wave of anger to crash over me. I suck in a deep breath, welcoming the blaze of fury that stomps out the attraction that sizzles in the charged air.

I plant my fists on my hips and growl, "How so?"

"We're stepsiblings."

"No, we aren't. Our parents are no longer married." The last part is tacked on because I know it'll burrow under his skin and piss him off. And right now, that's all the artillery I have in my arsenal. "Now, your dad? He's still my family."

His jaw tightens, the muscle ticking a mad rhythm as he grits his teeth. "But I'm not?" There's a beat of uncomfortable silence as he searches my eyes. For a second, I wonder if I've actually inflicted pain. "Is that what you're trying to tell me?"

Guilt reluctantly blooms inside my chest.

When I fail to respond, he advances, invading my personal space and sending my senses into a tailspin. Even though I'm tall at five foot nine, it becomes necessary to tilt my chin in order to hold his steady gaze. In the velvety darkness that blankets us, I'm in danger of drowning in his golden depths.

Why him?

Why is he the one guy who has set up residence inside my brain, refusing to be evicted?

It's frustrating. Especially when I'd prefer to feel absolutely nothing where Ford Hamilton is concerned. As much as I want to turn tail and run, I refuse to back away. Instead, I hold my ground.

Not to mention, my breath.

"Answer the question." His voice is deceptively calm. "I'm not family?"

I glance away, focusing on the small pockets of people toking up in the yard. The skunky scent of weed hangs heavy in the chilled air.

"Carina?" he snaps.

It's only when all of my chaotic emotions have been locked down tight that I force my gaze back to his. "No, we're not."

Hurt flickers in his eyes before it's shuttered away behind a smirking mask of indifference. "Unfortunately for you, I'm not that easy to shake loose."

Isn't that the truth.

It would be so much easier if he were.

Everywhere I go, there he is. The guy is like an incurable STI.

A nasty, pustulous one that oozes.

Unable to stand another second of our close proximity, I take a step in retreat. Just as I'm about to take another, his hands shoot out, locking around my upper arms before dragging me forward and crushing me against the steely strength of his chest.

Air gets clogged at the back of my throat as I stare up at him with wide, disbelieving eyes. "What are you doing?"

Once upon a time, I allowed Ford to touch me whenever he wanted.

I reveled in the feel of his hands.

That's no longer the case.

As much as he enjoys provoking me, he normally keeps his hands to himself.

His heated gaze drops to my lips. "I'm not sure."

The confusion lacing his voice is enough to make my heart stall. Just when it feels as if I'll expire from lack of oxygen, it's jumpstarted before beating a painful tattoo against my ribcage.

For years, I've worked hard to shut down my emotions where he's concerned. The last thing I need is for him to break through the walls I've erected to keep him firmly at bay. There's no way in hell I'll allow him to destroy the little bit of self-preservation I have. It's the only thing that allows me to sleep peacefully at night.

In a surprise twist I didn't see coming, he whispers, "Truth or dare."

Nerves explode inside my belly as his warm breath ghosts over my parted lips.

I can only stare in shock.

It's a game we used to play in high school. Stupid dares and truths that I would never have revealed to anyone but him. After he iced me out and pushed me away, he never revealed any of my secrets.

It's strange—even when we're taking jabs at each other, I trust him not to pull out the information I shared to use against me. It's always stayed in the vault.

He arches a brow. "I'm waiting, pretty girl. What's it gonna be? Truth or dare?"

Pretty girl.

That's what he used to call me all those years ago.

I suck in a shaky breath, knowing it would be wise to break free of his grip and leave before anything else can happen. We're treading on dangerous territory. I can almost hear the ice cracking beneath our feet. Spidering. Weakening. Any moment, it'll shatter and we'll both plunge into the murky depths, never to be heard from again.

"Dare."

Stupid.

Stupid.

Stupid.

I'm playing with fire, and I know it.

"Wrap your arms around me and pretend that I'm the only one you've been thinking about."

My mouth turns bone dry.

When I remain frozen in place, he rasps, "I've never known you to turn down a dare."

Don't do it.

Walk away while you still can.

Instead of listening to rational thought, my palms settle against the hard lines of his chest before sliding upward and tangling around his neck as if I'm holding on for dear life.

Our gazes cling under the silvery moonlight as people laugh and chatter around us. I'm pressed so tightly against him that I feel every sharp rise and fall of his chest. It's a shock to find that he's not unaffected by what's unfolding between us.

"Fuck, Carina," he murmurs, gaze dipping to my lips.

My heart picks up its tempo as his face looms closer. Just when I think he'll close the distance between us and kiss me, his name is shouted.

I startle, jumping out of his embrace. Our gazes stay locked as my fingers fly to my lips.

"Carina!"

I spin on my heel and fly back to the house.

To safety.

My fingers drift over my lips for a second time. I can't believe that almost happened. Just as I wrench open the door, Ford's deep voice cuts through the night air, stopping me in my tracks.

"Stay the fuck away from Justin. Understand?"

Instead of responding, I do the only thing I can and slip inside.

CHAPTER TWO

FORD

I lift the brown bottle of beer to my lips and take a long swig as my gaze stays locked on the feisty blonde. Instead of heeding my warning, she's been glued to that douchebag's side the entire night.

Hell, she's probably with him because I shot off my big mouth and told her to stay away.

I shouldn't have said jack shit.

If there's one thing Carina enjoys, it's being contrary.

Especially when it comes to me.

If I say up, she'll insist it's down all day long.

If I say black, she'll claim it's white.

When she waltzed through the door with Justin in tow, I told myself that I'd keep my distance.

But it's difficult.

So fucking difficult to see her with other guys.

Especially when all I want to do is get my hands on her.

I take another pull from my bottle as Justin drags her close. I have to flex my fingers and crack the bones in my neck to relieve a little bit of the built-up pressure so I don't end up blowing a gasket. It takes every ounce of self-restraint not to haul ass over there and punch that motherfucker in the face.

That guy isn't anywhere near good enough for Carina.

I've been friends with Demi Richards since sophomore year. She dated him for a while earlier in the semester and caught him getting a BJ at a party. Needless to say, their relationship came to an abrupt halt. It wasn't long after that the pretty soccer player started dating Rowan Michaels, her father's star QB.

He's a pretty good dude.

Even though he plays football, we've always been friends.

We lived on the same dorm floor freshman year.

"I hate to break it to you, but if you're looking to get laid tonight, that expression isn't gonna cut it," Colby McNichols says. "You're scaring away all the honeys."

With a snort, I take another swallow. Any attempt on my part to drown my sorrows isn't working. I'm still pissed off. "Who said I was looking to get laid?"

He grins and his dimples wink and flash. The girl standing a couple feet away from us gasps. If I had to guess, I'd say her panties just got incinerated.

I roll my eyes.

They don't call him the baby-faced assassin for nothing.

I've never seen anyone get as much pussy as Colby.

He's the pied piper of it.

One flash of his dimples and chicks fall right onto their backs and spread their legs wide, no questions asked.

Does he take advantage of his boyish charm?

Every chance he gets.

And why shouldn't he?

He's been single since I've known him. It's doubtful he'll ever jump into a relationship. If there were a competition for biggest player on campus, this guy would win the award hands down.

When Colby flashes a charming smile in her direction, both dimples on display, she just about swoons.

"You're really fucking shameless, you know that, right?"

His smile widens as he lifts the beer to his lips and takes a long swig. "Gotta give the fans what they want."

"Unbelievable," I mutter.

"Hey."

I glance at Bridger. He tugs the ballcap lower so you can barely make out the upper portion of his face.

"What's up with you? You look like you're incognito." As soon as the question flies out of my mouth, I remember the texts that have been popping up on the university message system that gets pushed out to all Western students and staff. The last time it happened, he got his butt chewed out by the chancellor who also happens to be his father.

He was in a shit mood for days afterward.

Bridger has always been a private person. Until that happened, I never realized what a dick his father was. He's quietly asked a few tech-savvy friends to look into the issue. So far, none of them have been able to figure out who's hacking into the system and broadcasting his personal life all over campus. A message turns up every week like clockwork. I feel bad for the guy. It's a crap situation.

His lips thin, wilting at the corners. "Yeah, something like that."

"Sorry, dude. I wasn't thinking."

He shrugs off the apology before glancing around the party that is now in full swing. I get the feeling that he's assessing each person as a potential suspect.

I do the same, searching each face to see if they're staring in our direction. "You think they could actually be here right now?"

"Not sure. That's what I'm hoping to figure out before another message pops up."

"Any idea who it might be?"

He flicks a steely gaze to mine. The look in his eyes is one that I've only seen on the ice when we're playing conference rivals. "I have a few theories."

"Care to share?"

"Not until I have more evidence."

"Sounds like you've got a real Scooby Doo mystery on your hands," Colby cuts in.

Bridger elbows him in the ribs.

Hard.

That's all it takes for Colby to dissolve into laughter.

Hayes sidles up to the group along with Maverick McKinnon.

"Save that shit for the ice," Hayes says.

"More like save it for Garret Akeman," Maverick adds. "That guy is such a dick."

"Seems to be the general consensus," I agree.

I glance across the room only to find the guy we're discussing attempting to put the moves on a girl. She's pretty, but not someone I recognize.

I jerk my chin toward Garret as he steps closer, crowding her personal space. "Looks like Akeman is trying to get laid tonight. Twenty bucks says he gets kneed for his efforts."

"Who the fuck would be stupid enough to take that bet?" Hayes shoots back.

I shrug. "Hey, I was just hoping to make an easy twenty."

Hayes snorts as Maverick narrows his eyes.

I glance at the girl in question. "Do you know her?"

Mav flicks his gaze at me before it zeroes in on the girl again. "Yeah. She's in one of my classes."

Sensing a tender spot, I shift as a smile slides across my face. "Great. Then you wouldn't mind introducing us? She's exactly my type."

Can't say that the muscle ticking a mad rhythm in the younger player's jaw isn't satisfying. "Fuck off, Hamilton. Go find your stepsister." He smacks his forehead. "Oh, that's right. She brought another dude with her tonight. Ouch. That's gotta sting."

The smile falls clean off my face.

Motherfucker.

Before I can say anything else, Mav cuts a path straight to Akeman and the girl he's intent on bagging.

"Looks like you just got your ass handed to you," Hayes says with a laugh.

I give him the finger.

Although, he's not wrong. I must be seriously off my game if I allowed Maverick McKinnon to get the best of me.

My gaze reluctantly slides to Carina and our eyes collide. Awareness sizzles through every fiber of my being.

Yup…definitely off my game.

And it has everything to do with the hot blonde.

The one who burrowed deep under my skin years ago.

CHAPTER THREE

CARINA

I slide into my seat for my nine o'clock class near the center of the room and unzip my backpack before pulling out my computer. A romance novel falls out and I quickly stuff it back inside. Just as I'm firing it up, a guy settles next to me. I glance over and find Cameron Lee.

A smile tugs at the corners of my lips. We've had a couple of classes together throughout the years and I've always enjoyed them. Our professor will be partnering people up today for a project, so I'm glad he decided to sit next to me. The guy is hilarious, and I could use a little levity.

"Hey, Carina. How's it going?"

I swivel on my chair and scan his face before snorting. He looks like he's been put through the wringer. "Better than it is for you, apparently."

A slow grin spreads across his lips. "Yeah, I might have knocked back one too many last night."

I jerk a brow. "On a Tuesday? That's pretty hardcore. Even for you."

Just as he's about to respond, a deep voice cuts him off. "Up, Lee."

Cameron flicks an annoyed glance at Ford. "Seriously, dude?"

"Yup. Move it or lose it."

Cameron drags a hand through his messy hair before scooping up his books and vacating the area. "Catch you later, Carina."

"Yeah." I glare at Ford as he drops down onto the newly vacated chair. "What's your issue?"

"No issue," he says easily, as if he didn't just chase another guy off. One side of his mouth hitches.

Grrr.

Before I can tell him to get lost, Dr. Betsworth clears her throat and smiles from the podium at the front of the room. Her gaze skims the small lecture hall before landing on Ford.

When her face brightens, I roll my eyes. I don't care if she sees me do it. This is exactly the effect Ford has on the fairer sex. Even the professors who should be above this kind of ridiculous behavior. I remember several teachers at our old high school making googly eyes at him. Or sidling up to him in the hallway and laying a hand on his bicep.

Trust me, it was vomit-inducing.

And Dr. Bets is just as bad. Maybe even a little more brazen with her attention. She can be downright flirty in front of the entire class. It's like she doesn't give a damn how unprofessional she appears.

From the corner of my eye, I watch Ford, wanting to see his reaction. I need to reconfirm that he's nothing more than an attention-seeking manwhore who eats this shit up like sugary cereal in the morning. He'll probably flash her a high-wattage smile and use it to his advantage. He's in it for the high mark she'll reward him with.

Instead of doing the expected, he gives her a polite smile in return.

Hmmm.

Interesting.

When she realizes he isn't going to flirt back, she says in a chipper voice, "Good morning! At the end of last week, we discussed the new project we'll be delving into. Today, I'll assign partners and you'll have the remainder of class to discuss the rubric and generate ideas."

Before the last word leaves her lips, Ford wraps his larger hand around mine and jerks them both into the air.

"I'll partner up with Carina."

I gasp and attempt to drag my arm away.

"Excellent."

What?

No!

Abso-fucking-lutely not!

Isn't it enough that we're next-door neighbors in the same apartment building and got stuck together in this class?

Being partners with him is the last straw.

No matter what I do, the universe continues to conspire against me. I can't get away from him.

Ford Hamilton is everywhere.

And that includes all up in my business.

Dr. Bets has the audacity to wink at me. "Lucky girl."

My guess is that the pinched expression on my face says otherwise.

Ford leans close enough for his warm breath to ghost across my flesh as he whispers, "She's right, you know. You're incredibly lucky to be working with me."

I turn just enough to bare my teeth and growl before straightening and doing my best to ignore him.

This guy seriously brings out the worst in me.

Unfortunately, ignoring him is easier said than done.

Especially when he stretches out his long muscular legs, manspreading like the ass he is until his knee bumps mine. Hot licks of awareness ripple through me like a wave, and I quickly shift, moving as far from him as I can get. Then I refocus my attention on our professor as she goes through the rubric.

"If you keep moving away, I'm going to end up with a complex and think you don't like me."

Ignore him.

Do.

Not.

Engage.

"Is that what you're trying to do? Make me work harder for your attention? 'Cuz I can—"

A hiss of air escapes from me as I turn and growl, "Shut the hell up! I'm trying to pay attention and you're making that impossible!"

"Carina? Is there a question?"

I swivel toward Dr. Bets and shake my head. "No. Sorry." My face heats as our classmates turn and stare.

"We all understand that you're eager to work with your partner, but let's finish discussing the expectations first."

I press my lips into a tight line. If I open my mouth to argue, I'm liable to lose my shit and that's the last thing I want to happen.

From the corner of my eye, I watch as Ford's shoulders shake with silent laughter.

That's the moment I realize there's no way I'm going to make it through this project without strangling him.

CHAPTER FOUR

FORD

The second our professor releases us for the day, Carina jams her computer into her backpack and shoots out of her seat like her damn ass is on fire.

"Hey," I call out, knowing it'll annoy her but unable to stop myself. "Aren't you going to wait for me? We're not finished discussing our project."

She gives me a withering stare. One that could shrivel my balls if I weren't made of sterner stuff.

My gaze dips to the rounded curve of her ass as she stalks from the room. Once I shove my crap into my bag, I take off. Carina should realize by now that there's no way to outrun me.

Not when my sights are locked on her.

It's been that way since the day our parents introduced us, and in all these years, it's never changed.

"Ford, do you have a moment?" Dr. Bets asks.

My shoulders tighten as I flick a glance at my sports watch. "Sorry, I have a meeting scheduled with Coach. Can we do this another time?"

Her lips curve into an understanding smile. One that's meant to be sexy. "Of course. I'll see you Friday."

Yeah, that's a lie. There isn't a meeting. Unfortunately, if I give Carina too much of a head start, she'll melt into the thick crowd of students moving across campus.

"Yup."

And then I'm gone, sliding into the flow of traffic that congests the hallway. Since I tower a couple inches over six feet, I'm able to crane my neck and search the corridor for her blonde head.

Just as I turn the corner, I spot her pushing through the glass door into the weak morning sunlight that's attempting to filter through the leaden-colored clouds. That's all it takes for me to pick up the pace and force my way through the press of bodies.

As she reaches the concrete pathway, I pull up alongside her. "If I didn't know better, I'd think you were actually trying to leave me in your dust."

Her spine stiffens as she stares straight ahead.

Her blatant disinterest only makes me hungrier for her attention.

"Weird. What gave you that idea?"

"Oh, I don't know. Maybe the way—"

She grounds to an abrupt halt before swinging around and slamming her fist into my chest. Barely do I feel the punch.

"Fuck, that hurt," she mutters, shaking out her hand as laughter sits on the tip of my tongue. I'm well aware that if I allow it to bust loose, she'll wallop me again. Only harder. The last thing I want is for her to hurt herself. It'll just be another transgression she holds against me.

"What was that for?" It takes a concerted effort to keep a straight face. Especially when her glare turns lethal. She's on the verge of ripping me to shreds with her teeth.

"You know damn well what it was for! You're the last person I want to be partnered up with." A low growl vibrates from her chest. "And now we're stuck together for the next month."

"Ouch." I pretend to wince. "That's not very nice."

"Yeah, well...I'm not feeling very nice right now. Thanks to you."

I tilt my head and give her a considering look. "You would've seriously rather been partnered up with Cameron?"

"Anyone, Ford," she grumbles with a huff. "I would have rather worked with anyone other than *you*."

"You realize that he would've made you do all the legwork and then write the entire paper, right?"

I can tell by the way she smashes her lips into a tight line that she understands that my assessment of the situation is spot on, otherwise she'd argue.

"He's a nice guy," she finally mutters.

"He's a high guy," I shoot back with a laugh.

She rolls her eyes before swiveling around and stalking away. "You're like a stubborn rash that refuses to clear up no matter how much steroid ointment I use."

Another chuckle slips free as I flash a grin. "You spend a lot of time thinking about me, don't you?"

She shakes her head, refusing to answer.

"So, about tonight—we'll take off after practice?"

Her only response is to raise her hand and give me the finger, letting me know that I'm number one in her heart.

Exactly where I want to be.

CHAPTER FIVE

CARINA

I reluctantly set the bookmark in my paperback and slip it into my purse as Ford drives his cherry red Corvette Stinger up the long, weathered brick road before pulling into the circular drive and easing off the pedal.

The first time I caught sight of the stone mansion with its turrets and portico was the summer before freshman year of high school. It was the kind of place I'd only read about in the romance novels I'd started to devour.

Mom met Crawford at the restaurant where she worked. It was love at first sight followed by a whirlwind courtship and engagement. Eight weeks later, they slipped rings on each other's fingers and promised to love one another until death do they part.

Then we moved in with Crawford and Ford and voilà—instant blended family.

Unlike the books I'd read, everyone got along great. Crawford had been widowed for more than a decade. His first wife, Sandra, drowned in a freak swimming accident. It had been him and Ford ever since.

Ford...

To this day, I'm still embarrassed by my reaction to him. It had been so cliché. My breath caught at the back of my throat and my chest constricted until sucking air into my lungs felt agonizing. I'd had the weirdest feeling that we'd met before. And then it hit me that I'd drooled over him in advertisements for a high-end teen clothing brand. The one where they barely wore anything at all.

I learned that in addition to playing hockey, he dabbled in modeling.

When we first moved in, I'd worried that Ford would despise me. After all, who wanted some teenage girl and her mother to take over a house that had been a bachelor pad for the last decade?

But that wasn't the case at all.

Ford was friendly and nice. He made me laugh and actually wanted to spend time together. When the school year began, he took me under his protective wing and introduced me to all of his friends.

Since Ford was popular—I mean, duh, of course he was—I was accepted without question.

Before the marriage, Mom and I scraped by, living paycheck to paycheck. I was able to take a dance class or two by helping out with beginner level ones as a way to pay for them. Once Mom and Crawford tied the knot, I was able to immerse myself in lessons and took them five days a week for hours at a time.

It was utter bliss.

After my new stepfather discovered how important dance was to me, he built a private studio in the basement. It was open and airy with wood floors and mirrored walls. I spent all my time there and it quickly became my happy place.

Within a matter of months, Ford's father felt like my own. It was devastating when they split up five years later. I was terrified that Crawford would turn his back on me the way my own father had.

As soon as Ford cuts the engine, I blink back to the present and pop open the door, relieved to escape the stifling confines of the vehicle before slamming it shut.

He trails after me as I jog up the wide stone stairs.

"Not even going to wait for me, huh?" he calls out, humor

simmering in his deep voice. It's like the guy is trying to burrow as far as possible under my skin. "How rude."

It's tempting to flip him off for a second time but I'm trying to limit myself to one bird a day where Ford is concerned. Trust me, it's not easy. Plus, I'm well aware that he takes perverse pleasure in riling me up.

The guy is like an overgrown child.

He'd prefer negative attention to no attention at all.

My fingers wrap around the intricate silver door handle before thrusting it open. I whirl around as Ford saunters up the stairs as if he doesn't have a care in the world. His gaze stays pinned to mine the entire time.

Just as he reaches the porch, I slam the door shut in his face.

Then I twist the lock.

A smile curls around the edges of my lips. That was almost as satisfying as flipping him off earlier this afternoon.

I don't take more than two strides inside the double-story foyer with its massive crystal chandelier that hangs from the ceiling as Crawford peeks his head out of his home office.

As soon as he catches sight of me, a genuine smile lights up his features. With his salt-and-pepper hair and clean-shaven jaw, he's a handsome man in his early fifties. After Mom took off, I assumed it would only be a matter of time before another woman snapped him up—after all, the man is a real catch—but that never happened.

I have the sneaking suspicion he's still in love with Pamela.

Poor bastard.

He never should have married her in the first place.

At the end of the day, I love my mother. But she wasn't cut out to be the wife of a politician.

What she loved most was the financial security Crawford provided. And continues to provide with fat alimony payments that are directly deposited into her account every other week. It allows her to continue living the lavish lifestyle she quickly became accustomed to.

"How's my girl doing?" Crawford asks, opening his arms wide.

That's all the invitation I need to fly into them. My eyelids feather closed, and my muscles loosen as I sink into the warm embrace. I inhale a deep breath of the sandalwood cologne that clings to him. There's something comforting and solid about his presence.

It's now impossible to imagine my life without him filling it.

"I'm fine. How about you?"

"Oh, can't complain. I'm glad you two are here for dinner. It's a welcome break."

"You work way too hard," I scold. Between his congressional duties and the construction business he owns, he's constantly burning the candle at both ends.

The front door swings open and Ford saunters in.

"Hey, son," Crawford greets, a smile lighting up his face.

For just a moment, I wonder what it would be like to have a parent who actually enjoyed being around me. As soon as that thought slithers into my brain, I shove it away. My mother is who she is and no amount of wishing otherwise will change that fact. It's taken time for me to come to terms with that hard truth and lower my expectations.

"Dad."

When I reluctantly draw away from Crawford, he slips an arm around my waist. "You guys ready to eat? Sarah made beef wellington along with steamed green beans."

Ford's eyes light up as he pats his toned belly. "My favorite."

Crawford flashes him an easy smile. "She made it especially with you in mind."

The three of us head down the long stretch of hallway to the formally appointed dining room. The glossy walnut table is large enough to seat up to twenty guests comfortably.

And it has.

Crawford holds fundraisers and dinner parties a couple times a month. At first, I enjoyed dressing up in fancy gowns and having my hair styled and makeup professionally applied by a glam squad. But after a while, it got old. You end up having the same conversations on repeat while you smile, fielding questions regarding Crawford and his political agenda.

Now that Ford and I are in college, we're not around for as many of them. Although, every once in a while, Crawford will ask me to accompany him to an event. After everything he's done for me, there's no way I would turn him down. Within months of him and Mom getting married, he set up a college account in my name and said that no matter what happened, it would be mine to use for higher education.

I owe this man everything.

Sarah greets us before serving the piping hot plates. The rich aroma is intoxicating. She was a head chef in a Michelin star restaurant before Crawford coaxed her into working exclusively for him. I nibble at my steak as the two men discuss the upcoming election.

"And what about you, Carina? How's your solo coming along for the Winter Showcase?"

"There are still a few things that need to be cleaned up, but it should be perfected by mid-December."

He flashes a smile. "That's my girl. I'm excited to finally see it."

After another ten minutes, I set my utensils down on my plate. "Would you mind if I use the studio for a bit?"

"Of course not. That's the reason I built it." His thick brows tug together as he glances at my plate. "You barely touched your dinner. Wasn't it to your liking?"

"It was delicious. Guess I'm just not that hungry."

"Would you like Sarah to package up some leftovers to take home?"

"That would be great. Thank you."

With that, I rise from the high back chair and shimmy around the table before brushing a quick kiss across Crawford's cheek.

As I do, I scowl at Ford.

That's all it takes for a wide grin to break out across his face.

Jerk.

Then I hightail it from the room and down the staircase to the walk-out basement. Once I arrive at the studio, I slip into the small changing room where I keep extra shorts and athletic tops.

As music fills the space, I take my position in the middle of the room and block out everything that attempts to push in at the edges.

And that includes my ex-stepbrother.

CHAPTER SIX

FORD

My gaze stays pinned to Carina as she walks out of the room. Unable to help myself, it drops to the rounded curve of her ass.

Damn, she's got a fine one.

High, tight, and muscular.

Her body is like a fine-honed instrument from years of dance.

It's a work of art.

There's an Olympic-sized swimming pool out back and in the summer, she spends a lot of time out there. The sight of her in a teeny tiny bikini is both heaven and hell.

It's only when my father clears his throat, reluctantly drawing my attention back to him, that I force those thoughts from my brain. One brow lifts as if he knows exactly what kinds of dirty fantasies are rolling around in my head.

Well, hell.

I'm usually careful to keep my true feelings under wraps when it comes to Carina. I brace myself, afraid he'll broach the topic. I fucking hate the way he looks at me. Like I'm a predator just waiting for the opportunity to take advantage of her.

It's a relief when he asks instead, "Is the new coach giving you any problems?"

I relax against the antique chair. "Nope. He's chilled out since the beginning of the season. He was more up Ryder's ass than anyone else. Kind of felt bad for the guy."

"I've been following the school's social media feed. Seems like your friend is doing well."

I nod in agreement. "He is."

If all goes according to plan, Chicago will pick him up after the season, and his goal of playing in the NHL will become a reality. It would be a dream come true for any of my teammates.

I'm probably the exception to the rule. I've always known that my future would take a different path. Dad drilled it into my head from a young age that once I graduated from Western, I'd work full time for his construction company, eventually taking it over.

As soon as school ends each spring, I spend roughly sixty hours a week working for him. Instead of kicking my feet up in the office and learning the business side of things, I'm part of the crew and treated like any other lower tier employee. He doesn't want anyone to think that I've gotten to where I am without earning it from the bottom up. By the time I head back to Western every fall, hockey and classes feel like a well-deserved break.

Dad jumped into the political arena about fifteen years ago, running for a local city council position before being elected to Congress. His partner, Peter Bowman, has taken on more of the lion's share of the company's responsibilities. In May, I'll have to jump in and hit the ground running.

It's not like I don't realize how lucky I am to have a path forged for me, but sometimes I wonder what it would've been like to have a choice in my future.

For a long time, I was the only heir, and everything rested on my shoulders. Now there's Carina. Since she's also a business major, Dad wants her involved in the company as well. I don't have a problem with that. In fact, if he can convince her to work for him, then at least she'll be forced to stick around.

With graduation looming on the not-so-distant horizon, it feels like this chapter of my life, one that has been filled with Carina, is slowly coming to an end. When I think about her moving to LA or New York and trying to make a career for herself in dance, a pit the size of Texas takes up residence at the bottom of my gut.

I hate the idea of her being so far away.

Out of my reach.

It's only a matter of time before someone wins her heart. I'm surprised it hasn't happened already. Even though I've steeled myself for the inevitability, I still run off the guys who aren't worthy.

Which, in case you're wondering, is all of them.

Especially that fucking moron, Justin Fischer. He and I had a private convo the other day. Needless to say, he now sees things my way.

"I'm hoping to make it to your next game," Dad says.

"It's not a big deal if you can't." He spent years schlepping me to the hockey rink five days a week for practice and games up until I could drive myself.

The guy's schedule is always packed full. He's self-made and doesn't know how to slow down and relax. Or even enjoy himself. It's one of the reasons Pamela pulled the plug on their marriage.

While she seemed to enjoy the finer things he was able to offer, she got fed up with him being a workaholic. She isn't the kind of woman who likes to be left to her own devices. I can't blame her for finding someone else, but the way she went about it sucked.

"I'll let you know if anything changes." Before I can tell him that he shouldn't bother, he circles back to the one topic I have zero desire to discuss with him. "Carina seems to be doing well."

I shrug, pushing back in my chair and attempting to keep my posture relaxed. "Yup."

With a nod, he studies me carefully. "So, you don't see her around very much?"

"We have a marketing class together but other than that, not really."

It's a little white lie meant to put his mind at ease.

"That's probably for the best." Even though the response seems casually thrown out, the intended meaning strikes a nerve.

Irritation explodes inside me and my fingers curl around the polished arms of the chair, my clipped nails biting into the smooth surface. "It's for the best that we don't interact very much?"

His expression shifts as if he finally found what he was searching for and isn't happy about it. "You know exactly what I mean." There's a brief silence before he adds in a lower tone, "You're siblings."

Is he out of his mind? What I feel for Carina isn't at all sisterly-like. It never was. Not even when we were fourteen years old.

"No, we aren't," I snap, immediately regretting the outburst.

"In all the ways that matter, you are. You'll be family for the rest of your lives. It doesn't matter if Pamela and I are no longer married. Carina is like a daughter to me."

I gnash my teeth.

There's no point in arguing with him.

When I continue to silently stew, he says, "There are plenty of girls out there. Find one of them. In fact," he leans forward, the sleeves of his perfectly pressed button-down resting against the table, "if you're interested in settling down, you should take Jaclyn out sometime. She's been asking about you."

Jaclyn Bowman is a gorgeous girl who has long, sable-colored hair and eyes to match. She's petite and curvy. Not to mention, outgoing. She's been learning the ropes at Hamilton Bowman Construction for as long as I have. Although, with her working in the office and me out on construction sites all day during the summer months, we don't run into each other very often.

As likeable as she is, Jaclyn doesn't hold a candle to Carina.

"I'm not interested in your partner's daughter," I say with a grunt, unable to believe he's playing matchmaker.

"Perhaps you should reconsider. She's grown into a beautiful and poised young woman. If you ever decide to follow me into politics, she'll make the perfect wife. And then your children would inherit the company."

"Dad…" My voice trails off on a frustrated groan. This isn't the first time this conversation has reared its ugly head. Unfortunately, it probably won't be the last. He seems stuck on shoving me in Jaclyn's direction.

It's almost a relief when his cell phone rings and I don't have to pull an excuse out of my ass to end this uncomfortable conversation. He picks up the sleek device and glances at the screen.

His mouth tightens into a thin line. "I need to take this."

I jerk my head into a nod as he rises from his chair and saunters out of the spacious dining room. A minute later, the door to his home office closes softly behind him.

Relief courses through me and my muscles loosen as I stare out the floor-to-ceiling windows into the swirling darkness that has now fallen. Throughout my life, Dad and I have always been close.

We rarely fight or have disagreements.

There's one exception to that rule and it's Carina.

He treats the pair of us like we're actually siblings when that's not the case. Maybe he's still holding onto hope that Pamela will change her mind and sweep back into his life.

There are times when I think back to senior year, and I wonder what would have happened had everything been allowed to play out without interference.

But we'll never know.

And that's the problem.

CHAPTER SEVEN

CARINA

My mind soars above the music as I leap from one foot to the other in a jeté. Then I repeat the movement. And then do it for a third time across the space. There's something about the required mental focus that allows me to turn my attention inward and forget about everything going on around me.

Dance has always been my escape. It's one I'm able to lose myself in for hours at a time. The physical exhaustion that seeps in afterward is always welcome. I can hit the sheets at the end of a long day and fall into a deep, dreamless sleep.

With my body fully extended, I raise one leg and leap off the other, achieving a full split in the air. For a second or two, I hang suspended before returning to the floor. My heart thumps a steady staccato as the last note reverberates throughout the air.

I squeeze my eyes closed and slowly return to myself, becoming more aware of my surroundings. My muscles are deliciously pliant as exhaustion creeps in at the edges. All of the sexual tension thrumming through my veins dissipates into nothingness.

It's the exact outcome I was searching for.

Lately, working my body over in the studio at school is the only thing that helps achieve a shred of inner peace. Not even my favorite vibe takes care of business completely. Afterward, I'm always left with a vague feeling of dissatisfaction. The sexual ache might be dulled but something's still there, clawing beneath the surface, desperately fighting to break loose.

It's terrifying.

The slow clap is what yanks me from those thoughts. My eyelids fly open only to find Ford sitting against the mirrored wall with his long, muscular legs stretched out in front of him.

The moment our gazes collide, my heartbeat explodes into overdrive. It only takes one look for all of the tension I'd just worked out of my system to slam back full force.

One second ticks by.

Then another.

The studio at Crawford's has always been my private domain. Ford has a weight room located on the other side of the basement. There's plenty of space to separate us.

I can't remember the last time I found him here.

In high school, I took great pleasure in dancing for him. I enjoyed the way his eyes would track every movement as I glided around the space. Back then, I wanted every bit of his attention focused on me.

I lapped it up.

Blossomed beneath his smiles, kindness, and praise.

As those thoughts slyly invade my brain, I shove them away, unwilling to get tangled up in the past. And the inevitable pain and confusion that was left behind in its wake.

I clear my throat, attempting to appear unfazed by his presence as my heart riots beneath my ribcage. It's as if the vast and airy space has shrunken around him, making it impossible to draw in breath.

"How long have you been here?"

Unable to stand still beneath the intensity of his scrutiny, I rise to my full height and beeline to the chair where there's a small towel and wipe the sweat from my brow.

"About ten minutes or so. You were too focused to notice me."

There's a moment of silence as thick tension ratchets up, permeating the atmosphere. "A bomb could have gone off and you wouldn't have realized it."

He's not exaggerating. My physical self might have been in the studio, but my mind was soaring free in the clouds.

When he says nothing more, I ask, "Is there a reason you came down here?"

His shrug is casual but there's a darker emotion buried within his golden depths.

I contemplate it for a second or two.

Annoyance maybe?

Anger?

His deep voice breaks the silence. "Dad received a call and locked himself in the office, so I came down to see what you were up to."

"Oh."

Just as I'm about to suggest that we take off, he says, "He's trying to work his matchmaking magic and set me up with Jaclyn."

The jealousy that flares to life within me is fast and furious. All-consuming. I quickly swallow it down before it can break loose and give me away.

Only then do I toss out what I hope sounds like a careless response. "Oh? And what did you tell him?"

I can almost feel the way his eyes sift through mine, attempting to pick through my innermost thoughts. "That I'm not interested."

It's only when my breath rushes past my lips that I realize it had become trapped in my lungs.

Before I can say anything, he tosses out a question.

"Truth or dare?"

My muscles still.

When I remain silent, his voice dips as he prods me into playing this game with him for the second time in a week. "Come on, Carina. What's it going to be?"

I swipe the towel over my face and watch him from the corner of my eye. The last thing I need is for him to chip away at my carefully constructed façade. Even though I realize it's a bad idea and has disaster written all over it, I can't seem to help myself.

"Dare."

A slow grin spreads across his face as if he's pleased with the decision.

I toss the towel on the chair as my palms settle on my hips. I'm irritated with myself for being goaded into playing with him. "Go on," I snap. "Get it over with. What's my dare?"

Anticipation gathers in the atmosphere like impending storm clouds darkening the horizon.

"I dare you to kiss me."

Surprise rushes through me as my brows rise across my forehead.

With a tilt of my head, I study him, attempting to figure out what the end game is. "Really?"

"Yup." Even though he appears relaxed, his muscles are coiled tight as if he's a snake waiting to strike. Only now do I realize that he's shed his sweatshirt from earlier. His chiseled biceps are showcased in the tank. It's enough to make my mouth water. "It's not like we haven't kissed before."

That's true. Quite a bit back in the day.

But it's been four years since we locked lips.

"And we'll kiss again." The casualness of his tone belies the intensity brewing in his eyes.

I fold my arms across my chest as if the protective stance alone will keep me from falling down the rabbit hole that is Ford Hamilton. "You think so?"

The tip of his tongue swipes over his lower lip. The small, barely discernable movement has heat gathering in the pit of my belly.

All right, so maybe it gathers a little lower.

"Yeah, I just dared you to kiss me, and I know how you can't resist one of those."

He's right, damn him.

My track record when it comes to dares is impeccable. I'm batting a thousand.

His gaze stays fastened to mine as I force my feet into movement, slowly narrowing the space between us. My heart picks up tempo until it pounds a steady staccato in my ears. When I'm standing beside him, he cranes his neck to hold my gaze. My hands shake as they settle tentatively on his shoulders. The heat of his skin singes my fingers as they reluctantly stroke over the broad expanse.

I've worked so hard to forget about our past and pretend it never existed. When I'm touching him, that's no longer possible.

My hands tighten around muscle and bone as I straddle his thighs and gradually lower myself onto his lap until we're facing one another. Our mouths are inches apart as our gazes stay locked. The minty freshness of his breath wafts across my lips. I have to stop myself from leaning closer and inhaling him like a hit. When his palms wrap around my waist as if to hold me in place, my arms twine around his neck, drawing him close enough for my mouth to ghost over his without ever quite touching.

When my movements stall, he growls, "I'm waiting."

My lips lift into a faint smile. Ford has never been known for his patience. Especially when he wants something. Anticipation builds within me as the room shrinks around us.

When I can't resist another second, I lower my face, allowing my lips to drift over his. It's barely a caress. More like a whisper of air. He tilts his head, angling his chin higher as if to close the distance between us. Instead of giving him what he wants, I retreat an inch or so.

"You're such a fucking tease," he says with a groan.

My lips twitch at the corners.

He shifts, pulling me tight enough against him to feel the thick swell of his erection. That's all it takes for my core to flood with arousal.

Our breath mingles, becoming one, as I nip his lower lip, tugging it with sharp teeth before doing the same to the top. His fingers curl, biting into the flesh of my hips. Instead of hurting, his touch grounds me in the moment unfolding between us. Every cell feels as if it's been sparked to life.

There've been boys in my past. Tons of them. But none have ever made me feel this alive. It's both addictive and frightening all at the same time.

Deep down in a place I'm unwilling to inspect, I'm terrified that all Ford is doing is ripping the lid off something I've spent years trying to keep contained. And yet, that knowledge isn't enough to stop this from happening. I'm not sure if there's anything that could tear me away.

And that's probably the scariest realization of all.

I shove those thoughts from my head and focus my attention on his mouth. I used to love the way he kissed me. Even in high school, he knew precisely what would drive me crazy and how to draw out the most pleasure.

His pupils dilate as I suck on the plump flesh before releasing it with a soft pop. When I've teased him enough, my lips slant over his. A groan rumbles up from deep within his chest as his grip tightens. I almost wonder if he'll take control instead of allowing me to set the pace, but he doesn't. His lips part just enough for my tongue to slip inside the warmth of his mouth to mingle with his own. Memories unfold inside my head, transporting me back to a time when slipping into bed with him and being held in his arms was a nightly occurrence.

He tastes exactly like I remember.

His fingers loosen as his arms snake around my ribcage, and he drags me close enough for my breasts to get crushed against the chiseled strength of his chest. I flex my hips, rubbing myself against his thick length.

He breaks away enough to growl, "Fuck, Carina. Keep that up and I'll come in my joggers."

Laughter rises in my throat. "I'd love to see that happen."

As tempting as it is to continue, if I don't pull back now, I won't be able to. I'll lose myself in the taste and feel of him and I can't allow that to happen. I can't allow myself to get sucked into his vortex like before.

With one final kiss, I unwind my arms from around his neck. His honey-colored eyes search mine for a long silent heartbeat before he sets me free. As soon as he relinquishes his hold, I pop to my feet and swing away on surprisingly unsteady legs. I need to put as much distance between us as possible.

"Come back here," he groans. The guttural scrape of his voice is like a straight shot to my core. Another burst of arousal explodes inside me before I snuff it out.

"You dared me to kiss you and that's exactly what I did," I say, tossing the words carelessly over my shoulder. "Now I'm going to change. I'll meet you upstairs and we can take off."

It's only when I close the changing room door behind me that I lean against it and squeeze my eyes tight, sucking a deep breath into my lungs before slowly releasing it back into the atmosphere.

I might have riled up Ford, but I did the same damn thing to myself.

Looks like my trusty vibe will be getting some action tonight.

CHAPTER EIGHT

FORD

The door reverberates on the hinges as I slam into the apartment I share with Wolf and Madden. An hour later and I'm still sporting a semi. I quickly adjust myself as I catch sight of them. Madden is perched on the edge of the overstuffed armchair. His gaze stays locked on the big screen, high-def television mounted to the far wall as his avatar dekes out a defenseman from the other team and shoots on goal. When it slides in, hitting the back of the net, he leaps from the chair and thrusts the controller in the air.

"Suck it!"

Wolf glares. "Seriously, dude. It's not that deep."

"You're only saying that because you're a loser." Madden drops back down onto the chair and his eyes drift my way before giving me a chin lift in greeting. "Sup?"

I grunt out an unintelligible answer before settling at the far end of the couch.

"How'd dinner go?" Wolf asks.

"It was fine."

I don't miss the smirks they shoot at each other. Normally, their sly glances don't bug me. For some reason, they do tonight.

"What's the issue? I said it was fine." Even as the words fly out of my mouth, I know I'm being churlish. That's the precise moment I realize that I've made a tactical error. I should have played it off the way I always do. They'll home in on my irritation like flies on a steaming pile of shit.

Wolf drags a hand through his short strands. It's barely an inch thick. "I don't know, man. Why don't you tell us what crawled up your ass and died."

"I think we all know what crawled up there," Madden snickers like the jerk he is. "Her name just so happens to be Carina."

"Actually," Wolf says easily, like I'm not sitting in front of him, listening to every word that comes out of his piehole, "I think his disposition would improve dramatically if that were the case."

My mouth falls open as Wolf's comment sinks in before I quickly snap it shut again. "What the fuck are you two yapping about?"

Madden arches a brow and shakes his head like I'm the one who's slow on the uptake. "Seriously, dude? You two have been dancing around each other since I met you freshman year."

"Excuse me?"

"You heard me," he fires back.

I cross my arms against my chest and glare, willing him to steer this convo in a different direction. These two are the last people on the face of the earth I want to discuss Carina with.

"Nope, don't think I did."

Madden rolls his eyes. "It's so obvious that you've got the hots for her. How about you do us all a favor and finally nut up."

I snort. "You're one to talk. When was the last time you were even with a chick, huh?" Every drop of humor drains from Madden's expression. "Like we don't all know what you're doing holed up in the bathroom?"

My roommate gives me the finger.

Not so funny when the shoe is on the other foot, now is it, motherfucker?

"Maybe you should find an actual girl instead of working your hand over so much," I continue, unable to stop myself.

The edges of Madden's lips sink. "There's no need to be a prick just because you've got a hard-on for Carina."

I drag a hand over my face.

He's right.

I'm being an asshole and she's the root cause of it.

Or, more accurately, my feelings for her are.

"Sorry." I allow my head to fall back until it can rest on the cushion as I stare sightlessly up at the ceiling. "That girl drives me batshit crazy," I mutter, forcing myself to say the words out loud.

From the corner of my eye, I watch as a slow grin spreads across Wolf's face. "Now we're finally getting somewhere."

"No, we're not." My father's comments from earlier ring hollowly throughout my head. "I'm wound tight and just need to get laid."

"Yeah, by your stepsister."

"She's not my stepsister," I grumble. "We're not even related."

Not really.

"Even better," Madden says with a smirk, my shitty behavior from minutes ago already forgotten. That's the great thing about him. He's never been one to hold a grudge.

"For what it's worth, I think you'd finally get her out of your system if you two would just smash," Wolf adds.

"That's a shit idea and never going to happen."

The only reason she locked lips with me tonight is because I dared her to do it. While some things change, others stay the same. Can't say it wasn't completely satisfying to see the challenging light spark to life in her pretty blue-gray eyes. Maybe she wanted to turn me down flat, but she couldn't bring herself to do it.

Wolf shrugs as Madden starts up another game and they both get sucked into the action playing out across the screen. Normally, listening to them shit talk while trying to outdo one another would be enough to lighten my mood.

Tonight, that's not the case.

All I can think about is Carina.

Even worse, Wolf's comments have weaseled their way into my brain and are gnawing away gleefully at the back of it.

He's probably right.

It would be a hell of a lot easier to move on if we just knocked boots.

Unfortunately for me, there's no way that will ever happen.

CHAPTER NINE

CARINA

I'm about to flip the page of the paperback I'm devouring when there's a knock on the door. With a frown, I glance toward the tiny entryway, debating if I can ignore the person on the other side. I just returned from work at On Pointe studio, and I've been dying to delve into this chapter all day. Things are just about to get spicy between the hero and heroine and I'm totally here for it.

Decision made, I refocus on the page. Whoever it is can come back when I'm not busy. Twenty seconds later, there's another, more insistent knock which I promptly ignore. Although, I'm not going to lie, the interruption is yanking me out of the story and ruining my vibe.

When I fail to answer for a second time, my phone chimes with an incoming message. I huff out a breath and reluctantly glance at the screen.

Open up. I know you're in there.

Ford.

Ugh.

I should have known it was him.

That guy can be such a pain in the ass.

Hmmm...unless he's stalking my every move, he has no idea that I'm here.

Another message pops up.

I saw you walk into the building ten minutes ago.

Yup. Definite pain in my ass. I'll be glad when this year is over and we graduate. He'll work for Crawford, and I can take off, going wherever I want.

Maybe New York.

Or LA.

If my heart clenches at the idea of leaving the only home I've ever known, I shove it away, refusing to dwell on it. Crawford is the one I'll miss.

Not Ford.

Never Ford.

Good riddance to him.

With a grumble, I set the paperback down and jump off the couch before stalking to the door and swinging it wide only to find my ex-stepbrother on the other side. A devilish grin lights up his face as if he's thrilled to have disturbed my solitude.

"About time you answered."

I bare my teeth and plant myself in the middle of the threshold, so he can't saunter inside. "What do you want?"

"I've got a little extra time before practice and thought we could get a jumpstart on the project. The end of the semester will be here before you know it and I'd rather get as much done as possible before we start hitting the road."

He's right, damn him. Practice for the winter showcase will only intensify the closer we get to the date.

"Fine," I mutter, wanting to make it clear that I'm not happy about getting stuck with him as a partner.

It's only when his eyes meander down the length of my body that I remember I'm wearing tiny shorts that cling to me like a second skin and an athletic bra.

How is it possible for the heat of his gaze to feel more like a physical caress? It's tempting to cross my arms over my chest to shield his view, but I'll be damned if I give him the satisfaction of knowing that he made me self-conscious.

His voice drops a few octaves. "Are you going to let me in or what?"

The deep timbre of it is enough to send arousal flooding my core.

My mouth dries as I jerk my shoulders into a careless shrug before reluctantly taking a step back and waving him in. He saunters past me into the compact living and dining room space. I make sure to give him a wide berth as I head to my bedroom to grab my computer and the handout that describes the project in more depth.

"I'll be right back."

It's only when I pick up the laptop from my desk and spin around that I realize Ford has followed me. His gaze travels around the room, taking in all the posters and photos that cover the walls. There are fluffy pillows on the queen-sized bed along with an oversized Squishmallow. There's a ton of makeup tubes, bottles, and compacts cluttering the top of the desk along with a pile of discarded outfits from the weekend thrown haphazardly over the back of the chair.

"Let's work at the table in the other room. It'll be more comfortable."

"Nah. Here is fine."

Before the last word leaves his lips, he throws himself onto the bed and stretches out, stacking his hand behind his head. I hate how much the movement makes his biceps pop.

I force my attention away as my pulse quickens. "Don't get too comfortable."

My grumbled-out comment makes his simmering smile turn into more of a slow grin. It's one that can melt the iciest of hearts.

Mine included.

I refocus my attention on the rubric. The sooner we get this over with, the quicker I can kick his ass out of here and get back to my novel. "We need to come up with a product and then develop a marketing plan that includes research, SWOT analysis, objectives, target market segmentation, strategies, an implementation plan, along with a way to measure and evaluate what we've done."

"Sounds easy enough."

I snort.

What it sounds like is a lot of work.

Even though I refuse to admit it to Ford, he's probably spot on in his assessment of Cameron. I would have got stuck doing all the heavy lifting. And considering that I have four other classes, and I'm still fine tuning my routine for the showcase, I won't have the time to take on a project of this magnitude alone.

My ex-stepbrother might be a lot of things, but a slacker isn't one of them.

"The first order of business is to come up with a product we can sell," I say.

Ford chews his lower lip as he stares silently at the ceiling. There's a slight furrow to his brow. The urge to smooth it out is so strong that I have to tighten my fingers, so I don't do exactly that.

The kiss we shared the other day nudges its way into my brain. I hate to admit just how much it's been lurking there.

Unaware of the dangerous thoughts circling through my head, he says, "What about a product for kids who play hockey? Like a rectangular board that's six foot in length and slippery. It can be utilized two different ways. One, you wear a pair of socks and work on lengthening your stride and two, you could use it with a puck to practice stick skills."

He turns his head just enough for his gaze to fasten onto mine.

"Remember the one Dad made? All my friends loved it."

My mind tumbles back to freshman year of high school. While my stepfather built me a private studio, Ford had an area in the basement where he could practice hockey and lift weights. If there was something they wanted that wasn't sold on the market, Crawford built it himself. Like hooking up a thick tarp to the basketball hoop where Ford could shoot pucks without worrying about them sailing fifty yards into the backyard. One broken window of the pool house was more than enough impetus to engineer just such a product.

It's not the worst idea in the world.

"Sure."

He flashes a grin. "See how well we work together?"

"Yeah...let's not get carried away."

Although, secretly, I suspect he isn't wrong. Especially when he stops trying to provoke me at every turn.

Needing to refocus my attention, I glance at the rubric before jotting down a few notes. "So, the next step would be to research the market and see if there are similar products and what their price points are."

"Yup. Sounds like a plan."

For the next thirty minutes, we do a deep dive on the internet. There are a few similar inventions, but all have slight variations. We take notes of the differences and brainstorm some ideas about how we can make ours stand out against its competitors.

When my back begins to ache, I rise to my feet and stretch. Ford sets his computer on the other side of the bed and rolls toward me before patting the mattress next to him.

"Come here."

My arms gradually fall back to my sides. Allowing myself to get too close to him is a shit idea. Especially after what happened the other day. I don't need our relationship to become any more complicated than it already is. My feelings for him have always been tangled and murky.

When he pats the comforter for a second time, I find myself gravitating toward him. It's gingerly that I settle at the far end of the bed. A smile twitches on his lips as if he understands my need for distance.

He sits up and inches closer. "How's Pamela doing?"

The question throws me off guard. I thought for sure he would bring up the kiss from the other day. That just shows you how much it's been taking up space in the back of my brain. And how much I need to exorcise him from my head.

Thoughts of my mother are enough to douse any flames that have been smoldering.

I jerk my shoulders. "Fine, I guess."

Ever since the divorce, Mom has flitted from one rich man to another in an effort to live her best life now that she no longer works for a living or takes care of me. It's embarrassing that she's so content to live off her alimony payments. She even asked Crawford for extra money when she wanted to jet off to Berlin with new friends.

Of course he gave it to her, no questions asked.

"When was the last time you saw her?"

With a frown, I swivel toward him.

If I'm being perfectly honest—this is exactly how I prefer my relationship with Mom to be.

One of absence.

So, it's not like I'm marking time, waiting for her to pop up and act all motherly.

I search my brain, wondering when I saw her last.

"I don't know…a couple months ago."

I think.

Maybe.

His hand rises to scratch his shadowed jaw. "Huh."

My gaze dips to the movement before I give myself a sharp mental slap and refocus my attention.

"What?" I search his eyes for clues as to what he's thinking. "What does that mean?" Even talking about Pamela makes me twitchy.

"Guess I'm just surprised. Dad mentioned they got together for dinner a couple weeks ago."

My nose scrunches at that bit of unexpected news. "They did?"

He watches me closely. "Yup."

"She never mentioned it," I mutter.

"You know Dad. He's always happy to spend time with her."

That hard truth makes the corners of my lips wilt. Poor Crawford. Even after the shit she pulled, he's still under her spell. Sometimes, I want to smack him upside the head and hope it knocks some sense into him where Pamela is concerned.

I'm almost afraid to ask but I have to know…

"Did he mention anything else?"

"Nope." He pops the P at the end of the word.

"Good." Relief radiates through me as the fist clenching my heart loosens just a bit.

Ford smirks. "Not interested in being steps again, huh?"

"Hell, no."

But it's way more than that. Crawford was devastated when Mom took off. For months, I lived in fear that my freshly ditched stepfather would announce that I was no longer welcome in his home.

Thankfully, that never happened.

But it's always been a concern.

One I can never quite banish.

Especially with the way she pops in and out of his life.

"Aww," Ford says. "Now you've gone and hurt my tender feelings."

I can't help but snort. "Tender feelings my ass."

He grins, one hand drifting to the middle of his chest, pulling my attention along with it. "What? It's true. I'm incredibly sensitive."

I roll my eyes.

If there's one thing I can say about Ford, it's that he's always been able to make me laugh. No matter what was going on in my life. It's one of the things that first attracted me to him. He has an easy-going personality that people automatically gravitate toward. Guys want to be friends with him, and girls want to belong to him.

For a night, a week, or longer.

I've watched that particular scenario play out hundreds of times before.

When he gave me his full attention, I felt special. Like he saw something in me that others couldn't possibly see. We'd hang out, talk, play games...

It's another reason why him icing me out had been so painful. I'd thought we were friends.

More than friends.

I'd thought it had been the beginning—

Those memories are all it takes for a thick protective coat of ice to harden my heart against the one person I've always secretly feared could crack it wide open.

There's no way in hell I'll allow Ford to hurt me for a second time.

Fool me once, shame on you.

Fool me twice and I deserve everything I get.

CHAPTER TEN

FORD

Say what you want about Carina, but the girl has never had a poker face. And she doesn't hide her emotions either. You always know where you stand with her. There's no subterfuge or games. It's one of the things I like most.

At this very second, numerous emotions are flickering across her expressive face, all trying to take precedence.

It's utterly fascinating.

And here I'd thought she would be happy about the possibility of our parents getting back together again but, if the pinched expression she's wearing is any indicator, that's not the case.

When she remains quiet, lost in the turmoil of her own thoughts, I allow my gaze to travel around her private space. It's a damn mess. There's makeup and clothing everywhere. Pictures and dance posters cover the walls. I pick up the smushy pillow with a face and stare at it.

Is it a cat?

A bunny?

Who the hell knows.

I drop it back to the bed before spotting a stack of paperbacks on the nightstand. I pick up the one on top and glance at the cover. The book is obviously beloved. Both the cover and pages are well worn.

Ever since I met Carina at fourteen, she's been an avid reader. The shelves in her bedroom at home are stuffed full of paperbacks. There have to be hundreds. She refuses to part with any of them. In high school, when I was out with friends, I'd stop at the local bookstore and pick one up I thought she'd enjoy. Then I'd leave it on her bed for her to discover. It's been a long time since I've done that.

Years.

Afterward, she'd always pop into my room to thank me. The expression on her face is what always killed me. It's like I'd given her the world.

I miss that.

Miss her looking at me that way.

I blink away those thoughts and stare at the guy on the cover. He's an okay looking dude…I guess. If you're into muscly guys with chests carved from marble and abs that border on the ridiculous.

Is this the kind of guy she's into?

Just as I'm about to take a closer look, the book is plucked from my fingers. My gaze shifts to Carina, who has scooched toward me.

I nod at the paperback. "I'm just as ripped as that guy."

"Yeah, I don't think so." She glances at the cover and studies it for a second or two. "I'm willing to bet *this* guy isn't even that ripped. The image is probably photoshopped."

"Bet?"

She arches a brow. "Huh?"

Her gaze flickers to mine as I roll from the bed and pop to my feet. My fingers grip the hem of my shirt. Her eyes widen as I yank it over my head and toss the cottony material onto the mattress. The muscles bulge as I flex my biceps. Ever since I was fifteen years old, I've been in the gym, lifting weights in order to get the body I want.

I'm proud of it.

Her gaze slides over my arms and chest before falling to my abdominals.

"All right," she mutters after a full minute of silent scrutiny. "So maybe you are."

A grin spreads across my face as I flex a few more times, wanting to keep her attention focused on me.

She points to the crumpled shirt. "You can put that back on now, He-Man."

Yeah…that's not going to happen. Especially with the way her pupils have dilated. The girl likes what she sees, even if she refuses to admit it.

When I bridge the gap between us with a single step, she lifts her chin to hold my gaze. I settle between her legs, forcing them wider. Her palms settle on my bare chest as her spine hits the mattress and I cage her in with my arms.

A potent concoction of confusion and lust swirl through her eyes as she searches mine for answers to questions that have yet to leave her lips. They're absolutely gorgeous in their intensity. Coupled with her long, blonde hair, toned athletic body, and smartass mouth, the girl is a fucking wet dream sprung to life.

I let it be known from day one when a few of my teammates mentioned what a hottie Carina was that she wasn't to be touched.

Or looked at.

Or spoken to.

All I had to do was headhunt a few guys during practice for it to sink in that I was in no way fucking around. It's been more challenging to keep the rest of the assholes at Western at bay, but I've done it.

Carina would probably kick my ass if she ever found out how many strings I had to pull to make certain she was not only on the same floor but right next door. It involved giving the apartment manager's kid a handful of private skating lessons as well as some Western Wildcats hockey merch.

Her breath catches, sounding as if it's become clogged at the back of her throat. "What are you doing?"

Instead of responding, I toss the question back at her. "What does it look like?"

She's a smart girl. She has to realize what's been brewing beneath the surface since the very beginning.

"Something we shouldn't."

My lips hover dangerously over hers. I can't stop thinking about the way she sat on my lap and rubbed herself against me like a cat in heat while we kissed the other night. Hands down, it was the single hottest kiss I've ever experienced.

And that's saying something.

It's not like I've led a chaste life up until this point. I've spent years trying to evict this girl from my head, but no other chick has been able to do it. I'm beginning to suspect that no one ever will.

I'm obsessed with Carina.

I always have been.

"And why is that?"

"Because…" Her whispered voice trails off.

Unable to resist the lure of her plush lips, my mouth drifts over hers in much the same way hers ghosted over mine in the studio. It's so damn tempting to take her the way I've dreamed about for years.

Fucking years.

"Because family and sex don't mix?" I ask.

A burst of surprised laughter escapes from her as humor flashes in her eyes. "Yeah…something like that."

I flex my hips until my hard length can slide against the V between her legs. It's a languid movement that has her pupils dilating until the black nearly swallows up the bright color.

"You got me pretty wound up the other day," I growl before nipping at her plump lower lip with sharp teeth. "I think you did it on purpose." When she remains silent, I grind against her for a second time. "Am I right?"

Instead of responding, her thighs widen, the long length of her legs tangling around my waist, anchoring me to her so that my cock is flush against her pussy. There's only a few pieces of clothing to separate us.

Fuck but her legs are muscular.

She could probably crack walnuts with them.

Why that image is so damn hot, I have no idea. I should be frightened. Not so turned on that I'm in imminent danger of going off like a shot.

"Maybe."

That's all the green light I need to proceed.

"Don't you think we should do something about all this pent-up sexual energy?"

When I arch my hips again, another wave of arousal crashes over me. The force of it nearly drags me to the bottom of the ocean where breathing becomes impossible. And the funny thing is when I'm with her like this, I don't care about propelling myself back to the surface. As long as Carina's in my arms, who needs oxygen to survive?

"Maybe I already do."

That's all it takes for my movements to still and my eyes to narrow. Even the thought of another guy laying his hands on her, touching her the way I dream about, drives me fucking insane.

"Who?" I bite out. "That fucko Justin?" If that turns out to be the case, I'll tear him limb from limb. It'll be an absolute pleasure.

Desire clouds her eyes when I grind myself against her again.

"No, I ended it after the party."

"Did you sleep with him? Did he touch you?"

"No."

"Good." A ridiculous amount of relief crashes over me.

"Are you hooking up with anyone right now?"

She studies me for a long moment, and I begin to wonder if she'll tell me that it's none of my damn business.

Which, technically speaking, is true.

"No." There's a beat of silence. "You?"

I can't stop myself from moving my hips again.

Fuck.

Fuck.

Fuck.

I want to tear off her clothing and drive deep inside the heat of her body. My cock is painfully hard.

Any second the tip will blow off.

"Nope."

Her expression turns skeptical. "No recent hookups?"

How the hell can I sleep with another girl when she's the only one who consumes me?

"It's been a while," I grudgingly admit. Before she can delve deeper and figure out how much power she holds where I'm concerned, I ask, "Truth or dare?"

There's zero hesitation on her part.

"Truth."

"Do you ever think about what it would feel like to have me buried deep inside your pussy?"

Other than the slight catch of her breath, she doesn't give anything else away. The longer she denies me a response, the more my nerves ratchet up.

When I can't take another moment, I growl, "Answer the damn question."

"Yes."

Just as surprise spirals through me, the door to the bedroom bursts open. There's a shocked gasp and then awkward silence as I remain in place.

"Daddy?" Ryder says in a voice that sounds ridiculously childish. "Why are you hurting Mommy?"

Carina squeezes her eyes tightly shut before swearing under her breath.

There's a thump. Ryder's grunt is followed by a soft chuckle.

"Sorry! I should have knocked," Juliette blurts before slamming the door closed again. Raising her voice to be heard from the other side, she says, "Go ahead and continue with whatever you two were doing!"

"Goddammit." Any arousal darkening Carina's pretty eyes is now long gone as she shoves at my chest and snaps, "Now look what you did!"

I reluctantly rise to my feet and point to the thick erection protruding from my jeans. "Maybe you should look at what *you* did!"

With a roll of her eyes, she grabs my shirt from the bed and tosses it at my chest.

One thing is for sure—the next time I see Ryder, I'll have to thank him for his untimely interruption.

With my fist.

CHAPTER ELEVEN

CARINA

With an aggravated huff, I shove Ford from my room and slam the door closed behind him. He can find his own damn way out of the apartment. Then I wait forty-five minutes, hoping Juliette and Ryder have taken off and we can talk about the unfortunate situation she walked in on another time.

Because I know damn well she'll have questions.

And comments.

Lots of comments.

Ones I don't particularly want to think about.

Or answer.

Ugh.

As the silence of the apartment settles around me, I crack open the bedroom door and creep into the hallway before peeking into the living room, which is exactly where I find Juliette camped out on the couch with a thick tome of a textbook spread open on her lap.

Damn. Looks like I won't be given a reprieve after all.

When her gaze collides with mine, she takes off her tortoiseshell framed glasses and sets them on the coffee table.

That's all it takes for awkward silence to descend. If it were possible to slink back into my room and quietly close the door again, I would. By the inquisitive look filling Juliette's eyes, that's not an option.

She'll hunt me down if it becomes necessary.

"So…you and Ford, huh?"

My shoulders wilt as I stalk into the tiny living room and throw myself on the chair parked across from the couch. "There's no me and Ford."

Can you even imagine such a scenario?

A thick shiver slides through me at the thought.

"Are you sure? Because that's not the way it looked to me."

"One hundred percent." I wave toward the scene of the crime, otherwise known as my bedroom. "We were studying, and one thing led to another."

She snorts out a disbelieving laugh. "Is that your story?"

Unable to sit still, I pop to my feet and pace the length of the couch. Juliette's gaze tracks every movement. "Yup. What you saw was nothing more than a lapse in judgement."

"All right, if you say so."

I spin around to face her, relieved that she isn't going to fight me on this. "I do."

"So…what would have happened if I hadn't barged in and interrupted?"

I can only stare as the casually-thrown-out question spins through my head like a top.

It's one I'm afraid to answer.

Especially when memories of the way he was able to rile me up so easily flood my brain.

But I can't tell her that.

Are you kidding me?

Of course I can't.

Barely am I able to admit it to myself.

"Nothing."

That's not what the voice at the back of my head is whispering.

All I can say is that the stupid, horny voice needs to shut the hell up.

"I need to get laid." My brows draw together as I mentally calculate how long it's been. When an answer doesn't immediately come to mind, I force out a laugh before dropping down onto the chair. "It's obviously been a while if I allowed Ford to lay his hands on me."

Except…it had felt so damn good.

Both times.

Do you ever think about what it would feel like to have me buried deep inside your pussy?

His question pops into my brain before circling around it viciously.

In a moment of weakness, I admitted the truth. I do think about what it would be like to have Ford buried inside my body. But there's no way I'd allow it to actually happen.

That would be the surest way to cause problems with Crawford. He's one of the most important people in my life and sleeping with his son would only complicate our relationship. It's bad enough that I have to worry about Mom fucking up the works at every turn.

That woman is a wildcard I have zero control over.

Now that rational thought has once again prevailed, the path forward seems perfectly clear. I need to keep my distance from Ford. It's not like I haven't been doing it for years. It was almost to the point where I could lock him in the back of my brain and forget about him completely.

For some unknown reason, that's no longer possible.

"Carina?"

I blink out of those thoughts and refocus on Juliette. "Yeah?"

Her expression softens as if she realizes I'm not only lying to her but myself as well. "You know I'm always here if you want to talk, right?"

I force a smile. "Of course. And I appreciate it."

When I say nothing more, she continues. "But there's nothing to talk about?"

The question hangs in the air between us.

For a heartbeat or two, I'm tempted to tell her everything before pressing my lips together and shaking my head.

"Okay." She reluctantly glances at the textbook on the coffee table. "Then I should probably get back to studying."

I pop to my feet, relieved this convo is behind us. "I'm heading over to the studio to work on my routine."

And if I'm lucky, I'll burn off some of this pent-up sexual frustration Ford stoked to life.

CHAPTER TWELVE

FORD

My gaze meanders to Ryder and Juliette who are seated across from me on the other side of the table. She's perched on his lap as they grin at each other like a couple of saps. Even though the music is loud, and the bar is packed to the gills, they're oblivious to it all.

It's only when a curvy body drops down on my thighs and slender arms loop their way around my neck that I blink back to the present and find Darcy Erickson smiling at me.

"You look entirely too serious for a Saturday night at Slap Shotz."

My lips quirk as I force a lightness into my tone that I'm not quite feeling. "Nah. Just taking it all in and letting my mind wander."

She presses closer until her warm breath can feather across my flesh. "We could always head back to my place if you're looking for a little peace and quiet."

Nope. That's definitely *not* what I'm looking for.

I shake my head and relax against the chair, attempting to create a bit of distance.

Darcy's a super nice girl. We've had a couple of business classes together and got to know one another. She'd park herself next to me during class whenever possible. Then she started turning up at our home games and the bar afterward to help celebrate.

I get the feeling that she's waiting for me to ask her out. Over the past few months, she's dropped a shit ton of hints. Like little breadcrumbs she's waiting for me to notice and pick up.

Except…I'm not interested in Darcy.

I'm not interested in anyone at the moment.

All right, that's not altogether true. There's one person I'm interested in. She just hates my guts.

And we're related.

Sort of.

"Thanks, but I'm good." I nod toward Wolf, who's lounging across the table. He radiates *leave me the fuck alone* vibes. "I'll never hear the end of it from that surly bastard if I take off early."

Disappointment floods her big brown eyes as she scrapes her lower lip with her teeth. I'm sure the look is meant to be sexy.

It has the opposite effect.

In fact, it's tempting to wrap my hands around her waist and physically remove her from my lap. There's only one girl I want taking up residence on my thighs and her name isn't Darcy.

That thought is enough to make me laugh.

Can you even imagine Carina perched on my lap and petting my chest like an overzealous groupie?

Fuck…that girl would be more likely to take a giant chunk out of me.

With her teeth.

We're talking full-on Hannibal Lector.

My gaze coasts over the crowd searching for the hot blonde. She showed up earlier with Ryder and Juliette. One look at me and she promptly spun on her heels and stalked away.

I shouldn't have expected anything less. She's been shaking her ass on the dance floor nonstop for the past hour.

I've always enjoyed watching Carina dance. I could—and probably have—done it for hours at a stretch. When we were in high school, I'd slip into the studio while she practiced. There was something about her graceful movements that never failed to soothe everything inside me.

She was like my own personal Xanax.

When I don't immediately find her, my brows pinch together, and I crane my neck, glancing around the bar.

"Ford?" Darcy presses closer, attempting to reclaim my distracted attention.

I force my gaze to hers. "Yeah?"

"Are you sure you don't want to get out of here?"

"Yeah, I am." As reluctant as I am to hurt her feelings, I don't want her to think I'm leading her on. "You understand that I'm not looking for anything serious, right?"

Her face falls as her gaze slides away. "Yeah, I do."

I've always tried to be upfront with girls when hooking up. Short of having them sign a disclosure form that states they fully understand this is a one-night encounter, I don't know what else to do.

And Darcy?

We've never actually screwed around because I know she's not looking for a couple hours spent between the sheets. She wants a boyfriend and for some reason, her sights are set on me. I'd almost feel better about the situation if she slept with a couple of the other guys on the team.

A flash of long blonde hair catches my attention and my head swivels so fast that I nearly give myself whiplash. Looks like Carina's hanging out at the bar. There's a bright smile on her face.

When was the last time she looked at me like that?

It's been years.

I'm so intent on staring at her that it takes a handful of seconds to realize that some dude is attempting to shoot his shot. Not only is he standing entirely too close, but he's playing with a lock of her hair, winding it around his finger as if trying to reel her in like a trout.

A punch of jealousy hits me square in the gut and nearly steals the breath from my lungs.

Oh.

Hell.

No.

Before I realize it, my hands wrap around Darcy's waist and I hoist her up, setting her on her feet before jumping to mine in one swift movement.

"Ford? Where are you going?"

This time, I don't bother glancing in her direction. I'm afraid if I take my eyes off Carina for one damn second, she'll disappear with this asshat before I can run interference.

And if that happens…

I don't even want to think about what I'll do.

Probably rip this town apart until I find them and beat him to a bloody pulp.

Fuck.

I drag a hand through my hair.

"There's someone I need to talk to. I'll catch you later."

And then I'm gone, pushing and shoving my way through the crowd. A few people call out my name, trying to catch my attention, but I ignore them.

I'm solely focused on Carina.

With the exception of the dick who's touching what belongs to me.

I wince. That thought is almost enough to stop me in my proverbial tracks.

But not quite.

As soon as I reach her side, I slip an arm around Carina and pull her close. I glare at the guy before reaching for his hand and tugging the thick strand free.

How dare he fucking touch her?

He blinks in surprise before his attention settles on me.

I give him a chin lift in greeting. It takes every ounce of self-control not to bare my teeth like a wild animal.

"What's up?" The question comes out sounding way more chill than I'm currently feeling.

"Ahh…nothing."

He's right about that. Absolutely nothing is going to happen here.

Eyes widening, he peers more closely at me before nearly shouting, "You're Ford Hamilton!"

My muscles loosen at the blatant hero worship that lights up his face. "Yup."

"You had one hell of a game last week! Didn't you score a hat trick?"

"Actually, it was just two goals," I correct modestly.

"That last one was sick! The way you deked out that defenseman and then hit the five hole." He shakes his head as if mentally reliving the play. "That shot won the game."

He's not wrong. That point was a tie breaker.

A slow smile curves my lips. Especially when I see the frown that morphs across Carina's face. He doesn't stop there either. He gives me an in-depth analysis of the last three games along with my stats and highlights. I should hire this guy for PR. He makes me sound fucking amazing.

Except…the more this guy gushes, the more irritated Carina gets. Her body has turned stiff as a board, which is a real contrast to how she felt lying beneath me the other night.

Unable to help myself, I turn my face just enough to catch a whiff of her floral scented hair before whispering, "Are you getting all this? Told you I was impressive."

"Please," she says with a grunt, attempting to untangle herself from my embrace. "You probably paid him to sing your praises."

My grip intensifies. If she thinks I'm going to release her now that I finally got my hands on her again, she couldn't be more wrong.

The look in her eyes confirms exactly what I suspected all along.

She's on the prowl.

Yeah, there's zero chance of that happening. I'll cockblock the shit out of her all night if I have to.

She turns her head enough to give me a full-on glare. "Can you please let me go?"

I slant a look her way before dropping a kiss against the crown of her head. "Absolutely not, pretty girl."

The guy glances at Carina in surprise as if he actually forgot she was standing with us before holding up both hands as if in surrender. "Sorry, Hamilton. I didn't realize she was one of yours. My bad."

Carina's eyes widen to the point of looking like they might fall out of her head as she opens her mouth to blast this idiot into next week. How it's possible for any guy to forget that this smoke show is standing next to them is beyond me. I couldn't be more attuned to this girl if I tried. All she has to do is breathe and I'm laser focused on her.

"No worries," I say, cutting in before she totally loses her shit.

Not that I wouldn't enjoy seeing her rip this guy a new one, but the last thing I want is Carina frothing at the mouth. She's already pissed that I've crashed her little party of two.

He shoots her a frown. "Why didn't you tell me that you're with Ford Hamilton? Not cool."

My grip tightens to hold her in place when her muscles stiffen. I'm half afraid she'll leap at him. "No worries, my guy."

That being said, he spins around and takes off, leaving us alone as a growl emanates from deep within her chest.

I rearrange her in my arms so that we're facing one another. "Now baby, you know I don't like when you flirt with other guys in front of me. It's disrespectful and hurts my feelings. We've already discussed how tender they are." I flick the tip of her nose with my finger. "Got it?"

When she bares her teeth, my shoulders shake with silent laughter. It doesn't take long before it spills from my lips.

"Dammit, Ford! That's not funny!" When her outburst only makes me laugh harder, she snaps, "You're such an ass."

"From where I'm standing, it's pretty damn funny. For a minute there, I thought I was about to witness a homicide."

"He's not the one I want to murder." Her narrowed eyes spark with irritation. "Why'd you cockblock me?"

That question is enough to have my good humor pulling a vanishing act as I drag her close enough for her soft curves to align with all my hard lines. "Because if you're looking for dick, it'll be mine."

"Are you seriously delusional? Why would you think that you

actually get a say in who I sleep with? The last time I checked, *I'm* the one who makes those decisions. Not you. *Never* you."

"We both know what's going on. You're still torqued up from the other day."

"The other day?" One brow slinks upward. "I have no idea what you're talking about."

"Nice try. I'm willing to bet we've both been thinking about it." There's a beat of silence. "I know I have." The admission is out of my mouth before I can stuff it back inside.

Surprise flickers across her expression before it's quickly shuttered away. If I weren't watching her so carefully, I would have missed it altogether.

"I'm going to be completely truthful with you." She reaches up onto the tips of her toes until her warm breath can drift across my lips. It's nothing short of intoxicating. "That sounds more like a *you* problem than a *me* problem."

"Is that so? Because it seems more like an *us* problem that needs to be solved pronto."

"Exactly how are we going to do that?"

My gaze drops to her lips. Any moment, the sexual tension shimmering in the air between us will explode, blowing the entire place to smithereens. "Why don't you take a guess."

Our gazes stay locked as she drops her voice. "We can't sleep together, Ford."

Desire rampages through my veins. It's so tempting to swallow up the little bit of distance that separates us. I want to hoist her into my arms and carry her out of here.

"Why not?"

"Because we're related."

"Actually, we're not." Then I tack on, "Not anymore."

"Crawford's like a father to me."

I jerk my shoulders, only wanting to shoot down every obstacle she attempts to throw in my path. "He doesn't have to know." There's a pause. "It can be our little secret. Just like when you used to sneak into my room at night and crawl into my bed."

Even in the darkness that floods the bar, it would be impossible to miss the color that stains her cheeks when I resurrect our past. It's never been something we openly discussed.

Especially afterward.

It's almost a surprise when she doesn't immediately shut me down. I was expecting more of a battle.

When she remains silent, I press forward, only wanting to secure her agreement. "It can be a strictly friends-with-benefits situation."

Her gaze flickers away and for a heartbeat or two, I wonder if I made a tactical error. But...

It's not like Carina wants to date me. Even the thought makes me want to laugh. She'd rather shank me in the eye than actually introduce me as her boyfriend.

Her cool gaze slices back to mine as she silently assesses me from under a thick fringe of lashes. Just as I shift beneath the relentless scrutiny of her gaze, she says, "Don't you mean frenemies-with-benefits?"

The easy-going grin I'd been wearing now feels forced and brittle around the edges. "You got it, sweetheart. That's *exactly* what it would be." I have no idea what propels me to take it one step further. I press my lips to her ear. "A little hate fucking could be cathartic for both of us, don't you think?"

Her body goes whipcord tight as she whispers, "Well, I do hate you."

If her response leaves me feeling hollowed out inside, I shove it away, unwilling to inspect it too closely. "So, we're on then?"

Anticipation coils deep inside me. All I want to do is lock her ass down tight. I want to know that for a few days, weeks, or whatever, Carina Hutchins belongs to me.

And me alone.

"I'll think about it and get back to you."

I pull away just enough to search her eyes. "No one else touches that pussy until I get an answer."

"You get to decide that as well, huh?"

"Yeah, I do. Do we have a deal?"

There's a long, drawn-out silence that ratchets up the thick tension between us until it becomes almost unbearable.

"I guess."

That's all it takes for my muscles to loosen and the air to leak from my lungs.

I'm one step closer to getting what I want.

One step closer to getting my hands on Carina.

CHAPTER THIRTEEN

CARINA

"How did I let you talk me into this?" I mutter as we walk away from the ticket booth.

Juliette throws an arm over my shoulders and tugs me close. "Because I promised to buy you a box of popcorn. And you're a whore for arena popcorn."

"You know me well," I reluctantly admit.

She flashes me a grin as her eyes dance with humor. My bestie is positively glowing and that has everything to do with Ryder McAdams. Her feet no longer touch the ground when she walks, and her head is always somewhere in the clouds. The girl is over the moon happy.

And who can blame her?

Ryder McAdams has always been a hot commodity on this campus, and she managed to lock him down tight.

Although, I'm pretty sure that it was the other way around. Ryder finally decided he'd wasted enough time and went after what he truly wanted.

Juliette.

His childhood neighbor.

My guess is that the blond defenseman had a secret crush on her for a while. Being teammates and best friends with her brother only complicated matters. But somehow, they worked through the obstacles in their way to find their happily ever after.

Am I jealous of what they have?

Nope. Not one damn bit.

All right, fine. That's a lie. I'm totally jelly. I've dated my fair share of guys during college, and none have lasted more than a couple of weeks. A month at the longest.

I've also had good sex.

But good sex and delicious orgasms can only take you so far. I've tried to make relationships purely based on phenomenal sex work. I've also learned the hard way that if you don't have much to say outside of the bedroom, it's basically like dragging a dead horse uphill.

Plus, I have the annoying habit of comparing the guys I date or sleep with to Ford.

They inevitably come up lacking.

As much as I've tried not to dwell on him, the guy is never very far from my thoughts.

If you're looking for dick, it'll be mine.

A tiny shiver dances down my spine as those words play through my brain on a constant loop.

That's probably the hottest thing anyone has ever said to me.

And it came from Ford.

My once upon-a-time stepbrother.

Am I tempted to take him up on the offer?

Of course I am.

Whenever we're together, the air around us becomes combustible and it's difficult to breathe. My core throbs a painful beat and my panties dampen. The urge to run my hands over him will pound through me.

His body is a work of art.

Chiseled and hard.

I might not have a problem lying to him, but the one thing I refuse to do is lie to myself. I've wanted Ford since the very beginning, and I've spent years tamping down those unwelcome feelings.

It's only when my bestie jostles me once we reach the rink that I relegate those thoughts to the back of my head. She waves to her family and her mom smiles, immediately rising to her feet and returning the gesture.

Juliette has the best parents. It's obvious that after all these years, they're still head over heels in love with one another. It's also equally obvious that their lives revolve around their children.

It's never been that way for me.

After how stressful my childhood was, I can't really blame Mom for wanting to focus on herself for a change. I just wish it didn't have to come at my expense. Those thoughts only make me realize how lucky I am to have Crawford. He came into my life when I needed him most and has been a solid presence ever since. He's the closest thing I have to a parent.

How could I even consider a choice that has the potential to damage that relationship?

That realization sinks inside me like a bolder.

"Hello, Carina! It's so good to see you again." Mrs. McKinnon pulls me in for a warm embrace. She's seriously the sweetest lady ever.

Her husband also gives me a quick hug. My guess is that Brody McKinnon is somewhere in his mid-forties. The man is seriously hot. There's just a bit of silver shot through at his temples.

Someone needs to explain why that's so sexy.

Because it totally is.

Once we settle in our seats, I lean closer to Juliette and whisper, "Have I mentioned lately just how foxy your father is?"

Her face contorts. Kind of like I just suggested we drown a sack full of kittens. It's the exact response I was aiming for.

"Please don't say anything like that ever again."

A smile blooms across my face. "What? I'm just saying that your mom's an *extremely* lucky lady."

"Ewww. I just threw up in my mouth. So, thanks for that." Before I can tease her any more, she threatens, "If you say another word about my father, I'm moving to another seat." When I open my mouth, she says, "I'm dead serious, Carina."

I shrug. "Sheesh. I was just trying to be complimentary."

"Well don't."

We both wave when Stella arrives with her father, John McKinnon. He also happens to be Brody's father, but there's a huge age difference between the half siblings. Which, in a weird little twist, makes Stella Juliette's aunt.

Since they're the same age and grew up together, they're more like cousins. Stella is besties with Riggs, one of the guys on the team, and attends most of the games along with the hockey parties.

Juliette nudges me just as the action is about to get underway. "Hey, isn't that your stepfather?"

My gaze slides around the packed stands until it lands on Crawford. I pop to my feet and wave, knowing how much it'll mean to Ford that his dad came to support him. As soon as he sees me, a wide smile breaks out across his face.

"Who's the older guy and girl with him?"

That's the exact moment I realize Crawford isn't alone. It doesn't take long for recognition to crash over me. Peter Bowman, his business partner. And the younger woman with sable-colored hair at his side is Jaclyn, his daughter. We've worked together in the office over the summers. We got along well enough and grabbed lunch most days. This isn't the first game they've attended, but it's been a while. Probably years. The reason for their sudden appearance at the arena hits me like a ton of bricks.

My eyes narrow.

Didn't Ford mention the other night that his dad is trying to hook him up with Peter's daughter?

That's all it takes for a tight fist to wrap around my heart until sucking in a full breath becomes impossible.

As they draw closer, I keep my smile pasted in place. I hug Crawford and shake hands with Peter. Jaclyn is busy glancing around the large space with interest. She's wearing a bright red jacket with a soft, inky-colored knit hat. Both her hair and makeup are perfect. It looks like she's been airbrushed.

She squeals before throwing her arms around me and hugging me tight like we're long-lost sisters. Both teams take their place on the ice and the puck gets dropped. Movement explodes as the centers fight for possession. Her eyes light up as Crawford points out his son.

I can't help but gnash my teeth before resettling in my chair.

It quickly becomes apparent that Jaclyn knows absolutely nothing about hockey as she peppers him with a ton of questions throughout the first and second periods. It's equally obvious from her over-the-top reactions that she's onboard with the idea of being set up with Ford.

Then again, what girl in her right mind wouldn't be?

From the corner of my eye, I take Jaclyn in for a second time.

She's totally his type.

Pretty with big boobs. And from what I remember, she loves to party.

These two are a match made in construction company heaven. They can have little Hamilton-Bowman Construction Company babies.

Ugh.

That thought gnaws at my insides and is enough to make me sick with jealousy.

And I hate it. Hate that he's able to affect me this way. I shouldn't care who Ford sleeps with or dates. I don't want to feel anything where he's concerned.

And yet…I do.

That realization is enough to rob the air from my lungs.

Why now?

Why is this happening now?

We've spent the past three years attending the same university, and I've been so good about keeping him at arm's length. Even when I discovered that we were next door neighbors.

I made it a priority to steer clear and for the most part, my efforts worked.

Family dinners with Crawford have been more sporadic during previous years. This fall, he's tried to set aside time on a weekly basis for the three of us to get together.

Instead of getting lost in the action unfolding on the ice, I continue to stew, barely paying attention when goals get scored. It's almost a shock when the buzzer rings throughout the arena signaling the end of the game.

"Damn. That was a real nailbiter," Juliette says. "Didn't you think so?"

I glance at the scoreboard to see that the Wildcats won by a single goal.

"Definitely," I say lightly, not wanting to admit that I've been stuck inside my head for the past three hours.

How embarrassing.

Not to mention pathetic.

For just a moment, I stare at my bestie and contemplate telling her about Ford's offer. My plan before the game had been to turn him down flat and then avoid him for the foreseeable future.

Now however...

My gaze reluctantly shifts to Jaclyn as she reapplies her lipstick before giggling at something Crawford said.

Christ...is she's seriously flirting with a man her father's age?

This girl has no shame.

That's the moment I realize that my plans have taken a one-eighty. A mixture of nerves and excitement explodes at the bottom of my belly.

It'll be just like he said—no-strings attached sex.

We'll do it a few times, get it out of our systems, and then it'll be over with.

I can just imagine what Ford will be like in bed. He's a pretty boy who's always been chased after. He's never had to work to get a girl's attention. He probably expects his partner—*or partners*—to do everything.

I've been with guys like that.

It gets old fast.

The last thing I want to do is get myself over the finish line *after* getting some dude off. The more I think about it, the more sense it makes. Deep down in a place I'm loath to admit, I've secretly wondered what it would be like to have sex with Ford. Now I can do it and put all the burning questions to rest.

I'm sure once or twice will be more than enough.

It takes a while for our group to filter out of the packed arena. The Wildcats hockey games are always popular and well attended. Not only with the students at the university but the town as well. People come from all over the state to watch the action. Most fans head out the double set of glass doors and into the crisp night air, but some hang around in the lobby, waiting for the players to get released from the locker room.

We stand in a loose group with Juliette's parents, Crawford, Peter Bowman, and his daughter. I probably should have expected them to stick around so they could say hello to Ford, but it still irritates me.

I just want them to take off.

My fingers twist together as questions flood my brain.

What if I'm too late and he changed his mind?

It's no secret that I've been dragging my feet about giving him an answer.

I saw Ford in class yesterday and in a surprising twist, he didn't press me for a decision. I thought that was kind of odd at the time but maybe...

Maybe he's over it.

Over me.

I nibble my bottom lip, all the while trying to figure out a course of action as the players filter out of the locker room. Air gets clogged in my lungs as I search each new face, looking for Ford.

It's only when all of the players have trickled out that I decide to take matters into my own hands.

CHAPTER FOURTEEN

FORD

I tip my face toward the hot spray of water and allow it to wash over me. As much as I tried to keep my attention solely focused on the game, it was difficult with Carina in the stands. The moment I stepped onto the ice, I spotted her blonde head.

I was so fixated on her that it took a while to realize Dad was also there.

Along with Peter Bowman and his daughter.

A disgruntled sigh escapes from me. I'm not looking forward to walking out of the locker room. I'll probably get roped into a late dinner. Even though I made it perfectly clear that I have no intention of getting involved with Jaclyn, I should have realized Dad would take matters into his own hands. He's been pushing me toward her for years.

"Get a move on it, Hamilton," Bridger calls out. "You're hogging all the hot water."

"I'll be out when I'm damn good and ready," I shout back.

My hope is that if I dawdle long enough, they'll take off without me.

It's probably wishful thinking on my part.

Dad has visions of cementing his business partnership with a marriage between their children and keeping everything in the family. It's fucking medieval, if you ask me.

It takes another five minutes for the rowdy voices to fade until there's nothing but the sound of running water to echo off the tile. Only then do I twist the handle and the heavy spray turns into more of a trickle. I thrust my hands through my wet strands, shoving them away from my eyes before grabbing a towel from the neat stack and drying my face. After everything else has been wiped down, I wrap the damp material around my waist.

I turn the corner and skid to a halt when I spot Carina loitering near a bank of black lockers. I blink, wondering if I've conjured her up out of thin air and it's nothing more than a fever dream. Lord knows I've thought about her enough over the past couple of days for my mind to play tricks on me.

Our gazes stay locked as the air around us turns charged. Expectant. I've never experienced this level of explosive chemistry with anyone else before and it's addictive.

"Yes."

That one word is like a punch to the gut.

No further explanation is necessary.

"When?" The question shoots out of my mouth and is more of an impatient bark.

With a jerk of her shoulders, she leans against the lockers. Unable to keep my distance, I prowl closer. It's as if there's an invisible string drawing me to her. The lure is impossible to resist.

Combustible energy wafts off her in suffocating waves.

It's so fucking intoxicating.

Enough to make my eyes cross.

And it goes straight to my dick.

Even though she remains in place, her eyes track every movement as I close the space between us. When I'm about three feet away, she straightens to her full height. Her posture is no longer casual. It's as if she suddenly realizes there's nowhere for her to go.

Nowhere to run.

She's trapped and at my mercy.

Exactly where I want her.

When I move forward, invading her personal space, she tips her chin upward to hold my gaze as her palms settle on my bare chest as if to hold me at bay.

Doesn't she realize that nothing and no one can keep me away from her?

Her voice dips. "If we're really going to do this—"

"Oh, it's happening."

There's not a fucking doubt in my mind.

She swallows, the delicate column of her throat working with the movement. "Then we need to have some rules in place."

"Rules?" The word comes out sounding foreign. I jerk a brow. "What kind of rules?"

When her tongue darts out to moisten her lips, my gaze drops to the movement. Unable to help myself, I nip at the plump flesh.

"This isn't a relationship. It's strictly dickly."

Even though I thought the same damn thing myself and presented it that way, I don't like hearing it from her.

"Fine," I reluctantly bite out. It's so damn tempting to argue. "Next rule."

"No having sex with other people while we're together."

I haven't slept with anyone in months. There hasn't been an urge. Well, there has but only for one specific girl. If I couldn't have her, there wasn't any point in fucking other people. I've spent most of college doing exactly that. It's only now that I realize it didn't work. Carina is like an infection running rampant through my bloodstream. I'm hoping a taste of her sweetness will be the antidote I need.

"Not even flirting," she tacks on, eyes searching mine.

Little does she know that I would have secured the same agreement from her. Otherwise, there'd be a lot of beatdowns going on.

Cameron Lee would have been the first on the list. The dickhead is still trying to get with her every class period.

"Yeah, fine."

"And we keep this on the downlow. No one else needs to know what's going on."

I flex my shoulders in an attempt to shake off the growing tension. "Why?"

"Because it's weird." She rolls her eyes as if I'm too dense for words. "Everyone thinks we're actually related."

"Who the fuck cares what everyone else thinks?"

Her expression flattens as she mutters, "We both know your father wouldn't like it. The less people who know, the better."

True enough. I suspect it's the reason why he's decided to push Jaclyn my way.

"Fine. So basically, I'll be your dirty little secret. Is that what you're telling me?"

Guilt stains her cheeks as she glances away. "It's not like that."

"Isn't it, though?" I press closer until my mouth can ghost across hers.

"No."

The way her warm breath drifts over my lips is enough to drive me insane. I haven't been able to stop thinking about the taste of her. When I can't stand another moment, I slant my mouth over hers and my tongue sweeps across her lips.

Once.

Twice.

Three times before she finally allows me inside.

And then we're fused together as I pin her body to the cold metal.

I don't like her rules one damn bit, but if it's the only way I can have Carina, then so be it.

It's only when it feels as if my lungs are on the verge of oxygen deprivation that I pull away to stare into her eyes. Her pupils look blown, and her eyelids have lowered to half-mast.

Fuck but she's sexy.

I bet this is exactly how she looks when she comes undone.

More specifically, it'll be the expression on her face when *I* make her come.

With my tongue.

And my dick.

And any other way I decide to get her off.

Only now do I realize how impatient I am to get my hands on her. Unfortunately, that's not going to happen in the locker room.

As tempting as it might be.

"Know what I'm going to do now?" When she shakes her head, I murmur, "Ruin you for all other guys."

The haze clouding her eyes dissipates as I take a reluctant step in retreat. If I don't, I'm liable to start something I won't be able to finish. The first time I have Carina won't be in a smelly locker room. And it certainly isn't going to be rushed for fear of getting caught. I'm going to take my sweet damn time and savor every inch of her.

She lifts her chin. "That's not possible."

With a smirk, I yank off my towel. "Challenge accepted."

CHAPTER FIFTEEN

CARINA

My gaze drops to his cock.

Holy shit.

He's huge.

And the more I stare, the longer and thicker his erection becomes.

"See something you like, pretty girl?"

I don't have to look at the expression on his face to know there's a smile curving his lips. It all but simmers in his deep voice. I open my mouth to snap out a pithy retort, but absolutely nothing comes out. I'm drawing blanks.

How embarrassing.

I'm usually quick on my feet and can give just as good as I get. My brain is screaming for me to look away but that's not going to happen anytime soon. It's like I've discovered a new species.

On Mars.

Before there's any real possibility of jumpstarting my brain, he wraps his hand around the thick length and slowly strokes himself.

My eyes widen.

My mouth turns bone dry.

And my knees grow weak.

Any moment, I'm going to sink to the tile floor.

A gasp may or may not have just escaped from me.

I've never seen anything so hot as Ford touching himself. I can't help but wonder what it would feel like to wrap my lips around the girthy head, drawing him into my mouth before taking him deep. The idea is more tempting than expected.

What would he do if I dropped to my knees and opened my mouth wide?

The way his tightly clenched fist moves upward before stroking down the hard length is nothing short of mesmerizing.

How often does he get himself off?

Does he think of me?

The ache building deep in my core turns almost painful.

When was the last time I was this aroused?

I don't remember, but it probably had to do with Ford.

Just when I can't take another moment of this sweet torment, his fist loosens, and he releases the stiff member. He looks excruciatingly hard.

Swollen.

The tip is a mottled purple hue.

As if he'll explode any second.

I can't believe how much I want to see him come undone by his own hand.

What could be sexier than that?

My gaze flickers to his in question as a whimper of need works its way up my throat. It's tempting to beg him to continue.

He jerks his head toward the metal door that leads to the hallway. "You should go."

What?

No way.

How can I leave now?

Better question—how can he just stop?

"Ford," I rasp, unable to help myself.

"Go." His voice turns gruff. "We wouldn't want anyone to see you coming out of the locker room, right?"

Some of my arousal recedes at the sharp edge that bleeds into his words.

He sounds angry.

What I don't understand is the reason for it.

Confusion churns inside me. I'd assumed he'd be happy about my decision. Hell, I'd thought maybe we'd get it on in the locker room. It's always been a fantasy. Hot, quick, and dirty against the lockers with the thrill of getting caught to heighten the experience.

My brows jerk together as I attempt to play mental catchup. At every turn, he's throwing me off my game. I don't like it.

"You want me to leave?" I wince at the disappointment that floods my tone.

"Yup. I need to get dressed."

Oh.

Um, okay…

My gaze reluctantly drops to his cock. It's still ridiculously hard. In fact, it's pointing right at me.

I gulp down my disappointment and force my feet into movement. It's tempting to close the distance between us and wrap my fingers around him, but there's no way in hell I'm going to do that.

I refuse to beg.

Especially Ford.

As I reach the metal door, his deep voice stops me in my tracks.

"Just remember, pretty girl—you belong to me now. That pussy is mine."

Another wave of arousal crashes over me.

I glance over my shoulder to meet his eyes. He has yet to move. He's still naked, every muscle coiled tight as if he'll spring into motion any moment. Is it pathetic that I'm standing here with bated breath, waiting for him to lay hands on me?

I smirk, wanting to provoke him into action. "You'll have to prove it. Many have tried but none have succeeded."

His eyes narrow.

Instead of waiting around for him to make a move, I slip from the locker room, abruptly ending the conversation. The cool breeze of the hallway slaps at my overheated cheeks. Only now do I realize how humid the air had grown inside the enclosed space. Although it has nothing to do with how inflamed I'm feeling.

That can be squarely laid at Ford's feet.

Who knew he had such a mouth on him?

Can't say I don't love a dirty talking hero.

I have to remind myself that Ford isn't the hero of my story. He's just a guy who I'm going to fuck.

Since my legs are still shaky, I lean against the cement wall beside the door and squeeze my eyes tightly closed, attempting to clear my head so I can once again think straight.

Except when I do, an image of Ford dances behind my eyelids.

A very naked Ford.

Thick and hard.

A groan works its way up my throat.

"Carina? Are you all right?"

Jolted from that disturbing image, my eyelids spring open and I find Juliette watching me with a concerned frown. Since my brain isn't exactly firing on all six cylinders, it takes a second or two to realize that she's patiently waiting for an answer.

I clear my throat, hoping my voice comes out sounding unaffected. "Yeah, it's all good."

She points to a door further down the hallway. "I was just on my way to the bathroom."

The ache between my legs continues to thrum an uncomfortable beat. Ford's unexpected dismissal has done nothing to stomp out that particular fire.

Unfortunately, there's only one way I'm going to find relief.

"Me, too. I need to rub one out."

She blinks before her eyes widen. "I can't tell if you're being serious or not."

"One hundred percent serious." I pat my little cross-body purse. "Thankfully, I brought my trusty vibe with me. See? What did I tell you about horny days and public restrooms?"

Her lips form a shocked little O as she retreats a step as if I'm contagious and she's trying to avoid the spread of infection. "You know what? I'm gonna hold it."

I shrug and push away from the wall. "Suit yourself."

With that, I hightail it to the bathroom.

If Ford is under the misguided delusion that I'm going to spend the rest of the night all hot and bothered thanks to him, he couldn't be more wrong.

CHAPTER SIXTEEN

FORD

I saunter into the lecture hall and immediately spot Carina in her usual seat before beelining in that direction and dropping down beside her. Cameron walks through the door a few seconds later and glares when he sees that I've already staked my claim. I flash him a gloating grin.

If he knows what's good for him, he'll finally get the hint and stay the fuck away from her. She gives me a bit of side eye but otherwise doesn't say a word. After the way I left her hanging in the locker room, I kind of figured this would be her reaction. She seemed surprised when I told her that she should leave.

Her list of rules pissed me off.

Should it have?

Probably not.

I'm not looking to announce to the world that I plan on boning my ex-stepsister. Although, it's not like either of us have anything to be ashamed of. We're consenting adults who can do whatever the hell we want.

Namely, each other.

When I glance toward the front of the room, Dr. Betsworth smiles before getting class underway. The woman has turned out to be a shameless flirt. Not to mention persistent. She keeps trying to get me alone after class and so far, I've been able to avoid it. I have the feeling that it's only a matter of time before my luck—and excuses—run out.

Carina grumbles something under her breath that I can't quite make out before straightening on her chair.

Is it possible that she's jealous?

Hmmm…it's an interesting thought.

It's almost tempting to flirt back with our professor just to see how much I can wind her up. Except, I've never been one to play games and I certainly don't want to start with Carina.

Instead, I stretch out my legs and manspread just enough for our knees to touch. A sizzle of electricity zips through me at the innocuous contact. Her wide gaze slices to mine. After a second or two, she shifts, moving away so that we're no longer resting against each other. The loss is instantaneous.

She sits coiled tight.

Her shoulders hunched.

It's tempting to reach out and massage them until she softens.

Midway through the class, her body finally loosens as she jots a few notes and continues to ignore me.

I fucking hate when she does that.

Carina is a lefty. Her other hand rests on her desk as her fingers curl ever so slightly. Her nails are neat and trimmed without polish. I like that she doesn't wear acrylics or anything fake. She's unapologetically herself.

I don't realize that I've reached out and wrapped my fingers loosely around hers until her gaze flickers in my direction. She scrutinizes me for a heartbeat or two as air gets clogged in my lungs waiting for her to pull away and leave me hanging.

It's a surprise when she doesn't.

When it comes to this girl, I tend to tread carefully and keep my hands to myself. She's like a chainsaw. The last thing you want to do is lose a limb because you've been fucking around.

As soon as Betsworth dismisses us for the day, Carina grabs her stuff and shoves it into her backpack. I do the same. Like hell I'll allow her to bolt. When she flees the small lecture hall, I'm right on her heels, dogging every step. It's a surprise when she wraps her fingers around my wrist and bulldozes her way through the crowded corridor. When we come across an empty classroom, she drags me inside.

Once we're alone, she releases her tight grip. Her palms press into my chest as she propels me backward until my spine hits the wall. Her glare turns ferocious.

Damn if it doesn't turn me on.

Is that perverse?

Probably.

There's absolutely nothing normal about my feelings for her.

There never has been.

With most girls, I have to stare down at them.

That's not the case with Carina.

All right, maybe a little bit. But the height difference isn't as great as some of the other people I've been with. There's about six inches to separate us instead of a foot or more.

I like the height on her.

I like the long, lean lines of her body. Especially the graceful way she's able to move them when she dances.

I blink out of those thoughts when she stabs a finger into my chest. "When are we going to sleep together?"

My brows shoot up at the unexpected question.

Is she actually *impatient* to have sex with me?

Has hell frozen over, and I'm the last to know?

I never actually thought this day would come.

Did I dream about it?

Damn right I did.

Most of the time, I don't think she can stand me.

Actually, it's probably way more than that.

The difference here is that she *wants* me.

Me.

The thought makes me a little bit giddy. Her eyes narrow when a chuckle slips from my lips.

"Don't worry, pretty girl. Your pussy will get exactly what it needs but that doesn't mean I can't drive you a little crazy before I take you." My voice drops as she sways closer. "When you're all achy with need and crying for relief, only then will I fill you up until you can't take another damn inch."

Her nostrils flare at my dirty words. Her voice is breathless when she mutters, "Then I'll just use my vibe."

My hands shoot out, wrapping around her elbows before tugging her forward until the tips of her breasts are smashed against my chest. Electricity zips through me at the points of contact. I angle my head until my mouth can ghost over hers without ever quite touching. Her breath catches as she tips her face toward mine as if trying to swallow up the distance between us.

We hover in suspension until thick tension crackles in the air.

Instead of leaning into the touch, I retreat.

That's all it takes for a whimper of need to escape from her.

"Did you really think you could throw out all those rules and I wouldn't come up with one of my own?"

The thick haze filling her eyes dissipates.

"You ready for it?" There's a pause. "No masturbation while we're together."

"What?" Her mouth drops open in shock. "No way! You can't do that."

"Sure, I can." I drag her just a bit closer until I can feel the hammering of her heart. "If you want to masturbate, it'll be in front of me." As if that's not enough, I add the clincher that will really send her temper skyrocketing, "But only when I give you permission to do it."

"You're out of your damn—"

I shake my head. "Sorry, that's the way this little arrangement is going to work, pretty girl." My voice drops a few octaves. "I bet after the other night, that's exactly what you went home and did."

"Actually, I took care of myself in the bathroom at the arena."

That image alone is enough to give me wood.

"Damn, I would have loved to see that."

She juts out her chin. "Too bad. You don't get to watch me masturbate."

A slow smile curves my lips. "Oh, we'll see about that."

When she grumbles, I release one of her elbows and snake a hand between us until it settles against her pussy. When her pupils dilate, I stroke my fingers against the seam of her lips.

"I agreed to your rules. Do you agree to mine?"

Another whimper explodes from her.

"Don't worry, it'll be worth the wait. *I'll* be worth the wait."

When she presses her lips together, refusing to answer, I nip her bottom one between my teeth, tugging on the plump flesh before sucking it into my mouth as I continue rubbing her center. It's a constant barrage of pleasure that will only fan the flames of her desire.

"I need an answer, Carina. Or you can forget about my dick."

When she arches into my touch, my fingers fall away, leaving her bereft.

Her body sags against me as if she no longer has the strength to hold herself up. "I think you're trying to torture me."

Damn straight I am. By the time I'm finished, she'll be owner specific.

"All you have to do is tell me what I want to hear."

"Fine."

"Good girl."

She inhales sharply as her pupils dilate.

This girl couldn't be more fucking perfect if she tried.

It shouldn't surprise me that she likes to be praised. As fiery and scrappy as Carina can be, at the end of the day, she needs someone to gently stroke her hair and tell her what a good girl she is.

And I'm just the man for the job.

When I'm confident that she won't sink to the floor, I release my grip on her arm before slipping around her and taking a quick step in retreat.

She turns to watch me. "So…that's it?" Her voice bristles with indignation. "You're just going to leave me hanging *again*?"

Our gazes stay locked as I continue backing away. Once I reach the threshold, I pause. Her cheeks are heated and even though she's agitated, arousal sparks from her eyes. It takes every ounce of willpower not to shove her against the wall and take her right here in the empty classroom. I don't care who walks in and sees us. My desire for this girl borders on the obsessive.

If I don't claw back a small shred of control, she'll walk all over me.

"Yup, that was the plan."

"You're a real jerk," she snaps, eyes spitting fire.

"Probably." I flash a grin. "But I'm a jerk you want between those pretty little thighs."

A small screech erupts from her as I slip from the room.

It's better to escape before Carina finds an object to throw at my head. Say what you want about her, but she's got one hell of an arm. If she wasn't so passionate about dance, she probably could have played softball. Luckily for me, the hallway is deserted, so no one's around to witness me adjust my junk.

I never realized just how much I enjoy winding her up.

The unintended consequence is that I'm doing the same damn thing to myself.

And there's only so much more I'll be able to take before finally claiming what's mine.

CHAPTER SEVENTEEN

CARINA

Holy crap.

Did that actually just happen?

I can only stare in disbelief at the empty doorway Ford disappeared through.

Exactly how did he gain the upper hand in this relationship?

I wince.

This is in no way a relationship.

It's screwing.

Plain and simple.

Well…at some point in the not-so-distant future, that's what it'll be.

I hope.

Right now, it's a whole lot of pent-up agitation.

When was the last time I felt like this?

I rack my brain, but nothing immediately jumps to mind. In the past, when I wanted to sleep with someone, I did it.

What's the point of waiting or playing games?

And when the relationship inevitably ran its course, I moved on. Although, I have to admit, there's something to be said for the anticipation that's flooding through me, ramping me up, turning my insides to a quivering mess. Then again, it would probably be best to sleep with the guy and just get it over with.

All right…maybe not *get it over with* per se.

But it would be in our best interest to douse the flames that continue to flare to life and get back to what we should have been from the very beginning—stepsiblings.

Or ex-stepsiblings, as the case may be.

Even when we were fourteen years old, there was something that simmered between us. As we became friends and spent more time together, the sexual tension grew until it turned oppressive. I'd assumed he snuffed it out senior year of high school. Little did I realize that it's been clawing beneath the surface this entire time, waiting to burst free.

And here I'd thought that Ford would jump at the chance to fuck me. Especially after I gave him the green light to proceed in the locker room.

But no.

My brows draw together.

I don't like this.

Not one bit.

It takes another handful of minutes to fight my way free of the sexual haze that's fallen over me and glance at my watch.

Ugh.

Now I'm late for class.

Damn Ford.

I hustle over to Wilson Hall, where the music, dance, and theater classes are housed. It's right next to the auditorium. When I rush in late, huffing and puffing, my instructor shoots me a look full of displeasure. I flash an apologetic wave and strip down to my leotard before getting to work. Two hours later, my muscles feel malleable, and my mind is blissfully clear. That's exactly what dance does for me. I'm able to work my body over until it's exhausted and in the process, it frees my mind, allowing it to soar.

It's what helped me through my childhood when I'd stress about where we were living, Mom's job at the restaurant, or our finances. Dance saved me. It never failed to transport me to a magical place.

As I slip into my jacket and glance at my phone, a message from Juliette pops up, reminding me that we're supposed to meet for lunch at the Union in five minutes. I swear under my breath before asking her to pick me up a sandwich. Then I grab my bag and race out the door, down the hall, and into the bright sunshine. Even though there's a distinct chill in the air, the cool breeze feels good against my overheated cheeks.

It takes another ten minutes to haul ass across campus before I step foot inside the Union. Since it's noon, the place is alive with activity. Everyone is buzzing around, searching for a table to settle at.

My gaze combs over the sea of students, landing on a bunch of rowdy guys from the football team. Well...maybe that's not altogether true anymore. Once upon a time, they were nothing but womanizing players. Ever since senior year started, they've fallen one at a time, slowly becoming domesticated.

Who would have suspected that when we came in freshman year, that they'd all get snatched up?

Trust me, the girls on this campus cried their little hearts out when Rowan Michaels, Brayden Kendricks, Easton Clarke, Carson Roberts, and Crosby Rhodes were taken off the market.

My attention settles on Brayden. No one can deny that he's a real heartbreaker. He's hot enough to give Ford a run for his money. The thought is enough to make me smile.

Sydney Daniels, his soccer-playing girlfriend, flashes a grin and waves when she catches sight of me. We had a business class together freshman year and lived on the same floor in the dorms. I make a mental note to give her a call sometime soon so we can get together. I miss hanging out with her.

After returning the gesture, I search the crowded area for Juliette. Just as I catch sight of her dark head, our gazes lock and she gives me a cheery smile. As I beeline in her direction, a few other girls gravitate toward the empty table. Stella, Viola, and Fallyn. I've only met Viola and Fallyn recently. They're cousins who live together in an apartment off campus. Viola transferred to Western at the beginning of the school year.

From what I've noticed, she likes to keep a low profile and doesn't party. Unlike Juliette, who stays in and studies most weekends, I get the feeling there's something else holding her back. But I don't know her well enough to dig deeper. My guess is that she'll open up on her own when she's comfortable.

I greet the girls before dropping down onto a chair with a huff. Only now that I'm off my feet do I realize how exhausted I am.

"Hope you don't mind a turkey and Swiss on toasted ciabatta bread," Juliette says, sliding the sandwich and a can of sparkling water toward me.

"Have I mentioned how much I love you?" I say with a contented sigh. Already my mouth is salivating. After two hours of dance, I'm famished.

"Nope, not today," she says with a smile.

"Well, I do. And don't you ever doubt it."

I dig into my sandwich as the other girls do the same. We talk about classes and how the semester is half over, which seems crazy. Senior year is flying by. Before I know it, graduation will be here, and we'll all be moving on with our lives.

At least, Juliette, Stella, and I will. Viola and Fallyn are juniors.

Midway through lunch, Stella waves to a girl with gorgeous caramel colored hair that falls down her back in soft waves. She has bright green eyes that dominate her face. As soon as Stella grabs her attention, the girl flashes an infectious smile and beelines toward the table.

She gestures toward the newcomer. "This is Britt. She just started at Western."

We all introduce ourselves before Stella encourages her to pull up a chair and join us. Then we scootch over to make room. There are a lot of girls at this university who are cliquey. Juliette, Stella, and I have never been that way.

"It's nice to meet you, Britt. Are you a freshman?" Juliette asks.

My guess is that she's a transfer. She looks older than someone straight out of high school. As I study her more closely, I realize there's something familiar about her face, but I can't put my finger on it. I'm almost positive that we've never met. More than likely, I've seen her around campus.

"Technically, yes. I took a few years off after high school to work and figure out what I wanted to do with my life."

"That's cool," Fallyn adds. "What are you majoring in?"

"Psychology. I'd like to be a therapist."

"You know what they say about people who go into psychology—" Fallyn says, who's studying the same thing.

"That they're really just trying to figure their own shit out," Britt finishes for her.

They smile in understanding.

Already I can tell that these two will be fast friends.

"Yup," Fallyn says.

"Unfortunately, it's not a lie." The wattage of Britt's smile dims. "My family can be pretty extra. It'll take years for me to unpack all that baggage."

The other girl sobers. For just a second or two, darkness flickers in her eyes before it's immediately banished. "Same girl. *Same.*"

Before the mood can take an unexpected turn, Stella glances around the table. "Why don't we have a girls' night out? It kind of sounds like we could all use one."

"I'm definitely up for it," Fallyn says before glancing at her cousin. "What about you? Think you're ready to come out of hiding yet?"

Viola's eyes widen before she smacks Fallyn in the arm. "I am not in hiding."

"Sure, you aren't," Fallyn replies dryly.

Dull color seeps into Viola's cheeks. "The engineering curriculum here is more challenging than I expected. I'm still trying to find my bearings."

"Damn girl," I say. "You must be one smart cookie." I nudge Juliette. "Just like the brainiac over here. Thankfully, I'm done with all my general ed curriculum. The bio classes were almost enough to make my brain explode."

My bestie bumps me in return. "I'm in if you are."

"Sure, I could use a night out."

Especially after the way Ford heated me all up.

Stella beams. "Great. Let's plan to meet up at Blue Vibe on Friday."

CHAPTER EIGHTEEN

FORD

My gaze bounces around the first floor of the house even though I'm pretty sure I won't find who I'm searching for. There's no way she'd show up on her own.

Even if she was horny as hell.

Can't say that I didn't enjoy revving up her engine the other day. It only makes me impatient to get my hands on her again.

Shifting on the chair, I drum my fingers against my knee as tension continues to coil inside the pit of my belly. As tempting as it is to pull out my phone and fire off a text to find out where her ass is, I refrain.

Trust me, it's no easy feat.

For the first time when it comes to that girl, the ball is in my court. I want to savor it for as long as possible. I have no idea how I managed to wrestle control of the situation away from her, but thank fuck I did.

Can you even imagine Carina Hutchins practically on her knees, begging for my dick?

Me neither.

So yeah...I'm just going to sit back and enjoy this rare occurrence. I've never known Carina to beg a guy for anything.

The steady drumming on my knee continues as I scan a new set of faces, disappointed when I don't find the one I'm looking for.

Damn.

Where the hell is that girl?

No, seriously. Where is she?

I probably should have made that a rule. From now on, she discloses her location at all times.

I tilt my head to one side and crack the joints, hoping to relieve some of the pressure gathering like a storm inside me. When that doesn't work, I look for a distraction. Something that will get my mind off of Carina.

Tonight's turnout is lowkey. Instead of throwing a massive party, it's just a bunch of guys from the team hanging out, playing video games, and knocking back a couple of cold ones.

Coach Philips scheduled a team meeting after a freshman player got totally shitfaced and then proceeded to get busted by campus police. He skated everyone until five of the younger players threw up and the rest of us were on the verge of passing out. By the time I made it back to the blue line, spots were dancing in front of my eyes. Over my dead body was I dropping like a wet-behind-the-ears freshie.

Unfortunately for Clint Peters, his ass is now on probation, and he'll be riding the pine for the foreseeable future. Unless he's able to do a one eighty and turn things around, there won't be a place for him on the roster next year.

I glance at Ryder, who's sprawled out on a small loveseat, watching a couple guys play NHL. "Where's your better half?"

The question shoots out of my mouth before I can stop it.

The last thing I want is for Ryder to figure out why I'm asking.

Like I need to catch shit from this guy?

Nope, don't think so.

"Ewww," Maverick McKinnon, Juliette's younger brother says from the armchair shoved in the corner.

I snort. He's still trying to wrap his head around the fact that his best friend and teammate is now dating his sister. If I weren't so preoccupied by the blonde dancer, I'd take this opportunity to give him a little shit.

Ryder rolls his eyes. "You really need to get over it, man."

"I'm trying. But watching you two suck face doesn't help matters."

Ignoring the comment, Ryder glances at me. "She's out with the girls. No dudes allowed."

"Oh?" My brows rise at this newly gleaned bit of information. I had no idea.

I impatiently wait for him to add more details, but he remains silent, gaze locked on the television screen. This is where the situation gets tricky. As much as I'd like to interrogate the guy, I don't want to rouse suspicion.

So, I drum my fingers on my knee and give it a few minutes before casually dropping another question. "I assume Carina's with her?"

A slow grin moves across Ryder's lips as a knowing glint sparks in his bright blue eyes.

Busted

"Yup." He cocks his head. "Jules sent a few pics. Looks like they're having a blast at Blue Vibe."

Blue Vibe?

She'd better not be having too good a time.

"What was that?" he asks, popping a brow. His voice has turned positively giddy.

Fuck. I didn't realize I'd muttered the comment out loud. I really need to get my shit under control.

Attempting to buy a little bit of time, I tip the bottle of beer to my lips and take a long swig before responding. "Didn't say a word."

Ryder strokes his chin. "Huh. I must be hearing things."

"You should really get that checked out," I mutter.

He smiles like the asshole he is. "I'll be sure to do that."

"That club is a meat market. You're not worried about her?"

Damn.

I really don't know when to stop, do I?

"Nope." He pops the P at the end. "'Cuz I know exactly who she's coming home to at the end of the night." He taps his chest. "This guy."

"For fuck's sake," her brother grumbles from across the room. "Can you just stop? I liked it better when you two ignored each other. This shit is brutal."

Colby breaks away from the girl he's kissing long enough to say, "If I'd known it would bother you so much, McKinnon, I would've made a play for her years ago."

Maverick gives him a one-finger salute. "Like she'd give your ugly ass the time of day. The girl has standards, and you don't meet them."

"Bet?" He glances at Ryder before grinning. "You know I don't mean it, McAdams. I'm just giving McKinnon a little shit."

All of Ryder's previous humor dies a quick death. "Say another word about Juliette and we can take this up on the ice."

Unperturbed by the threat of bodily harm, Colby goes back to making out with the raven-haired chick sitting astride his lap. Five minutes later, a brunette settles beside him and attempts to get in on the action. I'm half wondering if a fight will erupt when one girl pulls the other toward her for a long lip lock.

Colby grins as he runs his hands over both of them.

I can only shake my head before glancing around the living room. He's certainly not the only guy getting busy. And there's more than one couple who've already shed their clothing. Some of these people have no problem putting on a show. And hey, if that's what you want to do and it's consensual, go for it.

I'm not going to lie—it's one of the reasons I avoid the couch. The damn thing would probably glow like a Christmas tree under a black light.

Even the thought grosses me out.

When I catch Bridger's gaze, he gives me a chin lift. Instead of kicking back with a cold one, he's nursing a bottle of water.

I don't bother to ask what his deal is.

I already know.

Hell, everyone at the university does.

Last weekend, Bridger laid low and there was still another message blasted out Monday morning. After his ass was chewed out by his father, Coach pulled him aside to discuss the situation. I feel bad for the guy. Bridger's always kept his nose clean when it came to shenanigans. Whoever's behind the text messages must have a real ax to grind with him because it's causing a shit ton of problems.

Those thoughts are cut off when one of the girls Colby is making out with moans.

And that would be my cue to call it a night.

Alone.

CHAPTER NINETEEN

CARINA

"Here's to being a bunch of badass bitches," I shout, attempting to be heard over the pulsing beat of techno as we clink our shot glasses of tequila together before tossing them back. The liquor burns a fiery trail as it slides down my throat.

"Holy crap, that's terrible!" Juliette sputters, coughing as tears gather in her eyes. "Don't ever make me do that again."

With a laugh, I immediately order another round. My bestie brings the second one to her lips before slyly throwing the golden liquid over her shoulder when she thinks no one's paying attention. She's lucky it doesn't land on someone.

Tonight is turning out to be epic. All the girls showed up. Even Viola who, according to Fallyn, can give Juliette a run for her money in the studious department. Those two have spent a lot of time talking about the STEM courses they've taken throughout the years. Once it gets too deep, I shut them down before they officially kill the buzz I've been working on.

I twisted Juliette's arm and poured her into a little black dress that hugs all of her curves. Her hair has been straightened and her makeup is on point. Her newly minted boyfriend is going to lose his mind when he sees her at the end of the night.

You're welcome, Ryder McAdams.

Since I don't have anyone to go home to, I'm hoping to relieve some of the pent-up sexual tension brewing inside me by dancing my ass off. In hindsight, it was a mistake to give into Ford's little game of truth or dare. I've unwittingly been drawn into a frenemies-with-benefits situation where I've yet to get any D.

How's that for ironic?

It's the reason I'm wearing a short, sparkly dress that clings to every curve. I'm not nearly as voluptuous as Juliette but that doesn't mean I'm not gonna shake what my mama gave me. My hair is all long and loose and floats around my shoulders in soft waves.

I glance at Fallyn, Viola, Stella, and Britt. They all look seriously hot. And I'm certainly not the only one who thinks so. There's been a ton of guys sniffing around, offering to buy us drinks and trying to pull us out onto the dance floor.

After the way Ford left me hanging in the classroom, it's exactly the balm I need.

We've turned down all the shots, not wanting these dudes to take that as a silent invitation to join us and have only danced with a select few.

When a popular song with a great beat comes on, I grab Juliette and Stella's hands and drag them to the dance floor. "Come on! Let's get out there!"

The six of us shove our way through the crush of bodies before carving out a space for our group. It doesn't take long before my hands are rising above my head, and I lose myself in the music. My eyelids feather closed as I tip my face upward, enjoying the sensation of letting go and allowing my mind to wander.

It shouldn't be a surprise when Ford pops into my thoughts. As soon as I realize that he's slyly snuck into my mental space, I shove him away and refocus on my friends and the good time we're having. This isn't something we do nearly enough.

One song bleeds into the next as we continue to shake our asses. At one point, I grab Juliette's hand and twirl her around. A smile lights up her face as she laughs. I know how challenging her course load is and how hard she works to earn top grades each semester. It's nice to see her cut loose and have fun for a change. Now that she and Ryder are together, it happens with more frequency. He's drawn her out of her shell, and she seems happier. There's more of a balance to her life.

After about thirty minutes, Britt, Viola, Stella, and Fallyn head to the bar for something to drink. A couple songs later, Juliette disappears to use the restroom. It doesn't take long for her to get swallowed up by the writhing mass of bodies. And then I'm alone.

The club is a large, dark space with strobe lights that flicker from high above. It's difficult to tell whose limbs belong to whom. The music reverberates off the cavernous walls before slowly seeping into my bones. It's all too easy to lose myself in the rhythm as the DJ mixes beats. Alcohol rushes through my system, making me feel alive and free.

If only it were possible for this feeling to last forever.

Or, at the very least, until the end of the night.

My eyes fly open when large hands settle on my hips and drag me against a hard body. I twist around only to find a burly guy I don't recognize. He invades my personal space until the strong scent of alcohol is enough to knock me out.

"Hey, can I borrow a quarter?" The question comes out sounding all smushed together and barely coherent.

If there's one thing I can't stand it's drunken assholes.

Before I can tell him no, he slurs, "I wanna call my mom and tell her that I just met the girl of my dreams."

I roll my eyes and shove him away.

"Not interested," I yell over my shoulder before turning my back to him.

If I'm lucky, that'll be enough of a—

His hand locks around my arm, the fingers biting into my bare flesh as he spins me around.

The smile curving his lips falls away. "There's no reason to be a bitch. Can't you see that I'm trying to be nice?"

This is him *trying* to be nice?

Ugh. Sometimes I just don't understand the male species.

Like at all.

"Apparently there is," I shout to be heard above the insistent thump of the music. "I'm not interested in you or your cheesy pickup lines. So…we're done here." I shoo him away with my hand. "Now be gone."

His mouth twists into a snarl. When he attempts to drag me closer, I jerk my arm, trying to break his iron hold. It's like I'm caught in a steel trap. Had I been smart, I would have kept my big mouth shut and quietly slipped through the crowd, but this kind of behavior is tiring.

I'm not someone who enjoys causing a scene, but I will if I have to. And this has definitely turned into one. As I wind up to punch this guy in the face, a deep voice says from behind me, "If you value your life, you'll release her right the fuck now."

My gaze swivels toward the familiar voice, only to lock eyes with Ford. Not that I couldn't handle this jerk on my own, but a wave of relief crashes over me that I don't have to.

Drunk dude glances at him before scowling. "This doesn't involve you, buddy. So beat it."

A steely glint enters Ford's eyes as he straightens to his full height, which is just a few inches taller. The murderous expression on his face is one I recognize. There have been a half a dozen times, especially in high school, that he's given the same look to other guys who couldn't take no for an answer. Some of those confrontations ended in beatdowns. He always came out on top, but that didn't mean he didn't get scraped up in the process. At the end of the night, we'd go home, and I'd carefully tend to his wounds.

Not wanting the situation to escalate into a physical altercation, my palm settles on his chest in order to keep him at bay.

Ford's arm snakes around my waist before he hauls me against the solid strength of his body. "That's where you're wrong. She already told you that she isn't interested and for some strange reason, you're unwilling to accept that answer."

When Ford closes the distance between them, drunk guy has to lift his chin to maintain eye contact. His fingers burn through the thin fabric of my dress as he holds me close. It wouldn't surprise me to find his handprint singed into the flesh beneath.

A permanent reminder of him.

As if that's necessary.

I've done my damnedest to evict him from my brain and nothing has ever done the trick.

"Now, if you'd like, I'll back off and let her finish this. But I can tell you what will happen in case you're interested— you'll either get smoked in the face or she'll go for your nuts." Ford jerks his chin toward me. "She's not the type of girl who'll put up with shit from a drunk asshole."

The guy's lips flatten into a tight line as he glares at Ford and then me. "Are you calling me an asshole?"

I didn't think it was possible for the slurring to get worse.

Apparently, I was wrong.

"If you can't figure that out for yourself, then it's time to call it a night."

Drunk guy staggers a couple of paces before shaking his head. "Fuck this. No pussy is worth this much hassle."

I blow out a relieved breath as he stumbles off through the gyrating crowd. "What a jerk."

He snorts as the tension gripping him finally loosens. "Yup."

Now that it's just the two of us, Ford repositions me until I'm crushed against his front. I can't help but inhale the scent of his woodsy cologne.

"You look fucking hot, Carina. I really hope you didn't come here looking to get laid," he growls in my ear before nipping the delicate flesh with his teeth. "We had a deal. Do I need to remind you that there are rules in place?"

I pull back just enough to meet his eyes. "I came to dance."

He presses me so close that I feel the thickness of his erection against my lower belly.

"Anyone could see us," I murmur, glancing around. There are tons of students from Western who frequent this club.

"I don't give a damn. I just need to hold you. It drives me insane when other guys lay their hands on you."

His possessiveness sends a sharp thrill spiraling through me, and I give into the urge, slipping my arms around his neck.

"That dress should be illegal," he growls in my ear.

The press of his body against mine feels so damn good. It would be all too easy to lose myself in him. None of the guys I danced with made my belly flutter the way Ford does.

Always has.

His fingers splay wide across my backside, sinking into the material. "We should get out of here."

Deep down inside, I know that leaving the club with Ford is a terrible idea.

One I'll regret in the morning.

Instead of telling him no, I hear myself say, "Okay."

When he pulls away, the warmth of his body disappearing, a strange sense of loss crashes over me. His larger fingers lock around mine as he tows me through the sea of gyrating people. As we leave the dance floor behind, I spot my friends at the bar. It's a relief when none of them notice us slip away.

I'll shoot Juliette a text and let her know that I took off, so she doesn't worry.

I'm not ready to answer questions about Ford.

Mostly because I have no idea what to say.

CHAPTER TWENTY

FORD

With Carina's hand locked securely in mine, I wind my way through the crowd and head to the exit at the back of the building. I'm still pissed off about the guy who was harassing her.

It was so damn tempting to give him a beatdown that he wouldn't soon forget, but I knew it would upset Carina and I didn't want to go there. Even though there've been times in the past when I stepped in to defend her against clowns who were getting overly aggressive, I know she's more than capable of taking care of herself. I've seen her in action. Back in high school, she kneed a dude before I could punch him in the face.

I've never been prouder of anyone in my life.

Chilled night air wafts over us as we're swallowed up by the darkness. When the Corvette comes into sight, I click the locks before opening the passenger side door and hustling her inside the vehicle. Only then do my muscles loosen.

After rounding the hood, I slip in beside her and punch the ignition button. That's all it takes for the sleek sports car to roar to life. And then we're zipping out of the crowded parking lot and onto the street before heading toward campus. Carina relaxes against the plush leather as alt rock fills the cabin. Even though my gaze is trained on the ribbon of road beyond the windshield, I couldn't be more aware of her presence.

It just feels right.

Like she belongs here with me.

My gaze flickers to the short sparkly dress and the way it rides up her thigh. A couple of inches more and I'd be able to glimpse her panties.

Fuck.

Even the thought makes me pop wood.

Her long legs are toned and muscular. I can't imagine what they'd feel like wrapped around my waist as I drive deep inside the welcoming heat of her body.

Or maybe I can and that's always been the problem.

Because I shouldn't be.

She's always been off-limits.

Before I realize it, my hand settles on her bare leg, the fingers wrapping possessively around it, sinking into the warm flesh. When she glances at me, I wonder if I've made a tactical error, and she'll knock it away.

A heartbeat passes.

Then another.

Tension gradually leaks from my body when that doesn't happen. Instead, her thighs part ever so slightly. It's so damn tempting to slide my fingers upward, yank her panties to the side and bury my fingers in her tight heat.

It doesn't take long before I'm swinging into the parking lot of our building and cutting the engine. When I shift, I find her steady gaze already pinned to mine. Even in the darkness, it feels like I could drown in her liquid blue-gray depths. The way she stares, studying me as if she sees way more than I'm comfortable with. More than what I project to the outside world. Even my teammates, who I consider brothers, don't know me the way this girl does.

There's something about that undeniable truth that both calms and terrifies the hell out of me.

"Be honest. Did you go to Blue Vibe looking for a hookup?"

There's a moment of silence. "No. I just wanted to dance and have fun."

Everything loosens within me. "Good."

I fucking hate the idea of anyone else touching her.

Touching what belongs to me.

Her gaze dips to my lips as she angles her body toward mine before pressing closer. The moment our mouths brush, electricity hums through every cell of my being, making me feel more alive than anything else ever has.

Even hockey.

It wouldn't take much for this fire to burn out of control.

I pull away just enough to say, "We should probably head inside."

She blinks in surprise before narrowing her eyes. "Know what I think?" She doesn't give me a chance to reply before answering her own question. "That you're deliberately trying to torture me."

I huff out a laugh. The idea that I turn her on or could drive her so crazy is hilarious.

Her brows pinch together when she realizes that I'm serious. "Why can't we just take care of business?"

"Business, huh? Is that what this is?"

"Aren't you the one who said this would be a friends-with-benefits situation?"

That's exactly what I said.

Instead of acknowledging the truth, I volley the question back at her. "And I believe you're the one who said it was more of a frenemies-with-benefits kind of thing."

She slants a brow. "Well, isn't it?"

Maybe she considers me a frenemy, but that's never been the case for me. Pushing her away and keeping her at a distance was the only way to cope with the loss of her.

"I don't think so."

Before she can ask any more questions, I exit the vehicle. She does the same and we meet on the sidewalk before heading to the entrance of the building. When she wobbles in her sky-high heels, I slip my arm around her. I'll latch onto the flimsiest of excuses to keep her close. There's something about the feel of her willowy form pressed against me that just feels right.

Silence descends as we take the elevator to the third floor. Every second that ticks by has the sexual tension intensifying until it feels as if it'll blow us both to bits. When the doors finally slide open, I steer her into the hallway.

The place is surprisingly quiet for a Friday night.

When we arrive at her door, she pulls out the key from her purse before slipping it into the lock and twisting the handle. Instead of heading to my own apartment, I trail in after her. It's like there's an invisible string connecting us to one another. After all these years, I've never found a way to snip it. I don't know if that's even possible or if I'll be tethered to her forever.

Her purse gets tossed on the table in the combo dining/living area before she steps out of her heels. My mouth turns cottony when her fingers slide through the long mass of her silky hair, and she arches her back before meeting my eyes. A sly smile tips the corners of her lips.

"Who's trying to drive who crazy now?" I ask, surprised by the rasp that fills my voice.

Her smile morphs into more of a mischievous grin. "Only trying to do us both a favor and hasten things along."

The sultriness of her response has my cock stirring in my jeans.

She reaches around and fiddles with the clasp on her silver necklace before setting it down on the table next to the glittery little purse that matches the dress. The dangly earrings soon follow.

She gives me the long line of her back before glancing over her shoulder until our gazes collide. "Help me with the zipper?"

A groan rumbles up from deep within my chest as I eat up the distance between us. "Yeah."

My fingers shake as I sweep the thick length of her hair to the side before wrapping them around the tiny silver zipper and slowly dragging it downward. The grind of metal teeth is all that can be heard in the shadowy silence of the apartment. Air gets clogged in my lungs, making it difficult to breathe. My greedy gaze licks over her freshly exposed skin the second it's revealed.

It's like unwrapping a much-anticipated gift on Christmas morning.

As I reach the middle of her spine, I realize that she isn't wearing a bra. There's nothing but smooth, unblemished flesh as far as the eye can see. By the time I reach the small of her back, I'm so fucking hard that I could punch a hole through the wall.

My hands tighten as I force myself to retreat. The urge to rip the tiny dress from her body pounds through me like a steady drumbeat until it's the only thing I'm cognizant of. She must feel the thick tension that vibrates off me in suffocating waves as she steps away, just out of reach before throwing another sly look over her shoulder.

"Thanks." Her voice is light and airy as if she's completely unaffected.

Before I can pounce, she silently pads into the bedroom. I can't help but track her every movement. There's nowhere she could lead that I won't follow.

It's no longer a conscious choice on my part.

Maybe it never was.

As soon as I step over the threshold, she releases her hold on the sparkly material and lets it fall. The fabric slithers down her body before puddling at her bare feet, leaving her in nothing more than a sexy black thong.

"Truth or dare," I rasp, teetering on the edge of insanity.

When she turns toward me, I'm treated to a full view of her body.

Fuck but she's gorgeous.

As much as I want to keep my gaze pinned to hers, that's impossible. My attention dips to her breasts. They're high and tight with tiny, blush-colored nipples. My mouth waters for a taste. I want to lick and suck them.

"Dare," she says, just like I knew she would.

"You want a little relief?"

Her pupils dilate as she notches her chin upward. "You know I do."

"Okay." I jerk my head toward the queen-sized bed. "I want you to use your vibrator in front of me."

She stills as her expression freezes. "What?"

A slow smile lifts the corners of my lips as I wrestle back a tiny bit of control. Knocking Carina off balance has always been a pleasure. "You heard me the first time. I want to watch you come."

"You…don't want to have sex?" Confusion bleeds into her tone.

"Of course I do, but not just yet." I need to draw this out as long as possible. What I'm most afraid of is that she'll cut everything off between us as soon as I pull out.

That's not something I can allow to happen.

She releases a steady breath. A mixture of emotions flash across her face. She's so damn expressive.

I love it.

Love when I force her to think and feel.

"I've never done that in front of anyone else before," she says cautiously.

Good.

"There's a first time for everything, right?"

Carina gnaws her lower lip before her gaze resettles on mine. "Fine."

Straightening her shoulders, she beelines for the nightstand before tugging on the slender drawer and taking out a small black case. Once it's been popped open, she plucks out a slim, tube-like device that's a couple inches in length with a rounded head. Then she settles on the mattress before reclining against the stack of pillows.

Her gaze stays locked on mine the entire time. For just a moment or two, we hang in silent suspension.

Barely am I breathing.

My gaze slides down her body to the part of her that's still covered by a thin scrap of black satin.

"Take off the thong," I growl.

My voice is nothing more than a croak.

The vibrator gets set on the nightstand as both her hands drift to the slender band circling her hips. She slips both index fingers beneath the elastic strip before making an arcing motion.

A potent concoction of impatience and anticipation swirl through me, heightening the need that claws at my insides.

My fingers tighten, the short, clipped nails biting into the flesh of my palms. Three strides would have me at the bed. It's tempting to rip the damn thing off her body myself. Before I can do the honors, she slips the fabric down her hips and thighs before tossing it to the side. And then she's gloriously naked.

My gaze arrows to her core as she spreads her legs wide.

The sight is almost enough to bring me to my knees. She's more beautiful than I imagined. Her pussy is shaved perfectly bare. She hasn't even touched herself yet and a tortured groan rumbles up from deep within my chest.

"Fuck, Carina…"

She smirks. "I'd love to, but you keep turning me down."

A snort escapes from me. She has no idea just how much restraint that requires.

Her thighs fall open even further until her lower half resembles the shape of a butterfly as her knees touch the bedspread. "If I didn't know better, I'd think you didn't want me."

"Nothing could be further from the truth," I rasp. "I want you more than anything."

Doubt flickers in her eyes before it quickly vanishes, leaving me to wonder if it was there in the first place. I've only ever known Carina to be strong and confident. A force to be reckoned with. It's one of the qualities that drew me to her. There's a sexiness about someone who understands their own self-worth and refuses to accept anything less than what they deserve.

That's Carina Hutchins in a nutshell.

Her hands stroke over her inner thighs. "Still want me to use the vibe?"

"Yeah."

Fuck, no. I want to slide right inside her and stay there forever.

Without another word, she rolls to the side and grabs the slim device before clicking the button. A low hum fills the air as her hand drifts past her toned belly to the V between her thighs. She runs the slender wand down one side of her lips before stroking up the other to the top of her mound. With a light touch, she buzzes her clit before repeating the maneuver for a second time.

On the third pass, she dips the black device inside her pussy. Her spine arches as her eyelids feather closed and moisture glistens on her delicate pink lips.

My mouth waters for a taste of her sweetness.

Just one damn taste.

Then I could die a happy man.

I don't realize that I've closed the distance between us until I'm sinking onto the mattress near her outstretched legs. Unable to resist the urge any longer, my fingers stroke up one muscular calf before repositioning it so that I have an unobstructed view of her core. Her eyelids spring open and her gaze fastens onto mine.

"Do you like watching me?" Her voice comes out sounding breathless. Already I know that it wouldn't take much to nudge her right over the edge and into oblivion.

The truth is out of my mouth before I can stop it. "There were times in high school when I'd hear you in your room, getting yourself off. Listening to you come always made me so damn horny. I'd go in the bathroom and rub one out. I'd imagine what you looked like with your legs spread while you played with yourself."

I've carried that around with me this entire time like a dirty little secret. It feels good to finally come clean.

Her pupils dilate as she spreads herself wider. Years of dance have made her limber.

Flexible.

The way she's able to contort her body is enough to make my head explode.

Both of them.

"Show me how you'd touch yourself," she whispers.

I groan, unsure if I'll be able to hold back from sinking inside her body if I actually do it. It would be like teetering on a razor thin edge. And yet...

I'm so fucking hard. My cock throbs a painful beat in my jeans.

And I want to.

I want to share this moment with her.

Decision made, I flick open the button before dragging down the zipper. My fingers delve into the cotton of my boxer briefs, yanking down the material until my erection can spring free. A hiss of breath escapes from me at the slightest touch.

When was the last time I was this hard?

I can't remember.

Although, I'm sure it had to do with the girl spread out like a fucking feast in front of me.

Her gaze drops to my shaft as she uses the little black vibe to pleasure herself. I shove the jeans down farther, needing room to maneuver. A groan breaks free from me as my grip tightens and I slide my palm along the thick length.

The entire time I touch myself, my gaze stays pinned to her slick lips.

A whimper escapes from her as she arches off the mattress. The movement has her breasts thrusting upward. The sound is like a shot straight to the dick and my balls tighten against my body.

Barely have I stroked myself and already I know that it won't take much for me to—

When another cry falls from her lips and her pussy spasms, flooding with moisture, I rise to my knees and thrust my hips forward as thick ropes of cum erupt from the tip of my cock, decorating her lower abdomen. A guttural groan tumbles from my lips as my head falls back and an avalanche of pleasure crashes over me, nearly burying me alive.

It's so damn intense.

Any moment, I'll black out.

My orgasm seems to last forever as her breathy sounds fill the room.

When the last little shudder racks my body, my muscles slacken, every bit of energy drained away. It takes a herculean effort to lift my head and meet her gaze.

The deep satisfaction that fills her heavy-lidded eyes only reinforces my own. My attention drops to the thick white cum that paints her toned belly. Something primal floods my being that I've finally marked this girl as my own. I've spent years wanting to do it. It's a mental snapshot that will live in my memory until the day I die.

Nothing will ever erase it.

Possessiveness rushes through my veins, infiltrating every cell of my being.

To see her covered with my jizz is almost enough to have me stiffening up again.

I don't realize that I've reached out to run my fingertips through the mess until she sucks in a shuddering breath. My movement stills as my gaze slices to hers. For a second or two, neither of us dare to breathe as she bows her naked body as if making a sacrifice of herself.

A growl falls from my lips as I smear the cum around her skin before scooping up a small dollop and leaning forward until I can reach her breasts. I massage the thick cream around one nipple before doing the same to the other. I want to coat her entire body with it.

I want every guy she comes into contact with to scent me on her and know that she's taken. It's a fucked-up thought, but it's there just the same.

My finger returns to her belly to collect the last precious drop before lifting it to her lips. Her gaze stays pinned to mine as they part without prodding. I slide the digit into her mouth. As soon as I do, she clamps down on my finger, her tongue swirling around it, sucking every pearly drop.

This is exactly what it would feel like if those plush lips were wrapped around the head of my cock. It wouldn't take much for her to suck the cum right out of the tip. Hot licks of need burst to life inside me. It doesn't matter if I've just blown my load. Already I'm stirring to life and stiffening up. My dick wants inside that drenched pussy. I want to fuck until I can extinguish the blinding desire that riots beneath the surface.

But I refuse to give into the need that's consumed me for years.

At least not yet.

I want to draw this out until I'm so fucking wild that when I finally take her, it blows both of our worlds apart. Only then will I be able to relegate Carina to the back of my brain where she belongs and move on with my life.

CHAPTER TWENTY-ONE

CARINA

In silence, Ford rises to his feet and tucks himself back inside his jeans before taking a hasty step in retreat. I'm still coming down from that amazing release, floating somewhere in the stratosphere. Even though he wasn't buried deep inside my body, it was still one of the most intense orgasms I've ever experienced. My brain is still fuzzy around the edges, making it impossible to think straight.

It's the only reasonable explanation as to why that one word pops out of my mouth as he takes another quick step toward the bedroom door.

"Stay."

His feet ground to a halt and his brows slant together. His gaze stays locked on mine as he carefully sifts through it. Surprise flickers across his face. I'm sure my expression mirrors his own.

It's carefully that he asks, "You want me to stay the night?"

Air leaks from my lungs as I turn the question over in my brain. It only takes a second of introspection to realize what I want. Deep down, I miss the way it used to be. All the nights I'd sneak into his room after our parents went to bed. The way he'd wrap his arms around me. My head would be pillowed against his chest as I listened to the comforting beat of his heart. With the velvety darkness blanketing us, we'd talk about our hopes and dreams for the future. I never felt safer than when I was held securely in his arms.

In hindsight, it seems strange that I would feel that way since Ford was only eighteen years old. But I can't deny the truth. I knew he'd never allow anything bad to happen to me.

And he didn't.

A heavy silence falls over us.

When he doesn't immediately agree, it occurs to me that I made a mistake.

Is there anything worse than sounding like a needy bitch?

Ugh.

Why did I have to open my big fat mouth?

I should have allowed him to quietly slip from the room.

Just when I'm about to tell him to forget it, his fingers settle on the hem of his T-shirt before he drags it up his chest and over his head. He drops the material to the carpet before flicking open the button of his jeans for a second time tonight and lowering the zipper. The thick denim gets shoved down muscular legs until he's standing in nothing more than a pair of black boxer briefs.

My gaze licks greedily over him.

How could it not?

Ford has the body of a Greek god. He's sun kissed and sculpted from hours spent on the ice and in the gym.

I don't bother with pajamas as I slide beneath the sheet and comforter. He settles beside me before stretching out and pulling me to him. It takes a moment for my muscles to loosen as my head settles against his chest. The scent of his woodsy aftershave wraps around me, cocooning me in the past.

If I closed my eyes, I'd be right back there again.

To a place where we were friends.

Our relationship always teetered on the edge of something more, bursting with possibilities.

At least, that's the way it felt.

The mere sight of Ford could send my pulse skyrocketing and my hormones into a tailspin. We spent hours kissing and touching, never pushing the limits, but I always assumed that Ford would be my first.

I wanted him to be my first.

But that never happened.

It was like the flick of a light switch. One day we were close and the next, he was cold and distant. He refused to talk about what prompted the change, leaving me to figure it out on my own.

End of story.

After that, I never allowed another guy to know me the way he did.

The way he probably still does.

"Tell me what you're thinking about," he whispers, warm breath stirring my hair.

My gaze stays pinned to the far wall filled with hundreds of pictures from high school and college as memories of our past crash over me like a wave. It's tempting to lie, but there's something about being held securely within his arms that compels me to be honest.

"That it's been a long time since we've done this."

"February of senior year." His voice turns somber as if I'm the one who pushed him away and broke his heart.

"Yeah."

"I've missed holding you," he admits softly.

I squeeze my eyes tightly closed and try to keep my voice level. "I've missed it, too."

Questions flood my brain. They sit perched on the tip of my tongue. Instead of allowing them to burst free, I bite them back and swallow them down again.

There's no reason to bring them up.

This isn't anything more than sex.

If I'm lucky, we'll knock boots and that'll be the end of it. We can put all this behind us where it belongs.

"Carina—"

"After all that dancing, I'm really tired. Do you mind if we just go to sleep?"

There's a moment of hesitation before he tugs me even closer. "Yeah. Sure."

That's exactly how I drift off.

Locked up tight in his arms while listening to the steady thump of his heart.

CHAPTER TWENTY-TWO

FORD

It's the bright sunlight filtering through my eyelids that has me gradually surfacing from the best sleep I've had in a while. It's only when I shift that I become aware of the warm body curled up against mine. I rack my brain, wondering what the hell happened last night and who I took home.

Well…not home.

Because I don't bring girls back to the apartment. If I fuck, it's at their place. Or a room at a party.

Another thing?

I never stay the night. That sets a bad precedent.

Maybe I'll stick around and cuddle for fifteen minutes or so, but as soon as they fall asleep, I sneak away like a thief in the night and hope like hell that when I run into them on campus, there aren't any hurt feelings.

I'm not going to lie—sometimes there are. I've had my ass chewed out in front of a handful of people on more than one occasion.

It takes effort to pry my eyelids open. It's like they're cemented shut. One glance around the room and I realize exactly where I am, which is a shock to the system. That's all it takes for last night to slam into me at lightning speed. Images flash through my brain one on top of another before I'm fully able to process them.

Sitting around the house.

Showing up at the club and searching for Carina.

And the gut punch when I found her in that slinky silver excuse for a dress that barely covered her ass and somehow made her legs look even longer and leaner than usual.

My dick stirs to life at the mental image.

Then I drove her home.

And dared her to masturbate in front of me.

That's the thing about Carina—she's never been able to resist a challenge. It was always easy to steer her in the direction I wanted if I dared her to do it.

Like kiss me.

Damn right I did that a ton of times when we were in high school. I spent years tap dancing on the line without actually crossing it. Especially with my father watching like a hawk, making sure I wasn't acting anything other than brotherly.

I glance at the blonde cuddled up against me, one leg thrown haphazardly over mine in sleep. It's been a while since we woke up in the same bed. There was a time when Carina would sneak across the hall to my room and slip between my sheets every night. It became a habit I looked forward to. After a while, I couldn't sleep unless she was snuggled up against me.

To wake up to her again after all these years feels more like a dream. I can't stop staring. She's so beautiful with her thick mass of golden blonde hair spread out on the pillow. She never bothered to put clothes on after the show she treated me to after the club.

Hottest.

Fucking.

Thing.

Ever.

And then coming on her belly...

And her sucking it off my finger.

Just thinking about it makes my dick throb.

My gaze drops to the now tented comforter at my waist.

Exactly.

This girl has always been a wet dream.

My wet dream.

No matter how much time passes, I can't imagine that changing.

Fuck.

The thoughts circling around in my head like hungry sharks are dangerous.

If I were smart, I'd slip from the bed and sneak out of her apartment before the situation becomes any more complicated.

Although, it feels much too late for that.

"You look like you're planning an escape."

Her sultry voice, more roughed up in the morning, has me blinking out of those thoughts. My gaze slices to hers only to find her watching me steadily as if waiting for me to hightail it from the room.

I pop my shoulder. "You caught me. I was contemplating the possibility of gnawing off my own arm to get away."

Instead of getting offended, she smirks. "That would certainly make hockey more of a challenge."

"It would make a lot of things more of a challenge. Hockey's the least of them. Once the season ends, I'll hang up my skates." The thought of not playing the sport I've loved my entire life is a bittersweet one. Normally, as soon as the notion fills my brain, I shove it away, not wanting to dwell on the eventuality of it.

Carina moves closer, stacking her hands on my chest before resting her chin on them. Her clear blue-gray eyes stay fastened to mine. She's the only one who's ever been able to sift through my innermost thoughts. I couldn't keep her out even if I wanted to.

"Are you ready for that chapter of your life to be over with?"

"Does it really matter?" I shoot back. It's much too early in the morning for such a serious conversation. One that'll probably end up tanking my entire day.

She contemplates the question for a handful of seconds. "Of course it does. I can't imagine not dancing. It's part of who I am. How I express myself and deal with stress."

I can't imagine her not dancing either. Corny as it sounds, the girl is poetry in motion. Her body and soul were made for it. She's able to convey so much emotion without speaking a single word.

How many people have the ability to do that?

Dance is like the very air she needs to breathe.

I'm not sure if hockey is the same for me.

Don't get me wrong, I love the sport.

Have always loved it.

I laced up my first pair of Bauers when I was five years old. And in all the time that's passed, I've never *not* skated. But the difference is that I always knew I wasn't good enough to turn pro. No matter how much time and energy I poured into it. Some people have raw talent and innate ability that shines through and propels them forward.

I don't have that spark.

My future was always going to be working alongside my father.

I came to terms with it a long time ago.

But that doesn't mean I'm not sad that part of my life is coming to an end.

I sift my fingers through the long strands of her hair. It feels amazing to have her draped across my bare chest.

Right.

Like the tumblers of a safe finally clicking into place.

I could stare at her for hours, getting lost in her fathomless, blue-gray depths. They've always had the uncanny ability to see too much.

I clear my throat and force my thoughts back to the conversation at hand. "We both know I was never good enough to play professionally."

Her expression turns thoughtful. "Want to know what I think?"

Only wanting to lighten the mood, I say, "That feels more like a rhetorical question. I'm pretty sure you're going to tell me regardless of my answer."

Her eyes narrow as a huff escapes from her.

She really is fucking adorable.

Especially with the way her disheveled hair tumbles around her face and naked shoulders. She has so much of it. I used to fantasize about winding it around my hands while sinking deep inside her body.

"I think it was easier to tell yourself that the future was already set in stone rather than take a chance on something you actually wanted only to end up falling short."

My heart hitches for one painful beat before thrashing against my chest.

When I remain silent, she murmurs, "Am I wrong?"

I expel the air slowly from my lungs. "No."

She tilts her head and studies me in a way that strips me bare. "It's never too late to go after what you want."

Our gazes cling and part of me wonders if we're still talking about hockey.

Or something else entirely.

My hands slip under her arms before dragging her on top of me so that her lips hover inches above my own. She feels so damn good stretched out across my length. Her hair tumbles around her face in soft waves, shielding us from the world beyond the four walls of her bedroom. No longer am I thinking about the reasons we aren't supposed to be together.

In this moment, they don't matter.

Nothing matters except for Carina.

One hand snakes down her backside before cupping a taut cheek, squeezing the firm flesh until my fingers sink into the muscle. The other tangles in her hair, dragging her head closer until my lips can settle over hers. I flex my hips so that my thick erection can slide against the V between her thighs.

When a whimper of need escapes from her, I swallow down the sound.

Her legs widen to cradle me. The only thing standing in my way of slipping inside the welcoming heat of her body is a thin layer of cotton. It's tempting to free my erection so I can do exactly that.

I'm so damn hungry for her.

Famished really.

"I want you to fuck me. Haven't we waited long enough?"

A tortured groan escapes from my lips, knowing that it won't take much for my self-control to crumble because she's right. We've waited so damn long. As much as I want to draw this out, I can't do it any longer.

"Do you want my cock, baby?"

"You know I do. I've made that perfectly clear."

"Then show me. Show me exactly how much you want *me*. Grind that sweet little pussy against me. I want you to drench my boxers with your cream."

Before the last word escapes from my mouth, she flexes her hips. The pleasure that reverberates throughout my body is enough to make my eyes cross.

The way she dry humps me is so damn good.

Well…there's nothing dry about it.

One hand tightens around the back of her head, holding her securely in place as the other bites into the rounded curve of her ass.

"That's it, baby. Ride me until you're sobbing for my dick."

Her breathing turns labored, growing frantic. "I need you so much. My pussy is crying for you."

The tortured sound of her voice is the last straw and what finally shreds the little bit of willpower I've been holding onto.

She gasps when I roll us over and land on top of her. I yank down my shorts just enough for my erection to spring free. One hard thrust is all it takes for me to slide deep inside her tight heat. It's only when I'm buried balls deep am I able to suck in a lungful of fresh oxygen. It feels as if I've been holding my breath for years.

The way her inner walls clench around my girth makes me realize that I won't last long.

How can I when I've been dreaming about this moment since I first laid eyes on her?

I've spent years fantasizing about it.

The reality of this moment blows all of those fantasies out of the water.

When she squirms beneath me, I flex my hips, dragging my thick length from her body before plunging back inside, seeking her warmth. A moan escapes from her as her eyes roll to the back of her head and she arches her spine.

"Please tell me you're on the pill," I mutter, only now thinking about protection.

"I am."

Thank fuck.

But still...

This situation isn't ideal. I've never fucked anyone without a condom. It's another rule I live my life by. Just like screwing girls off premises and never spending the night. I should have realized long ago that Carina would be the one who made me chuck them all out the window.

There's an unexpected level of intimacy when you're inside another person without the thinnest layer of latex to separate you.

And part of me fucking loves it.

Revels in the softness that surrounds me.

It feels fitting that the first time I have sex without a condom should be with her.

When Carina's inner muscles contract and a low moan slides from her lips, it breaks the last of my self-control and I come even harder than I did last night. The sweet sounds that fill the air only spur on my own release.

We couldn't be more in sync with one another if we tried.

Just like going without a condom, it's not something I've ever experienced before.

We ride the wave until every last shudder has been wrung from both of our bodies. My muscles loosen and it feels like I've just finished a two-hour practice. My heart is on the verge of exploding from my chest.

Instead of pulling out and rolling over, thinking about ways to extract myself from the situation, I rest my forehead against hers and stare deep into her eyes, searching for signs of regret.

It's a relief when I don't find anything other than the fading remnants of pleasure. I have the feeling that the same sentiment is echoed in my eyes as well.

That's the moment I realize fucking her once or twice will never be enough to satiate the deep well of need that lives inside me.

CHAPTER TWENTY-THREE

CARINA

I glance down at my phone and scroll through a few messages as the elevator doors slide open. I just got home from teaching two back-to-back dance classes at the studio. Those little five- and six-year-olds are seriously adorable. Especially with their tap shoes.

As soon as I step into the hallway, the sound of male voices greets my ears, and my gaze fastens onto Ford's golden depths. That's all it takes for the air to get knocked from my lungs as an avalanche of shivers cascade down my spine.

Even when I try to ruthlessly stomp out the attraction I feel for him, embers continue to smolder at the bottom of my belly.

Ugh.

This is bad.

The last thing I want to do is develop feelings for the guy. In fact, that's what this entire friends-with-benefits situation was supposed to alleviate.

His teammates—Wolf, Madden, and Ryder—greet me before jostling their way onto the elevator.

There's a moment of silence as everything around us falls away and Madden clears his throat. "Are you coming or what, Hamilton?"

"Coach will rip us a new one if we're late," Wolf adds.

Ford's penetrating gaze never deviates from mine. "I'll meet up with you in the parking lot. I need to talk to Carina."

"Suit yourself," Ryder says. "If you're not down in five, we're leaving without you."

"I'll be there. Don't get your panties in a twist."

Wolf snorts and mutters something under his breath that I can't quite decipher before the metal doors slide shut. This is the first time we've been alone since sleeping together. On Monday, I snuck into class late and sat toward the back of the small lecture hall. Our gazes collided several times when he'd turn and stare like he knew exactly what I was doing and why. The wolfish smile that overtook his expression set fire to my panties and the knowing look in his eyes made me think he was remembering what it was like to be buried deep inside my body.

The big jerk.

Before I can throw out an excuse and dart away, his hands lock around my upper arms as he forces me backward against the wall next to the elevator.

"Ford…"

My voice comes out sounding ridiculously breathy. This isn't the kind of girl I am, and it irritates the hell out of me that he's able to elicit just such an unwanted reaction.

"What?" He flicks a glance up and down the hallway. "The place is empty. We're all alone." There's a moment of silence. "Or would you prefer for us to be surrounded by people? Then you could continue avoiding me."

Heat suffuses my cheeks. "Don't be ridiculous. It's been busy."

But yeah…I've been totally avoiding him.

I need all the strange feelings he rouses within me to settle before we see each other again. There was a tiny part of me that wondered if maybe this would be a hit-it-and-quit-it kind of thing. Ford has always been a player. I don't want to be all like- *let's hook up again* and he's like- *thanks, but no thanks. I've had my fill.* And then I end up looking like a clingy puck bunny.

No way.

Not for a second time.

I'm knocked from the tangle of those thoughts when he nips at my lower lip. There's no other choice but to refocus my attention on the man pinning me to the wall.

Because that's exactly what he's turned into.

A man.

When I met Ford at fourteen, he was tall and lanky. Muscular from playing hockey but he still looked like a young teen. One who needed to grow into his body. Fast forward seven years and he's packed with muscle. His shoulders are broad, his chest wide, and hips lean. The sight of him naked is enough to turn any woman's insides into a pile of mush.

Even though I've tried to fight the attraction tooth and nail, I'm guilty of the same.

"Has it?"

"Yes. I've been spending a lot of time in the studio."

He searches my eyes for a long silent moment before his tone lightens. "Good to know."

My muscles loosen with relief that he dropped the topic so easily.

I avert my gaze, unwilling to get sucked into his vortex. "You should probably get moving or you'll get your ass chewed out."

"I don't give a shit about that. It was more important to clear the air with you." His gaze drops to my lips. "And I wanted a kiss for good luck."

Before those words can fully register, his mouth crashes onto mine. His tongue licks at the seam of my lips, weakening my freshly fortified defenses, until I have no other choice but to capitulate and open. That's all it takes for him to delve in and make me forget that we're standing in the middle of the hallway where anyone could see us. His hands remain shackled around my upper arms. The thickness of his erection digs insistently into my lower abdomen, and I can't help but squirm against it as memories of Saturday morning flood my brain.

I've never come so hard in my life.

With barely any foreplay at all.

A half dozen strokes was all it took to send me careening over the edge and into oblivion. It must have been the culmination of years of pent-up sexual tension simmering between us. What other explanation is there?

The way his hungry mouth roves over mine is enough to make me forget my own name. If he weren't pinning me to the wall, my knees would buckle, and I'd melt into a puddle of goo.

Just when I grow lightheaded from lack of oxygen, he pulls away enough to ask, "You're coming to the game, right?"

"Sorry. Wasn't planning on it."

Lie.

Juliette secured my promise the other day. And I was secretly happy to let her believe she twisted my arm in the matter.

He nips at my lower lip, tugging it with sharp teeth before sucking it into his mouth. My eyes nearly cross as another punch of arousal hits me square in the gut.

Or maybe it hits a little lower.

With his gaze locked on mine, he releases the plump flesh with a soft pop.

"I want you there, sitting in the stands, cheering me on."

"Maybe I have other plans that don't involve hockey." Another lie. "Ever think of that?"

A growl vibrates in his chest. "That better not be the case."

He kisses me again before his mouth trails possessively down the column of my neck.

"I'll…think about showing up."

"No thinking necessary. Just be there."

When he retreats a step, I press myself against the wall and lock my knees.

"Or what?" It's a surprise when my voice comes out sounding so steady.

"Or you'll find that pretty little ass spanked." With a smirk, he swallows up the distance again. His gaze slides down my length before flicking back to my eyes. "Although, I have the feeling you'd probably enjoy it."

With one final kiss, he turns away, hustling down the hall to the stairwell that leads to the lobby. It's only when the metal door slams shut behind him that I release the pent-up breath from my lungs.

Holy cr—

"Was that as hot as it looked?"

My head jerks to the side so fast that I nearly give myself whiplash. A girl I recognize from the floor leans against her door with her arms crossed against her chest.

"Hotter," I reluctantly admit because it's the truth.

She fans herself with her hand. "Yeah, that's exactly what I thought."

It takes effort to push myself away from the wall and walk to the apartment. My panties are such a damp mess that I could probably wring them out.

It's so tempting to grab my vibe and use it to relieve the sexual tension Ford stirred to life with a kiss and some dirty words but…

I promised that I wouldn't.

Damn him.

I'd feel a lot more relaxed if I could get off on my own. Especially if I'm going to be spending more time with him. At this rate, I'll sneak into the locker room just so I can fuck his brains out. And I won't give a damn who's watching.

That thought is almost enough to stop me in my tracks.

This is bad.

Really, really bad.

I need to figure out a way to regain the upper hand in this situationship.

Part of me wonders if that's even possible.

Two hours later, Juliette and I are settled in our seats at the arena. Her parents are there along with other hockey families. I don't think Mr. and Mrs. McKinnon have missed a single one of Maverick's games.

Even the away ones.

As I reach for the box of popcorn my phone dings with an incoming text. I slip the silver device from my jacket pocket and glance at it.

Your ass better be in the stands.

A smile tugs at the corners of my lips.

Maybe. Maybe not.

Looks like someone wants to be spanked.

Go ahead and try it, buddy. See where it gets you.

Tell me you're here to watch me and we'll take that off the table.

My fingers hover over the keys. It's so damn tempting to tell him what he wants to hear.

I decided to work on choreography instead. Sorry. Not sorry.

Three little bubbles appear on the screen and my insides clench with anticipation, waiting for a response.

Why do I love pushing Ford's buttons so much?

Then again, the same could be said for him.

We're like two powder kegs, intent on setting one another off.

"What are you smiling about?" Juliette asks, breaking into my thoughts.

I've been so intent on the phone that I forgot she was beside me.

I almost groan at that private admittance.

She leans closer, attempting to catch a glimpse of the screen before I press it against my chest.

Her brows skyrocket into her hairline as she searches my eyes. "It's like that, huh?"

Dull heat creeps into my cheeks.

Why am I making such a big deal about this?

I should just admit that Ford and I knocked boots, and it meant absolutely nothing. It was a hookup. A frenemies-with-benefits situation.

But not a single sound leaves my mouth.

"It's nothing," I finally mutter.

Her eyes widen. "Oh my god, if you're actually trying to convince me that it's *nothing* then it has to be *something*." She points to the phone. "I don't think I could pry that thing out of your cold, dead fingers."

Unfortunately, she's not wrong.

"It's, ah, just someone from dance."

"Wow." She shakes her as if in wonder. "Now you're lying to me?"

I huff out an embarrassed breath and break eye contact. My gaze slides over the sheet of pristine ice before landing on Ford, who loiters near the player benches. That's all it takes for my heartbeat to hitch before thrashing against my ribcage. His eyes pin mine in place as he jerks a brow. A knowing smile lifts the edges of his lips. A second later, he swings away, disappearing into the locker room.

"Oh my god. You slept with him, didn't you?"

I wince and force out the truth. "Yeah. In hindsight, I'm pretty sure it was a mistake."

A long stretch of silence follows that admittance. Any moment, my nerves are going to snap.

"I wouldn't be too sure about that."

I blink, thrown off by her response. "Trust me, it is," I reiterate. "He's my stepbrother."

"Haven't your parents been divorced for a while?"

"Well, yeah. But Crawford is like a father to me." Then I blurt, "I don't want to do anything that would damage our relationship. It's not worth it. You know what Pamela is like. She's a non-existent presence in my life."

A sympathetic expression flashes across her face. "That's not true. She cares about you. In her own way."

"That woman is too damn busy jetting around the world to worry about me." Bitterness creeps into my tone. I've spent years trying to brush it off and pretend it doesn't exist. It's like revealing a weakness and I hate it. Even to my best friend.

She wraps her arm around my shoulders and tugs me close. "I love you and so does Crawford."

Thick emotion swells inside me. "I know."

"Ford cares too."

I snort.

"He does. I see the way he watches you."

"I have no idea what's happening between us. It was probably just a one-time deal."

"Or it could be something amazing."

A groan works its way up my throat. I've never felt more confused in my life. We've only slept together once and already the lines have become blurred.

Before I can share any other details, my phone dings with another message. I don't bother glancing at the screen.

I know who it's from.

"Can I assume it's Ford?"

I jerk my head into a tight nod.

When a second, then another ticks by, she clears her throat. "So… are you going to read the message?"

"Nope."

But I want to.

So bad.

"Not at all curious about what it says?"

"Nah."

Actually, I'm dying inside.

When Juliette's mother catches her attention and she swivels away, I peek at the screen.

Looks like someone won't be getting their ass spanked tonight. What a shame.

Air gets trapped in my lungs as disappointment settles like a heavy stone in the pit of my belly.

Oh god. Am I seriously disappointed at the prospect of not being spanked?

Please tell me that's not the case.

Looks like you owe me.

Is this guy seriously off his rocker?

Owe you? For what? Showing up to your game? Because I can always rectify the situation. Just say the word.

I'm about to pop to my feet and stalk out of the arena when another text rolls in.

How about we make things interesting?
Interesting? How?
A wager. If I score a hat trick, you blow me.

Air leaks from my lungs as I turn the prospect over in my head.

What do I get if that doesn't happen?

A laughing emoji appears on the screen before another message pops up.

Baby, I plan on scoring all three goals. I want you on your knees, staring up at me with your mouth full of cock.

His dirty text has my panties flooding with a ridiculous amount of heat. I squirm on the hard seat as an image of taking him deep into my throat dances behind my eyes.

That probably shouldn't turn me on so much.

My fingers shake as I type out a response.

That didn't answer the question.

You want me to lick that sweet little pussy? Done. You want me to fuck you nice and slow? Done. You want me to spank that perfect, heart-shaped ass? Done. Whatever you want me to do. Done.

I release an unsteady breath as my belly trembles. If I'm not careful, I'll come right here.

It wouldn't take much to shove me over the edge.

There are times when the chemistry that sparks between us feels as if it'll explode, blowing us both to smithereens.

I don't understand it. More specifically, I don't understand what it is about Ford that makes me feel this way.

Okay.

I tap in those four little letters and hit send, realizing that I've just sealed my fate for the evening.

And yet, I can't bring myself to regret it.

But…that doesn't mean I can't make things a little more interesting in my own way.

I wait until the game is just about to start and he takes his place on the ice. When his gaze locks on mine, I pop to my feet and unzip my jacket, revealing the jersey beneath.

His eyes narrow right before the puck gets dropped.

And then he's off, blades digging into the ice as he races for the black disc.

I sit perched on the edge of my seat and watch Ford throw himself into the action. Barely does he step off the ice for shift changes. And when he does, our gazes stay locked as he gulps down water before heading out again.

Toward the end of the third period, Juliette says, "Damn, Ford is really on fire tonight." She glances at the clock. "There's only two minutes left. Think he'll score for a third time?"

Actually, I do.

He's taken at least a dozen shots, but the other team's goalie is some kind of phenom, and his reflexes are lightning quick. It's as if he has a sixth sense regarding where each shot will land. If this were the same team the Wildcats played last week, Ford would have racked up at least five or six goals by now.

Maybe even more.

His determination and single-mindedness are almost impressive. He's a man on a mission. And I know exactly what that mission is. Anticipation hums in the cold air of the arena. Each time he makes a drive for the net and takes a shot, everything in me freezes as my heart thumps a steady staccato, threatening to pound right out of my chest.

I can't decide if I want him to score or not. I'd dearly love to rub it in his face that he didn't accomplish what he assumed would be so easy.

Although...the taste I got of him the other night wasn't nearly enough and I'd be lying if I didn't admit to wanting more.

Fun fact—he didn't taste as bitter as some of the other guys I've gone down on.

It makes me wonder if he's eating pineapple.

Or is that just the way he naturally tastes?

"Holy crap, he did it!" Juliette yells, jumping to her feet and shouting through cupped hands. "Ford scored a hat trick!"

I'm jarred back to the present when she reaches down and drags me up until I'm able to catch sight of the ice through the sea of cheering fans. I scan the sheet until my gaze lands on Ford, only to find his attention locked on me.

One look is all it takes for electricity to zip down my spine. The delicate hair on my arms and at the nape of my neck rises as his teammates slap him on the back, congratulating him. Instead of celebrating the moment with them, he continues to stare, holding me captive with the intensity of his golden gaze. Through the cage that covers his face, he beams a slow grin around his mouth guard.

His gloating expression is like a punch to the gut.

Juliette glances at me before shaking her head. "One-time deal my ass."

The pent-up air in my lungs escapes in a burst.

Yeah...that's exactly what I'm afraid of.

CHAPTER TWENTY-FOUR

FORD

As soon as I turn the corner to the lobby where everyone has congregated, my gaze scans the thick crowd until it lands on Carina's blonde head. Only then do my muscles loosen and I can finally breathe again. I'll admit there was a part of me that wondered if she'd stick around or if I'd have to hunt her ass down.

Because you damn well know I'd do it.

It's a pleasant surprise to find her here.

Know what's not a pleasant surprise?

Finding her in Maverick McKinnon's jersey.

My eyes narrow when I realize that's exactly who she's chatting with.

Not to mention, smiling at.

Hot licks of jealousy flare to life inside me before settling in the pit of my gut to simmer. No matter how much I attempt to stomp it out, it's always been like that with her. Watching Carina talk and flirt with other guys drives me batshit crazy. It makes me want to plow my fist into their faces.

Even the ones who are my friends.

Have I?

No.

Have I come close?

Yup.

Now that I've actually gotten a taste of her, been inside the heat of her body, made her shutter around me before moaning out her pleasure, it's even more so. I might have reluctantly agreed to keep what we're doing on the downlow, but I want all these motherfuckers to know that she belongs to me.

For the time being.

If that thought leaves a bitter taste in my mouth, I shove it aside.

My attention stays locked on her like a heatseeking missile as I shove my way through the crowd. People reach out, slapping me on the shoulder, congratulating me on the game. I remember what it felt like the first time I scored a hat trick as a mite.

Best fucking feeling in the world.

And you know what?

I still get the same rush fourteen years later.

But today, it meant even more.

When I'm about ten feet away, Carina turns, her blue-gray gaze fastening onto me. There's a spark of challenge in her eyes. I have the sneaking suspicion it has more to do with the name plastered across her back rather than the fact she now owes me a BJ.

Did this girl really think that seeing her in Mav's jersey would throw me off my game?

Yeah, that wasn't going to happen.

Not with a blowjob from Carina on the line.

Do you have any idea how many times I've fantasized about those pouty lips wrapped around my dick?

Too many to count.

Nothing was getting in my way tonight. Including that fucking goalie who seemed to catch every damn shot I fired off.

Except for three lucky ones that slipped in.

Barely do I give Mav the time of day before wrapping my fingers around her upper arm and steering her away from the group and down a long stretch of deserted corridor.

"Good talk, Hamilton," Maverick's voice echoes after us.

"Was it really necessary to drag me away like that?" she asks indignantly. "Maybe you didn't notice, but I was in the middle of a conversation."

"Yes, it was," I say voice strung tight. "And I don't give a fuck about your convo. We have several things to discuss."

"Oh?"

As if she doesn't know.

Ha!

We turn another corner before I grind to a halt and swing her around to face me.

She lifts her chin. The way her eyes glitter tells me that she knows *exactly* what's about to go down.

Her.

I release her long enough to grip the hem of the jersey she's wearing and drag it up her body before tugging it over her head. The purse and jacket she's holding gets dropped to the floor in the process. There's a pale pink cami beneath that hugs every slender curve. It's tempting to rip that off as well.

"What do you think you're doing?" More indignation wafts off her.

I drop Mav's sweater on top of her jacket.

"If you're going to wear someone's jersey, it'll be mine. You can add that to our growing list of rules."

Her chin rises another notch. "Is that so?"

"Damn right it is."

I step closer, backing her up against the concrete wall before nipping at her top lip and then the lower one. There's a faint vanilla taste from the balm she slicked on. It only stokes the flames of my desire and makes me want her more.

Although, it's doubtful anything could make me want this girl less.

Even seeing her in another guy's jersey.

Her breathing turns labored.

And I fucking love it.

Love that I'm able to affect her when she tries so damn hard not to give me a reaction.

"I believe you owe me a blowjob, pretty girl."

"Here?" Her face turns slack as her eyes widen. "Now?"

That wasn't the original plan but…

Why the hell not?

I glance up and down the hallway to reconfirm that it's empty. There's the faint hum of laughter and conversation that drifts from the lobby.

"Yup." I cock my head. "What's the matter? Afraid of getting caught with your mouth stuffed full of dick?"

Some chicks would slap me for saying something so vulgar. Carina isn't one of them. Instead, her pupils dilate in response, the black swallowing up the blue-gray color.

When she remains silent, looking uncertain, I drop my voice. "I dare you."

She squeezes her eyes tightly closed and gulps. The delicate column of her throat works, heightening my own excitement. It's like waving a red cape in front of a bull. When her lashes flutter open again, lust swirls through the glittery depths. It's so fucking intoxicating.

"You know that's one thing I can't resist."

A chuckle slips free. It's nothing more than a deep scrape of sound that resonates in the charged air.

That I do.

I've used that knowledge like a not-so-secret weapon, prodding her into doing things she normally wouldn't and giving her permission to do exactly what she wanted.

Needed.

Craved.

I know Carina. Better than she knows herself, because I've always been there watching.

Waiting.

Her palms flatten against my chest before she gives me a slight push. I retreat a step or two, giving her the space she wants. For all I know, she'll walk away and give me the finger.

It wouldn't be the first time. Although, I've never known her to back away from a challenge. Even if it's nothing more than a juvenile dare.

She shoves away from the wall and steps to the side. My attention stays locked on her as she strolls in a semi-circle before grounding to a halt. For a second time, her fingertips settle on my chest before forcing me to retreat until it's my spine that hits the rough concrete. Only then does she close the distance between us until her slender curves are pressed against my harder lines.

We're like two puzzle pieces.

Both a little jagged around the edges.

But somehow, we fit perfectly.

Carina reaches onto the tips of her toes. Even though the girl has height, she's not tall enough to reach my lips without stretching.

Instead of going for my mouth the way I expect, her teeth scrape across the scruff covering my jaw before sliding to the point of my chin. When she sinks further down the column of my throat, I tip my head and bare it in silent invitation.

There was a time in the not-so-distant past when doing so would have been much akin to taking my life into my own hands. She'd have ripped out my jugular and I would have choked to death in a gurgling puddle of my own blood. Then she would've stood and watched me bleed out before stepping over my cold, dead body.

When her sharp little teeth sink into my flesh for a second time, I wonder if maybe that's exactly how this scenario will play out.

The bite of pain feels good, like a shot of adrenaline straight to my dick. A groan rumbles up from deep within my chest as her hands slip under my hoodie and T-shirt to the bare skin beneath before stroking upward along my pecs.

Fuck, that feels good.

On her way down, her fingertips make lazy passes around my nipples and another guttural sound of pleasure escapes from me. She hesitates over the button of my jeans before flicking it open and dragging down the zipper. The sound of metal teeth grinding against each other fills the charged air as anticipation swirls through the atmosphere. Any moment, it'll explode like a powder keg.

Without another word, she slides down my body, sinking to her knees. I flick another glance up and down the corridor to make sure we're alone. The hum of conversation from the lobby has died away as people take off. The team will head over to Slap Shotz to celebrate another win.

I couldn't give a fuck about that.

The only thing that matters is the girl on her knees.

That's all it takes for my world to shrink down to the two of us.

Maybe it's always been that way.

My gaze refastens on her as she slips her hand into my boxers and drags down the cottony material until my thick erection can spring free. She stares at it for a second or two before the velvety softness of her tongue darts out to moisten her pink slicked lips.

Already my dick is like stone, swelling against her fingers. The brush of her plush lips against my tip is enough to have me inhaling a sharp breath.

Fuck.

Fuck.

Fuck.

That feels so damn good.

Better than that.

This girl hasn't even taken me into her mouth, and I might just die from the pent-up anticipation building inside me.

Her gaze falls to my erection as her tongue swirls around the bulbous head.

Not that I don't like her staring at my cock but…

"Eyes up here, pretty girl," I growl. "I want them on me when you take me deep inside your throat."

Satisfaction fills me when her blue-gray depths, the ones I could happily drown in, fasten onto mine. My fingers tangle in her thick blonde strands, slowly gathering them up until I can see her face.

I've spent too many years dreaming about this moment to not watch every drop of emotion that flickers across it. God knows I'll end up pulling out the memory to relive after it comes to an end. Not wanting to dwell on the lifespan of our arrangement, I shove it away and focus on the beautiful girl in front of me.

I've been blown more times than I can count and for most of them, I'd close my eyes and pretend it was Carina sucking me into her mouth and taking me down her throat.

Trust me, I'm more than aware of how fucked up that is.

I'm almost hoping that she can't suck a dick to save her life. Because if she can…this little obsession will only grow more out of control.

And that, I don't need.

My breath hitches and I steel myself as her tongue swirls around the head before she drags it down the shaft to my balls before sliding back up again to the tip and sucking it. A shiver of pleasure dances down my spine.

Watching my dick disappear between her pouty lips is so damn hot.

It's like having a wet dream you're wide awake for.

Movement catches the corner of my eye and I turn my head just a bit, only to realize that Wolf is standing at the entrance to the corridor. My fingers tighten in Carina's hair as she continues to lick me. We make the briefest of eye contact before he swings away, departing as quietly as he'd stumbled upon us.

I have to grit my teeth when she sucks the head deep inside before drifting down the hard length. Half my erection vanishes before my very eyes. Every time she slides to the head and then glides down again, she sinks lower, swallowing more of my cock until the tip nudges the back of her throat. Her hands slip around my thighs before drawing me closer.

If I'd secretly hoped that Carina wouldn't give good head, nothing could be further from the truth. The girl knows exactly what she's doing. She understands when to apply pressure and then back off, leaving me to want more. When my balls draw up against my body, I know I'm precariously close to losing it.

But damn, I want to stop time and make it last forever. The pleasure is so fucking exquisite.

With her eyes pinned to mine, she slides down so far that her nose brushes against my groin. A light sheen of tears gathers in her blue-gray depths, making them appear even more shiny and luminous than usual. When a single, crystal-like tear trails down her cheek, I can't resist reaching out and capturing it before bringing the wetness to my mouth and licking it away.

I don't think I've ever seen anything as beautiful as Carina on her knees, staring at me as if I'm the beginning and end of her fucking world with her mouth stretched wide, stuffed full of cock.

When she turns voracious, I tilt my hips and tighten my fingers in her hair, only wanting to hold her close. Our eyes stay locked as I splinter apart. The orgasm that rips through me is just as intense as the other night. It wouldn't surprise me if the tip blows right off.

A long, guttural groan escapes from me as I come down her throat. Instead of shoving me away, she milks my cock as her muscles convulse, making sure to swallow down every last drop as if it's precious. It's only when I soften that she presses a kiss against the tip. I quickly stuff my dick back into my jeans before hooking my hands beneath her arms and hauling her against me.

As soon as my lips collide with her swollen ones, my tongue delves inside her mouth to tangle with her own. The fact that she tastes like me turns me on more than anything. A strange contentment steals over me. It's impossible to imagine anyone else giving me this kind of peace.

That thought is enough to stop my mental gears in their tracks.

It's also the moment I realize just how screwed I am.

CHAPTER TWENTY-FIVE

CARINA

"Where'd you disappear to after the game?" Juliette asks. Ryder's brawny arm is thrown casually over her shoulders, holding her close. It's like he wants the entire world to understand that she now belongs to him.

It's adorable.

Straight out of a romance novel.

The enemies-to-lovers kind that makes you devour a book.

I pat my tummy and make a face that hopefully conveys pain. "The popcorn really did a number on me."

"Oh." Her expression turns sympathetic. "Are you feeling better?"

"Yup."

My gaze unconsciously wanders to Ford, who's seated at a bunch of tables that have been shoved together for the hockey team. There's lots of laughter and good-natured camaraderie going on. Even over the pumping beat of the music, they're giving each other shit.

Riggs is seated next to Stella. Much like Ryder, he has his arm tossed casually over his bestie's shoulder. They're both laughing at something Hayes is saying. Colby, Maverick, Wolf, and Madden are also seated at the table. There's a ton of puck bunnies buzzing around, searching for available laps to settle on. At this very moment, Darcy Erickson is trying to capture Ford's attention.

He has yet to spare her a glance.

In fact, he's not giving any of the girls the time of day. It's like they aren't even there.

Since we arrived an hour ago, his gaze has been locked on me. No matter where I am in the bar, I feel the heat of it as if it were an actual physical caress. I've never been more attuned to another person in my life than I am to Ford Hamilton.

There's something hot and needy that scratches beneath the surface of my skin, begging to be unleashed. Even now, I can taste him on my tongue. There was something so sexy about going down on him in the hallway when anyone could have turned the corner and stumbled upon us. The way it felt to be on my knees, staring up at him while I sucked him down my throat is enough to have my panties flooding with heat.

What I hate is the flare of jealousy when I meet his gaze and find all those girls touching him.

Talking to him.

Trying to convince him to take them home at the end of the night.

It's tempting to stalk over and stake my claim. Instead, I remain rooted in place, refusing to do what every instinct is prodding.

It shouldn't matter if every girl at Western flirts with the guy.

We're not together.

We're hooking up.

And once it gets stale, it'll be over.

Those are the terms we agreed to.

I blink back to awareness when a loud cheer goes up and I realize that Sully, the owner of the bar, has lumbered onto the stage.

He spears a beefy finger toward the crowded tables of hockey players. "Our boys brought home another win tonight and you know what that means!"

"Karaoke!" everyone screams in unison.

"You got it!"

Already people are hustling to the stage. They've been waiting for the chance to sing their little hearts out all night. The first performance is by a trio of girls who shimmy their asses across the platform and do a whole lot of unnecessary twerking. Then a couple of younger hockey players do the same—minus the twerking. They have surprisingly good voices.

Color me impressed.

Ryder drags my girl up there and they belt out a duet.

'Grenade' by Bruno Mars.

They're so barfy.

I love it.

Juliette deserves all the happiness in the world.

Is there a tiny part inside me that wishes I had someone who loved me just as fiercely?

Yup. I've been devouring romance novels since I was thirteen years old. Not only did I learn about love but sex as well. I've always held up those stories as shining examples of what a relationship should be.

When I fell for Ford senior year of high school, I'd believed I found it. Until my heart was crushed. And then I realized that's all they were...

Stories.

Meant to entertain and pass the time.

They weren't to be used as a measuring stick against real men who would almost certainly fall short every single time.

My gaze reluctantly flickers to Ford, only to find him watching me with a hungry look in his eyes. Even from across the crowded room, the heat sparking within them is almost enough to melt the panties off my body. It takes effort to stomp out the attraction attempting to leap to life inside me.

I'm afraid of what will happen if I allow it to go unchecked.

It's like a fire that will singe me alive.

And I've been burned before.

I should know better.

Once the notes die away, Ryder yanks Juliette into his arms and kisses her in front of the crowd. The bar goes crazy with whistles and applause. Even her brother, Maverick, smiles reluctantly before shaking his head.

When my phone vibrates, I fish it out of my pocket.

Dare you to get up there and sing.

My gaze slices to Ford.

He arches a dark brow in silent challenge.

Two dares in one night?

The blow job wasn't a dare. It was a deal. There's a difference.

When my fingers hesitate over the miniature keyboard, another message pops up on the screen.

Don't make me double dog dare you.

The corners of my lips lift as I consider my options.

What is it about a dare that I find so damn irresistible?

Or maybe it's the sender.

Instead of responding, I tuck the phone back into my pocket and head for the stage, weaving my way through the thick press of bodies. When Darcy Erickson moves in the same direction, I cut her off, arriving at the stage first. She glares as I beeline for the computer. I'm halfway through the list when the perfect song appears.

A smile hovers at the edges of my lips as I bring the microphone an inch or so from my mouth. I've never been shy. I've been dancing for more than a decade. I'm used to being on stage for solos and having everyone's attention focused on me.

But performing for a bar full of drunk college kids?

That's not something I do on a regular basis.

For just a heartbeat, I close my eyes and suck in a deep breath, attempting to center myself. The first few beats float on the air. Unlike the array of songs that have already been played, this one hits different. There's a distinct bass line and the melody is almost ominous.

Slow.

Erotic.

That's when the percussive elements come in. My tongue darts out to swipe across my dry lips as I sing Fiona Apple's 'Criminal'.

The tune is rich and soulful.

The bar grows silent as every eye in the place stays focused on me. Just like with dance, the way I'm able to command attention is a high. My gaze slides across the sea of faces in the dark room until it lands on Ford.

He's no longer lounging on his chair with a smug expression. Instead, he's perched on the edge of it. Even from across the distance that separates us, I feel the growing tension of his rigidly held muscles. It's as if he'll spring out of his seat any given moment.

Excitement coils in the pit of my belly as my attention stays locked on him while I belt out the song. I'm not a professional by any means, but I'm more than capable of carrying a tune.

Everyone else in the bar fades away until he's all I'm cognizant of.

Just him.

And me.

'Criminal' is a sexy song. Maybe this particular tune seems appropriate because I enjoy toying with him.

Or maybe it's because, deep down, I know what we're doing is wrong.

But if that's the case, why does it feel so damn right?

My grip tightens around the microphone as I hold it close and sway. The audience is eerily quiet. Not even the clink of glasses can be heard over the instruments and my voice.

As the last notes reverberate throughout the bar, there's a moment of absolute silence before thunderous applause erupts. A few guys jump to their feet, whistling and yelling my name.

My gaze unconsciously flickers to Ford.

His eyes are narrowed.

I can't tell if he's pissed by the song selection or not.

"Hey, Carina! How about you be a bad girl with me?" a guy shouts from across the bar.

Not bothering with a response, I slip through the crowd and head for the exit. I don't quite understand it, but I feel strangely vulnerable. Like maybe I revealed a little bit too much of myself up there. I'm used to leaving every drop of emotion on the stage after a performance, but that was different.

I need to take off before I say or do something I end up regretting. If I'm smart, I'll think long and hard about what's happening with Ford before this goes any further and blows up in my face.

If it hasn't already...

As I cross the darkened space, a hand reaches out. My heart thunders beneath my breast, hoping that Ford hasn't caught up to me.

"Carina?"

I spin around, expecting someone else. A weird concoction of relief and disappointment swirls through me when I find Fallyn.

"Hey," she says, nodding toward the stage. "You were amazing up there. I had no idea you could sing like that."

I force my lips into a smile. "Thanks."

"Are you heading out already? It's still early."

"Yeah." My gaze flickers over the rowdy crowd searching for one face in particular. "I am."

"That's too bad. I just got here. We'll have to do another girls' night soon. That was so much fun."

My mind tumbles back to the evening in question.

And Ford.

"We definitely should."

When there's a burst of laughter from the table where the hockey players are crowded around, we both turn and stare. Madden and Riggs are chuckling about something. A couple girls are hanging all over Colby, vying for his attention. All he has to do is flash his dimples and the ladies on campus instantly melt. Whether they want to or not. It's like he has a superpower.

Just as I'm about to look away, my gaze gets snagged by Wolf. Unlike most of the other guys on the team, he's tatted up. There's a quiet dangerousness about him. Almost broody. He's not as quick to laughter like some of the others. I've noticed over the years that he tends to hang back, observing everything and everyone first.

And right now, his sights are locked on us.

Or, more accurately, they're locked on Fallyn.

I flick a glance at the girl at my side, only to find her returning the stare with an equal amount of intensity. I wasn't aware they were acquainted. Although Fallyn and I just met, and we don't know each other well. Even though there's a ton of people milling around as the music reverberates off the walls, the tension between them continues to ratchet up, turning almost suffocating.

"Do you know Wolf?"

Her gaze stays locked on him as she shakes her head. "No."

Thrown off by the response, my brows snap together in surprise. "Really?"

My attention slices to him again. He's still staring. There's a strange expression on his face. As if at any moment, he'll leap out of his seat and stalk over here. What he'll do after he arrives is anyone's guess.

Except…that doesn't happen.

Instead, Larsa Middleton places her hands over his eyes as she stands behind his chair and presses her boobs against the back of his head. That's all it takes to break the spell woven around them.

Fallyn swings around, angling her body away from the table of hockey players.

"The heat you two just generated was almost enough to have me bursting into flames," I say lightly, hoping she'll open up and tell me what's going on. "You really don't know him?" Skepticism fills my voice.

Even in the darkness of the bar, it would be impossible to miss the dull color that crawls up her neck and cheeks. "No, I don't."

My lips quirk. "Do you want to?"

She shakes her head.

Hmm. Even more interesting.

Most of the girls on this campus have a thing for the guy and would jump at the chance to sleep with him. He's the broody bad boy of the team.

From the corner of my eye, I catch a glimpse of Ford shoving his way through the crowd and decide it would be best to hightail my ass into gear.

Cutting off our convo, I point toward the exit. "It was great running into you, but I've got to head out."

Disappointment crashes over her features. "Oh, okay. I'll text you later."

"Sounds good." With that, I swing away, slipping through the sea of drunken students to the back of the bar. Once the cool night air hits my cheeks, relief pumps through me as I beeline toward my BMW parked in the lot.

Even though Ford and I drove over together, he'll have to find his own way home.

CHAPTER TWENTY-SIX

FORD

"Dude, that hat trick was freaking awesome! With the number of shots you took on goal, you should have had at least three of them."

My attention flickers to the guy who just slid in front of me, effectively blocking my path to Carina.

"And then when that player knocked you into the boards…" He shakes his head.

"Yeah," I mutter. "It was a solid hit."

My gaze returns to the blonde as she slips out the back door.

Dammit.

"I couldn't believe it when you took that shot and it hit the crossbar before bouncing off it. That totally should have been a goal."

He's right about that.

I jerk my shoulders. "Well, what can you do?"

I'm hanging onto my patience by a thread. Every second that ticks by only makes it more unlikely that I'll catch Carina. It's tempting to shove this dude out of my way and make a run for the exit.

He shakes his head and shifts, looking as if he's settling in for a nice long convo.

Before he can launch into yet another play, I clap him hard on the shoulder. "It was great talking to you…" My voice trails off as I blank on his name.

"Steve," he supplies helpfully. "We were in the same marketing class last year."

I snap my fingers and point, even though that's not ringing any bells. "Right. Dr. Masterson."

His brow furrows. "No, it was Giddings."

"Sorry." I flash a tight smile. One that feels as if it'll crack into a million jagged pieces. "It's been a long day and I was just heading out."

"No worries."

"Have a good night."

That said, I slide past him, huffing out a relieved breath when he doesn't trail after me. A few more people clap my shoulder and call out my name. Instead of engaging, I stare straight ahead, ignoring them all.

There's only one person I have an interest in talking to.

More like getting my hands on.

Carina.

And that song?

Fucking hot.

It took less than thirty seconds of her husky crooning for my dick to give her a salute worthy of a five-star general. Unfortunately, one glance at all the dazed and slack-jawed expressions told me I wasn't the only one blown away by her performance.

By the time I make it to the paved lot and jog to where she parked the BMW, there's nothing but an empty space.

I plow a hand through my hair and contemplate my options before swinging around and heading back inside. It takes a solid twenty minutes to convince Wolf to hand over the keys to his Mustang GTO. The guy treats the damn thing like it's his baby.

Ridiculous.

Sure, I love my Vette. But at the end of the day, it's just a car. A really nice, shiny automobile that gets me from point A to point B. That's all I need it to do.

"Let me guess...did Carina take off without you?" he asks, a smile tugging at his lips.

He's probably thinking about the eyeful he caught in the corridor after the game.

I shoot him a glare and turn away without responding. His deep rasp of a chuckle chases after me.

Dick.

Once I slip behind the wheel and start up the engine, the muscle car purrs to life and I take off, roaring out of the parking lot. It takes less than ten minutes to reach the apartment building. I slide into a space and spot her sleek silver Beamer a few rows over. Something settles inside me that she came straight home.

As I stalk through the lobby, a gaggle of drunk girls waiting for the elevator catches my attention. They turn and stare, eyes lighting up when they spot me.

Oh hell no.

Over my dead body am I getting stuck with them in an enclosed space.

Two of them call out my name as I beeline to the stairwell and jog up to the third floor. Once I reach the landing, I shove through the door and head to her apartment.

Did she really think she could avoid me after that little performance?

Yeah, that's not going to happen.

I'd tear this damn town apart with my bare hands if I had to.

I rap my knuckles against the thick wood and wait a beat and then two. When I'm greeted with silence, I do it again, a little louder this time. I'm just about to pull out my phone and call her ass when the door swings open and Carina stands on the other side of the threshold wearing nothing more than a skimpy tank top and panties.

I jerk a brow as my hungry gaze roves over her length. "You always answer the door in your underwear?"

"Yup."

I flash a smile. "Works for me."

It only takes a couple of steps to eat up the distance between us and then my lips are crashing onto hers. As soon as they do, she opens and my tongue thrusts inside her mouth to tangle with her own. Her sweetness floods my senses, calming the raging beast that lives inside where she's concerned.

It's just enough to take the edge off so I don't fall completely apart at the seams.

Her arms tangle around my neck and my hands drop to the rounded curves of her ass, biting into the firm flesh. When I hoist her off the floor, her long legs wrap around my waist.

My mouth devours hers as I stride through the living area and then short hallway to her bedroom. I kick the door shut behind us before lowering her to the mattress and following her down. Our teeth scrape as our tongues continue to mate. Her legs tighten around me as if she's afraid I'll untangle myself from her, but I don't see that happening anytime soon.

I can't imagine ever getting enough of this girl, and that's a scary thought.

Watching her up on stage, knowing every dick in the joint was having the same dirty thoughts roll through their heads made me want to jump up there and drag her away.

Carina has a presence about her. She always has. Even in high school, I enjoyed watching her dance. On stage or in the studio my father built. I'd slip inside the room and sit against the mirrored wall, silently soaking her in for hours. There was something calming about the graceful sweep of her arms and legs that never failed to soothe the teenage angst that raged inside me.

She was like taking a hit and chilling out.

My own private drug.

Even when I tried to distance myself, that proved an impossible task. Carina was always there, simmering in the back of my mind, fighting her way to the forefront by any means necessary.

My mouth trails along the curve of her jaw before drifting down the slender column of her throat. My tongue laves the delicate flesh, nipping it gently with my teeth.

The primal urge to mark her thrums through me until it's all I can think about. If I assumed that fucking her once would dull the need burning inside me, I couldn't have been more wrong. In fact, it's been the complete opposite. One taste has only whetted my appetite for more. I'm not sure if it's even possible to satiate the deep well of need that burns inside me.

Unwilling to inspect that disturbing thought more thoroughly, I rip the tank from her body and toss it over my shoulder. Her breasts are small and firm. Utterly gorgeous with pretty little nipples that tighten as the cool air of the room wafts around them. My tongue darts out to lick one perky tip before sucking it into my mouth as her fingers tunnel through my hair, curling around my skull.

"Ford," she whimpers. "That feels so good."

Damn right it does.

When we're together like this, it's electric.

More than that—it's addictive.

I'm a fucking junkie for this girl.

I release her nipple with a soft pop before giving the same ardent attention to the other one. When she's writhing beneath me, I continue my descent, licking and kissing my way down to the elastic band of her panties. My teeth scrape across the silky material, pulling it away from her body before allowing it to snap against her hipbone.

I glance up at her face as my fingers slip beneath the slender band.

Thick tension crackles in the air.

"If you don't, I will," she says with a groan.

There's nothing funny about this moment, but that comment makes my lips twitch.

Just like with the tank, I tear the thin scrap of material away until she's gloriously naked. Even though it's not the first time I've seen her like this, air gets clogged at the back of my throat as my gaze licks over her with more care.

She's so toned and muscular. An athlete, just like me. The dedication she has for her discipline is so damn sexy.

As my gaze dips to her pussy, my hands settle on her inner thighs, shoving them apart until I can see every delicate inch. My mouth waters for a taste of her sweetness. I spread her wide with my thumbs before lowering my face.

The first lap is nirvana.

How did I go so long without tasting her?

Fucking addictive.

That's the only thought that reverberates throughout my head.

Her spine bows off the mattress as the tip of my tongue circles her clit before I drag it down her slit and then up again. I repeat the maneuver a handful of times until she's twisting beneath me, throaty moans of pleasure escaping from her, filling the silence of the room.

I'd like nothing more than to eat her up all night long, but there's no way she'll last that long. Already her muscles are tightening as her nails scrape across my scalp. Any moment, my dick will explode.

I shouldn't be this wound up.

Especially after she sucked me off.

I should be satiated.

Firmly under control.

And yet, I'm on the brink of losing it.

Years of pent-up need have finally broken loose and there's no way to tamp them down again. For better or worse, they're out there.

When I suck her clit into my mouth, she splinters into a million jagged pieces. The way she screams out my name is sweet music to my ears.

She doesn't even try to temper her pleasure.

She breaks apart beautifully beneath my mouth.

I continue lapping at her softness until her muscles lose their rigidity and she sinks into the mattress like a limp noodle. Her breath escapes in short, panting gasps as if she's run a marathon. I press a kiss against her soaked flesh before rising to my feet and stripping off my clothes.

When I stroke my erection, her gaze drops to the movement.

"You ready to come again, pretty girl?"

She spreads her legs wide in silent invitation. Her pussy is soft, swollen, and wet.

I fucking love that I did that to her.

All I have to do is lick her sweetness and she falls apart within a matter of minutes. Just like I do when she takes me deep inside her throat. Even the thought of her muscles constricting around my length is enough to make me throb with need.

Unable to wait another second, I settle on top of her.

It occurs to me that we should probably use a condom. I made sure to shove a few in my wallet after last time but as I stare into her gorgeous eyes, I realize that I don't want to. There's no way I can fuck her with a thin layer separating us.

I need her bare.

Just like before.

I hold perfectly still and grit out the question. "Are you good if I don't wear anything?"

"Yeah, I'm protected."

Thank fuck. If she wanted me to suit up, I would. I'd rather screw her with a condom than not at all. But there's something about being inside her without anything that feels so damn good. It adds another layer of intimacy to the act that I never anticipated.

She's the only one I'd do this with.

Just like last time, there's no preamble. I drive inside her tight heat with one smooth stroke. A tortured groan escapes from my lips as I squeeze my eyes closed, relishing the delicious feeling, wanting to somehow stretch it out and make it last forever.

If I thought the first time we had sex was some kind of strange anomaly, I quickly realize that's not the case. This girl has a unicorn pussy. That's the only plausible explanation. The way her inner muscles clench makes it feel like I'm moments away from blowing my load.

And there's no damn way—

Fuck.

Before I realize it, I'm going off like a shot.

Cum erupts from me as I force my eyes open and stare into hers. As soon as I do, her pussy clenches as her own orgasm takes hold and we come together. The way she moans out my name makes my release even more intense. She milks my dick until there's nothing left to give. When my muscles finally slacken, I hold myself up on my elbows and stare down at her, marveling at the bond that continues to strengthen between us, binding us together.

The thought that bothers me most in this moment of blissed-out introspection is how I'll get enough of her to last me for the rest of my life.

The uncomfortable silence that follows that question is nothing short of deafening.

CHAPTER TWENTY-SEVEN

CARINA

Ford's fingers absently play with mine as we drive to Crawford's house for our usual Wednesday night dinner. He's been toying with them ever since he pulled out of the apartment building parking lot.

And I've let him because I love it.

As soon as that sly thought sneaks into my brain, I wince.

I don't want to get used to the way he touches me.

Or come to expect it.

Only to be disappointed when he moves on.

Ever since last Thursday, he's been sneaking over after Juliette hits the sheets and staying the night.

We have sex. The first time is always quick and dirty.

Mr. playboy manwhore who has slept with his share of the co-eds on this campus can't seem to control himself. The only reason I don't tease him mercilessly is because no matter how fast he orgasms, I always come as if on command.

It's demoralizing.

Afterward, he'll huff out a breath and rest his forehead against mine before apologizing, muttering something about how he doesn't understand why he isn't able to last longer and how unusual this is.

Ha! Whatever you say, quick draw McGraw.

My sympathetic nods and pats on the shoulder are not appreciated. The way he frowns and narrows his eyes as color stains his cheeks is kind of hilarious.

Most of the drive has been made in silence. Every once in a while, he turns his head just enough to watch me from the corner of his eye. I can almost hear the questions churning in his brain. I keep my lips tightly pressed together because I don't have the answers he's looking for.

I'm just as confused about our situation as he is.

Tension continues to ratchet up between us until it becomes stifling. It's a relief when we pull into the gated subdivision with its sprawling mansions. Every property is perfectly maintained and manicured with trees that dot the rolling landscape.

The first time Mom drove us through the imposing iron gates and I caught a glimpse of our new home, I was worried that Crawford wouldn't be interested in Mom's baggage.

Namely, me.

But nothing could have been further from the truth.

Mom is no longer the person I call when I need advice or when something amazing happens.

Crawford is. He's become that stabilizing figure I spent my childhood searching for.

Ford squeezes my fingers, drawing me out of those thoughts. "Are you all right? You've been awfully quiet."

I force a smile, unwilling to share the concerns that eat at me. "Yeah, I'm fine."

More questions fill his eyes as he pulls into the driveway. As we near the two-story stone structure, my gaze lands on a sleek black Audi that I don't recognize.

"Who do you think that is?"

He shrugs. "I'm not sure."

"It's weird," I mutter. "Usually, it's just the three of us at these dinners."

"Maybe there's a new girlfriend."

I shoot him a look of horror. "What? Has he been seeing someone? Do you have insider info that I don't?"

Ford's lips quirk as he flashes a smile. "Not that I know of. Don't worry, you'll always be his best girl."

I roll my eyes and glare. That only makes him chuckle.

When Mom and Crawford announced their divorce, I was terrified he'd find someone to quickly replace her and whoever the woman was would be less than tolerant of having his ex's college-aged daughter hovering about. The one time he did bring a potential girlfriend around, she made no bones about asking why I was still part of his life. Crawford told her in no uncertain terms that I was his daughter and then promptly dumped her fancy ass.

I don't think I've ever been more relieved in my life.

We exit the sports car and meet around the hood. When Ford holds out his hand, I stare at it for a few heart pounding seconds.

Another smile twitches around the corners of his lips. "Are you afraid my dad is standing at the windows, watching us?"

Kind of.

Even though my stepfather has never come out and said anything specific, I get the feeling that he wouldn't be pleased with this new development.

As much as I want to resist the offer, my hand drifts to his until his fingers are able to wrap around mine, clasping them firmly as if he'll never let go.

A teeny tiny part of me doesn't want him to.

"Was that so difficult?"

"You have no idea."

He snorts and pulls me up the wide stone staircase to the eight-foot-tall mahogany door. As soon as he throws it open, I slip my fingers from his grip. He smirks as I glance around the entryway for Crawford. Normally, he's in his home office and comes out to greet us as soon as we arrive. I peek in the study only to find it empty.

Which is…odd.

As I swing around, my stepfather's laughter rings out from the family room off the kitchen.

My gaze slices to Ford's before he extends an arm as if to say *after you.*

Maybe he's right and his father *does* have a girlfriend. I mean, he did mention over the phone that there was something he wanted to discuss with us. I assumed it was about the upcoming election.

I straighten my shoulders as we head down the echoing corridor until we reach the double story space. There's a massive, stacked stone fireplace along with a sleek, cream-colored couch and matching navy armchairs upholstered in rich velvet.

As soon as Crawford catches a glimpse of us, he rises to his feet. There's a wide smile on his face as if he's bursting with excitement.

"We were just talking about the two of you," he says in a jovial voice.

I force a smile as my gaze skitters to the woman sitting in one of the armchairs. From this angle, all I can see is long blonde hair that tumbles down her back in loose beachy waves.

I guess Ford was right after all.

There's a new girlfriend.

My gaze slides over her, taking in the pink designer jumpsuit that clings to her curves and the pale blue Birken sitting on the end table.

It would appear that Crawford really does have a type.

When the woman finally swivels toward us, her blue-gray eyes lock on mine and I grind to an abrupt halt.

Pamela.

What the hell is she doing here?

My brows snap together at this unpleasant surprise. I would have preferred that it was some random woman rather than her.

"Mom?"

She tilts her head as husky laughter falls from her lips. "Who else would it be?"

That's all it takes for a heavy stone to sink to the pit of my belly as I glance at Crawford, attempting to figure out what her sudden reappearance in his life means.

Hopefully, nothing.

As much as I try to crush the concern now blooming inside me like a weed, that's impossible.

My gaze flickers to Crawford. His attention remains solely focused on Pamela. There's a besotted look in his eyes. He loves to tell the story about how he walked into the restaurant, took one look at her, and fell head over heels in love. And I tend to believe it because two months after she waited on him, they were hitched. It was a crazy, whirlwind affair.

At the time, it had all seemed so romantic.

Almost like Cinderella when Prince Charming swooped in to save her.

Crawford gave her anything and everything she asked for.

Whatever her heart desired.

Hence the Birkin bag.

Along with the three others she owns.

They're like her children. They actually have pet names she jokingly refers to them as. Although, I'm pretty sure the woman isn't joking. If there were a choice between rescuing her expensive purses or me from a burning building, I'd be toast.

Literally.

"Aren't you going to give me a hug? Or are you just going to stand there with your mouth gaping wide." She makes a tsking sound with her tongue. "Most unattractive, Carina."

I snap it shut and grit my teeth before forcing my feet into movement. She rises gracefully from the chair before extending her arms. I wrap mine loosely around her, wishing it didn't feel so awkward. It's like embracing a stranger.

She's thinner than the last time I saw her.

Or she's had work done.

Possibly both.

I'm sure Crawford would know since he foots the bill for everything. A mixture of shame and guilt pricks at me as that snide thought pops into my head. I've heard the ugly whispers that she married Crawford solely for his money and is nothing more than a gold digger.

She's heard the ugly rumors, too.

Instead of being embarrassed when people talk loud enough for her to overhear, she'll smile brightly and raise a crystal flute of champagne before bringing it to her lips and downing the bubbly contents.

It's the reason I insisted on getting a part-time job at the dance studio when I was a junior in high school. When I went away to college, I quickly found another studio to work at near campus. Even though I barely make enough to buy groceries each week, it's at least some small contribution.

No one can claim that I'm sponging off Crawford.

Deep down inside, I don't want him to think that I've stuck around all these years in order to mooch off him. I've told him on more than one occasion that I'd be happy to take out loans for college, but he insists I use the fund he set up as soon as he married Mom.

Relief washes over me once I untangle myself from her and take a hasty step in retreat. A cloud of Christian Dior perfume clings to me.

Her gaze shifts to her ex-stepson and she ups the wattage of her smile. "Ford, you're looking handsome as ever."

He gives her a quick peck on the cheek before taking up sentinel beside me. I have no idea how he understands that I need his emotional support now more than ever.

"It's good to see you, Pamela." There's a beat of silence before he adds, "I didn't realize you were in town."

She beams as her gaze slices to Crawford. The intimate look they share has my belly erupting with fresh nerves.

"We were going to make an announcement over dessert, but why wait?" he says, voice brimming with excitement. He cuts across the thick wool rug to where Mom stands before slipping his arm around her waist and dropping a light kiss against the crown of her head. "Pamela and I have been seeing each other for about a month now and we've decided to give our relationship another shot."

My wide eyes dart to Mom in shock. The calculating gleam that fills hers never wavers.

When I remain silent, my brain cartwheeling, she asks, "Aren't you happy for us, Carina?"

CHAPTER TWENTY-EIGHT

FORD

My fingers clench the leather steering wheel as we speed back to campus.

After Dad dropped his bomb, dinner turned out to be an awkward affair.

Throughout the hour-long production, I watched Carina withdraw into herself, toying with her food and barely contributing to the conversation. Immediately afterward, she shoved away from the table, saying that she needed to practice her solo for the showcase.

When Dad asked if she wanted dessert—tiramisu, her favorite—she shook her head and fled from the room as if the hounds of hell were nipping at her heels.

The fact that she wouldn't even glance in my direction only heightened my concern.

After demolishing the coffee-flavored sweet, I told them that I needed to use the john and never returned.

Not that they'd notice.

Or care.

Or maybe it would be accurate to say that Dad wouldn't notice. Throughout dinner, he barely glanced away from his ex-wife. It's as if she's the sun he revolves around.

It's been like that since day one.

Pamela, on the other hand, is more difficult to read. She doesn't wear her emotions on her sleeve the way my father does. Not even where her daughter is concerned, which is a damn shame. If there's one person who deserves both her time and attention, it's Carina. As far as I can tell, Pamela is more interested in herself than anyone else.

Instead of hitting the bathroom, I headed straight down to the studio, only to find the door locked.

Can you believe that?

Not in all these years has Carina locked me out.

I didn't even know the damn thing had one.

How's that for a kick in the balls?

So, I did the only thing I could and sank to the floor outside the room, giving her the space she craved. I slid a piece of paper under the door, letting her know I was there if she wanted to talk. An hour later, we walked upstairs together, and I told the parentals we needed to head out.

Carina shot me a grateful look.

Since she hasn't said a single word, I blurt, "I take it their relationship is a surprise?"

"Yeah." Her voice is flat. Monotone. "For you as well?"

"I knew they'd grabbed lunch together a couple of weeks ago, but nothing more than that." The last thing I want is for her to think I've been keeping secrets. The next question flies out of my mouth before I can stop it. "You really don't want them together?"

For some unknown reason, hurt pricks me. Which is stupid, I know. It would be far easier for us if our parents weren't together. As soon as that thought pops into my head, I realize it's exactly what I want.

To be with Carina.

Even though we've been pretending this was casual, it was never a friends-with-benefits situation.

Or, as she likes to say, a frenemies-with-benefits situation.

At least, it wasn't for me.

"No."

Only wanting to lighten the mood, I say with a snort, "You should really stop mincing words and just tell me how you feel."

She sucks in a lungful of air before slowly releasing it back into the vehicle. "I don't want Pamela and Crawford together. Ever. End of story."

Damn.

I flex my fingers, attempting to loosen the death grip I have on the leather steering wheel. "Why? What does it even matter anymore?"

She hunches her shoulders and swivels away, making it impossible to get a read on her expression. "I just don't."

I kick an idea around before it tumbles off the tip of my tongue. "Do you think Pamela's too good for my dad or something?" What else could it be? Why is she so adamant about them not being together?

"Are you serious?" She whips around and stares at me with wide eyes. "Of course not! It anything, Crawford is way too good for almost any woman."

Ahhh. Now we're finally getting somewhere.

"So…you think he's too good for your mother?"

She slumps on the leather and turns her head away again. "I don't want to talk about it, okay? I'm really tired. I just want to go home."

A frustrated burst of air escapes from me. I'm unsure how to get Carina to open up and tell me what's really going on inside her head.

Doesn't she understand that I just want to be there for her?

It's been that way since day one.

It was always her.

Even after I pushed her away.

It was her.

I spend the rest of the drive trying to draw her into conversation. Every attempt I make is met with stilted, one-word responses.

She won't even look at me.

As soon as I pull into the parking lot and cut the engine, she jerks the handle and jumps out of the car. I swear under my breath that she won't even wait for me. By the time I slam the driver's side door closed and click the locks, she's already yanking open the glass door and slipping inside the building.

I hasten my pace to catch up with her, even though it's fairly obvious that I'm the one she's running from. By the time I make it to the lobby, there's no sign of her. Instead of waiting for the elevator, I shove through the stairwell door and take the concrete stairs two at a time. Once I arrive on the third floor, I barrel through the metal door and burst into the hallway. I grind to a halt and glance down the long stretch where our apartments are located.

The space is empty.

Is it possible that I missed her?

Just as I take a step, prepared to bang on her door if necessary, the elevator dings and the metal contraption slides open. The moment Carina steps into the hallway, her gaze locks on mine.

Her eyes widen as she stumbles to a halt. She blinks a few times as if she can't believe I've materialized in front of her like a specter.

"Ford." Her voice is breathless as if she's the one who just ran up three flights of stairs instead of me.

"The one and only," I say calmly.

Her teeth scrape across her lower lip. "I'm sorry. I just want to be alone right now."

It's so fucking tempting to reach out and drag her into my arms. Instead, I keep my hands to myself. It's one of the hardest things I've ever had to do. "Just tell me what's going on, because I don't understand why you're so upset."

She glances away as color drains from her cheeks until they turn ashen. I swallow up some of the distance between us and drop my voice. "Is it because we're sleeping together and if they actually get married again, we're back to being stepsiblings?"

Something shifts in her eyes. "Yeah, that's exactly what it is."

Before I can pull any more information from her, she darts around me.

Instead of giving chase, I plow a hand through my hair and watch as she shoves the key in the door before sending one final glance my way and stepping inside the apartment.

CHAPTER TWENTY-NINE

CARINA

I close the door behind me and lean against it before squeezing my eyes tightly shut and sucking in a deep, calming breath. The entire way home, I tried to wrangle all of these out-of-control emotions back into submission, but Ford's presence made it impossible. It's hard to think straight when he's nearby. The heat of his gaze seared my skin every time it slid over me. The more questions he fired off, the more I shut down.

Maybe I shouldn't have been thrown off by Mom's sudden appearance. She might have walked away from Crawford without so much as a second glance, but it's obvious that he hasn't moved on. He brings her up in conversation any chance he gets.

It's like fingernails on a chalkboard.

How doesn't he realize that she's using him?

He's nothing more than a safety net.

I wish to hell that she'd stay away.

Why does she have to ruin everything?

Well…maybe not everything, because if she hadn't caught Crawford's eye in the first place, he wouldn't be in my life.

When the going got tough, instead of trying to work out their issues, she took off.

I'd love to believe that my mother has changed, but I don't think that's the case. My guess is that she'll stick around for a while and then, when he doesn't shower her with enough attention, she'll get fed up and leave.

She's selfish that way.

A prick of guilt hits me for thinking that about my own parent. Unfortunately, it's the truth. What I've come to realize is that my feelings for Pamela are complicated. They always have been. Part of me loves her dearly. The woman is my mother. But there's also another part that sees her for the person she truly is. A self-centered narcissist. She had me when she was seventeen and struggled to make ends meet until Crawford swept into our lives and saved us.

Instead of being grateful, she treats him like a puppy she can't shake loose. Everything in Pamela's life revolves around Pamela. I've learned over the years to accept her for the way she is (hello therapy) and stop expecting her to be the kind of mother I've always longed for.

That being said, I don't want her messing with Crawford. And I don't want her to hurt him to the point where he tosses me out of his life because he doesn't want any reminders of her lurking around his house.

Even the thought of that makes my blood run cold.

"Carina? Are you okay?"

My eyelids snap open and just like the past couple hours, I force a smile to my lips. "Yeah, I'm fine. Just tired. It's been a long day." Then I pushed myself in the studio, trying to burn off some of my excess emotion. Dance is the only thing capable of getting me out of my head.

Well…maybe that's not altogether true. Ford does it as well.

But not this time.

She points to the books and computer spread out on the tiny table in the dining area. "I have an exam tomorrow. I'm pretty sure inorganic chem will be the death of me."

I push away from the thick wood and swing into the compact

kitchen to grab a bottle of water. "Nah. You'll ace this test just like all the others. You're wicked smart," I say in my best Boston accent

"That remains to be seen," she mutters before rubbing her eyes.

"Girl, please. You'll probably wreck the curve for everyone else. It wouldn't be the first time."

She snorts before switching topics. "Hey, how did dinner go?"

If there's one thing I hate to do, it's lie to Juliette. Over the years, she's become one of my closest friends. Maybe we didn't grow up together and only found each other in college, but that girl is my soul sister. The frick to my frack. My sister from another mister. Normally, we talk about anything and everything. Even the vibe I found while rummaging around in her underwear drawer.

Let me tell you—the fact she actually had one and it was so dang cute was a pleasant surprise. The memory of her embarrassment is almost enough to make me smile.

But I don't necessarily want to discuss Pamela. The situation is embarrassing. Juliette's parents are like an institution, and the four of them are the perfect family. It's hard not to be jealous. Especially when I see how close she is to her mom and how much Natalie genuinely cares about her. Something in me longs for the same kind of relationship, even though I recognize that Pamela isn't capable of it.

"It was fine." I decide to give her a tiny bit of the truth, so I don't feel so guilty. "Mom dropped by for a visit."

Her eyebrows skyrocket. "Oh?"

She draws out the word so that it comes out sounding more like *ohhhhhh*.

"Yeah." My voice turns flat. It's impossible to pretend that I feel any kind of joy where that woman is concerned.

When I say nothing more on the subject, she asks, "How come?"

I jerk my shoulders, trying to loosen the growing tension that now sits between them. "She and Crawford might be getting back together."

There's a second or two of silence as she studies me more carefully. "Is that good news?"

Nope. It's the worst possible news ever.

"I don't know," I say with forced lightness. "Guess we'll just have to see."

How long it lasts, that is.

"So...what does that mean for you and Ford?"

That question is enough to have my heart slamming painfully against my ribcage. "Nothing. We're just hooking up. It's not that big of a deal." Pushing out that response leaves a bitter taste in my mouth, because nothing could be further from the truth.

"Are you sure?"

"Positive."

When I refuse to say anything more, she glances at her computer before rubbing her eyes. "I should probably get back to it. I've still got a couple hours to knock out before calling it a night."

"Don't stress. You're gonna kill it."

A smile curves her lips. "Thanks for the vote of confidence."

I blow her a kiss before heading to my room to change. Just as I'm about to pull off my shirt, something on the bed catches my attention. I step closer, trying to get a better look.

It's a paperback.

It's probably the one I loaned to Juliette last week. She's been devouring them lately. It might have taken a couple years, but I've finally managed to turn her to the dark and smutty side.

I pick up the book and inspect it with more care. My brows draw together as my fingers slide over the crisp cover. That's strange. It's not one I recognize. I flip it over to check out the blurb.

Wait a minute...I think it's from one of my wish lists.

A new release.

Aww, Juliette is the sweetest. She really is a good friend.

My step is a little lighter as I return to the living room and hold up the paperback. For the first time in hours, a genuine smile curves my lips.

"Hey, thanks for the book. I was looking forward to getting my hot little hands on this one."

She glances up from the computer screen. "Oh, that's not from me.

Ford dropped it off earlier this afternoon. I thought you saw it before you left for dinner."

I can only stare as my heart hitches. Seconds later, an ache blooms in the center of my chest before slowly spreading outward. It's tempting to lift my hand and rub at the spot.

He did?

That's something he used to do in high school. Every once in a while, I'd find a paperback waiting for me on my bed. It was that kind of thoughtfulness that had me falling head over heels for him.

"That doesn't really seem like something a guy would do if he's just hooking up with a random girl," she says softly, drawing my attention back to her.

Those words circle viciously through my head as I clutch the paperback to my chest. Unsure what to say, I clear my throat and avoid the questions that simmer in her eyes. "I'm, ah, going to bed now."

"All right. Good night."

"Night."

Once in my room, I change my clothes and slip beneath the covers before staring at the book again. Almost reluctantly, I flip to the first page. That's all it takes for me to get sucked into the story. This is a brand-new release from my favorite author. I've been dying to pick it up but just haven't had the time with everything going on. Sure, I could have downloaded the e-book, but there's something about the feel of a paperback in my hands.

After an hour or so, my eyelids finally grow heavy, and I set the book carefully on the nightstand before turning out the light and rolling over. If I'm lucky, I'll drift right off to sleep.

Except…

That doesn't happen.

Half an hour later, I flip over, hit my pillow a couple of times, and attempt to get comfortable. Then, I flop onto my back and huff out an aggravated breath as I stare sightlessly up at the ceiling. There's too much circling around in my brain, and I can't turn it off. Most of it has to do with my mother. Maybe I need to sit down with her and have an honest conversation. I can bring up all the reasons she took off in the first place.

It can't hurt, right?

Now that I've come up with a potential resolution in regard to Pamela, I squeeze my eyes closed and try to fall asleep again.

But still...

Nothing happens. I'm wide awake.

It doesn't take a genius to figure out that the other issue bothering me is Ford. Our situation was built on the premise of being straight-up sex. We knock boots a couple times and then go back to being frenemies who can barely tolerate one another.

I'm no longer sure that's possible.

As much as I'm loath to admit it, my feelings for him have changed.

Flourished into more.

Or maybe they were always there, simmering beneath the surface, waiting for the perfect opportunity to break loose. I've tried like hell not to let it happen.

But it's difficult.

So damn difficult.

My gaze settles on the dark stack of books piled next to the bed.

Especially when he does something so sweet.

The guy gets me.

And that's probably the scariest thing of all.

It's almost a relief when my phone chimes with an incoming message and knocks those disturbing thoughts from my head. I roll over and grab the slim device from the nightstand before glancing at the time on the screen.

It's almost a surprise to realize that it's well after midnight.

You up?

My belly swoops as I stare at those two words.

For a handful of seconds, my fingertip hesitates over the screen. It's so damn tempting to respond. But if I do, I'll become even more tangled up in Ford than I already am.

The more time we spend together, the more I feel myself falling for him.

And that's a problem. One I have no idea how to solve.

If I were smart, I'd set the phone on the nightstand and ignore the text.

Instead, I type out a quick response.

Yes.

I'm coming over.

What?

No way!

That'll only exacerbate the situation. What I need is distance. Time alone to get my head on straight. I can't do that when I'm with him.

Just as I'm about to tell him to forget it, there's a soft knock on the apartment door.

My eyes widen as I leap from the bed and race into the living area. It's a relief when I find it empty. Juliette must have already gone to bed. Although, it's possible she's still up and studying in her room. I don't want her to know that Ford is coming over this late at night.

I whip open the door and find him wearing nothing more than gray joggers that are slung indecently low across lean hips. My gaze unconsciously licks over the broad expanse of his chest and chiseled abdominals before dipping to the large bulge in the cotton material. It's obvious that he's not wearing anything beneath them.

That's all it takes for my mouth to dry.

He's so fucking big and I love it.

Love the stretch of his cock when he slides deep inside my body.

And the feeling of fullness that follows.

"You keep looking at me like that and I'll take you right here in the hallway. We won't even make it to the bedroom." His voice is nothing more than a low growl that vibrates in my core.

My wide eyes dart to his in shock. The heat that sparks and snaps from them is almost enough to have me going up in flames. When I remain silent, at a loss for words, he steps across the threshold before closing and locking the door behind him. In one swift motion, he lowers his shoulder before wrapping his arms around my thighs and hoisting me off my feet until I'm dangling upside down.

"Ford," I gasp. "What are you doing?"

When the flat of his palm lands on my ass, I hiss out a shocked breath.

"Better keep it down or your roommate will wake up." He squeezes the firm flesh beneath his hand. "Have I ever mentioned how much I love your ass?"

"No." I'm pretty sure I'd remember something like that.

His fingers curl into the muscle, and I can't help but squirm against him as arousal explodes in my core. One touch and I'm panting for him.

"Some guys are all about the titties," he says almost conversationally as he walks us through the short hall and into my room. "But I like a nice juicy peach." He squeezes me again before his fingers slip beneath the thin material of my panties, slowly tracing over the cleft. "Anyone ever fuck you here?"

"No," I say breathlessly.

"Maybe one of these days, I'll have to dare you to do anal. We both know you won't be able to resist that. Sometimes I suspect it gives you the permission you need to do all the things you secretly long to."

Oh god…

He's not wrong.

That's exactly what it does.

Especially where he's concerned.

Once inside the room, he closes the door before dropping me to the bed. I bounce on the mattress and stare up at him, wondering what will happen next. Actually, I have a pretty good idea what that will be. That's all it takes for excitement to build inside me.

A knowing glint enters his eyes as he smirks. "You're so damn needy, aren't you?"

Before I can deny the truth, he shoves the material of his joggers down to reveal his thick erection. A whimper escapes from me as I stare.

His dick is as beautiful as the rest of him.

"That's exactly what I thought," he says with a satisfied grunt.

Even though my panties are still firmly in place, my legs fall open. I didn't realize until now just how much I needed to be screwed. I don't want to think about how my mother's presence has the potential to mess with my life. I want Ford to fuck me into oblivion until I'm too exhausted to dwell on the consequences of her actions.

He shackles his fingers around one ankle and drags me closer before ripping off my panties. The moment his mouth settles over my pussy, my muscles turn to butter.

Is there anything better in this world than Ford devouring me?

He eats at my flesh, stroking his tongue along my slit. From the bottom to the top before circling my clit with the tip. Then he thrusts deep inside my center. My muscles clench around him, greedy for more. Somehow, he knows exactly how to drive me to the brink. It doesn't take more than a handful of minutes before I'm spiraling out of control. I clap a hand over my mouth to stifle the cries that rise in my throat.

"That's right, pretty girl. Scream your little heart out. Release it all. I know this is exactly what you need."

His muttered words only intensify the orgasm that rips through my body.

It's only when my muscles turn limp and I'm floating back to earth that he turns me over and drags me backward until I'm perched at the edge of the mattress with my ass in the air.

His large hands slide over my cheeks before giving one side a whack with the flat of his palm. There's a slight sting of pain before a surprising amount of pleasure blooms in its place. My eyelids drift shut as I relish the delicious sensations that reverberate throughout my being. I've never had anyone smack my ass before. It's almost a shock to discover just how enjoyable it is.

He palms my cheeks before his fingers slip back inside my body.

"So fucking wet," he says with a groan. "And here I thought I'd licked up all your cream."

Even though I just came, his dirty words have more arousal flooding my core.

With the side of my face pressed flat against the mattress, I'm unable to see what he's doing.

I can only feel.

He spreads my cheeks apart as he nibbles at me before spearing his tongue deep inside my drenched center. I can't help but arch into his touch, only wanting to get closer.

The warmth of his mouth disappears as he smacks my ass again. "I'm the one who decides just how much you get."

My teeth sink into my lower lip to stifle the arousal that spikes through me like sharp knives.

He whacks me again. The crisp sound echoes in the silence of the room.

"Are you going to be a good girl?"

When I remain silent, he smacks the other side. "I want an answer." His finger slides across my swollen lips before zeroing in on my clit and rubbing soft circles. The pleasure is enough to make my body hum.

"Yes!" I blurt, unable to hold it back.

He presses his lips against my pussy. "Good girl. I know what you need, Carina. Let me give it to you."

His soft words knock the air from my lungs.

I squeeze my eyes tightly closed, almost hating how strong my need is to bend to his will and hand myself over to him.

The prospect is a scary one.

His large hands gently stroke over my flank, hips, and back. The caress is so soothing. Comforting. He continues to nibble until I'm dripping and writhing against him. Only then does he dip a finger inside me.

Once.

Twice.

On the third time, he drags it from my over-sensitized body.

I wait for him to rise to his feet and plunge inside me like he always does. To take me hard and fast, fucking us both until we're mindless.

Instead, one hand settles in the middle of my back, pushing me further to the mattress until it becomes necessary to arch my spine. My breath catches as he spreads my cheeks and uses the same finger that had just been buried deep inside my core to circle my rosebud.

When he makes no move to penetrate the opening, my rigidly held muscles loosen as I sink into the mattress. After a while, my eyelids feather closed. There's something strangely relaxing about the massage.

"Does that feel good?"

"Yes." It never occurs to me to lie.

Every once in a while, he drifts over the tiny pucker. Each time he does, my breath hitches, bracing for more.

Wanting more?

I'm unsure.

There's something so taboo about what he's doing but I can't say that I don't like it. Or want to explore more of it.

"You're so fucking pretty. Everything about you is." There's a pause as his deep voice grows whipcord tight. "I want to be the only one who touches you. Do you understand what I'm saying?"

I do. And I'd be lying if I didn't admit that I want it too.

I want to belong to Ford.

And I want him to belong to me.

His finger drifts over me again. "Carina?"

"Yes."

"And you want that too?"

"I do."

"Good girl."

With that, his finger glides over my rosebud again. My body tenses as he teases the entrance, prodding the opening until he's able to slip inside. There's a slight burn as the muscles stretch around the intrusion.

"Your ass is so damn tight, baby. I can't imagine what it would be like to bury myself deep inside you. To take and own you this way."

A huff of relief escapes from me as he withdraws.

It's short lived.

In the very next breath, he presses his finger back inside, sliding deeper than before. I close my eyes and silently wait for him to withdraw, but that doesn't happen. His movements stall as blood thrums through my veins until a dull roar fills my ears. It takes a handful of seconds before my muscles lose their rigidity. Instead of trying to squirm away from this new intimacy, I sink further into it.

A sigh of pleasure escapes from me.

"That's it, baby," he croons. "Just relax and let it all go."

When I release a breath, he presses even deeper until he's fully seated and his palm rests along the curve of my ass. There's something so possessive about the hold.

It doesn't make sense that I would find this comforting, but there's no denying that I do.

Maybe it's because he demanded that I give myself over to him.

To trust him enough to let go.

And that's exactly what I've done.

As those thoughts run rampant through my brain, I realize that as many guys as I've fucked, I've never allowed myself to be intimate. I've never given myself over for safekeeping or allowed myself to be vulnerable.

It's so much more than physical.

It's emotional as well.

I can almost feel the silky webs tangling around me, binding me to him in ways I never dreamed possible.

If I were thinking clearly, I'd immediately distance myself. With his finger buried deep inside me, there's no way to do that. I'm raw and exposed. His for the taking. And there's nothing I can do about it.

More than that, there's nothing I want to do about it.

With his other hand, he smacks my ass. The quick slap isn't sharp or painful. It's just enough pressure to draw my attention back to him.

Back to the present.

"Stop thinking. I can practically hear your brain churning. There's nothing you need to think about when I'm playing with your body, giving you pleasure. Because that's what this is, isn't it?"

"Yes," I whisper.

"Good girl."

He massages the tender area before slowly withdrawing. Just when I think he'll slip free, he surges forward before once again pulling out. He keeps up a steady rhythm until I'm once again lulled to a strange place of contentment.

"You spread so beautifully, Carina. I fucking love seeing you like this. Ass in the air as you offer yourself up to me. The fact that you've never allowed anyone else to stroke you like this means everything. I won't break the trust you're placing in me. Do you understand?"

"Yes."

For a long stretch of silent minutes, he plays with my backside. No longer is there the bite of pain. My muscles have loosened. It's almost a surprise when pleasure begins to build. It's different from when he plays with my pussy. The effect is nothing short of drugging.

And I want more.

When I squirm, he says with a groan, "If I kept this up much longer, I bet you'd come for me. Especially if I stroked your clit. Is that what you want, pretty girl? To orgasm?"

The idea of coming like this turns me on more than I could have imagined.

His fingers grip my ass, stretching the flesh so that there's once again a slight burn before he slaps the cheek. That's all it takes for arousal to coil deep inside my core.

When he dips the fingers of his other hand into my pussy before sliding around to my clit and rubbing it with soft circles that leave me breathless, every muscle tightens with expectation. The one buried in my ass continues its slow, rhythmic slide. I can't help but press into his hand, greedy for more contact. The orgasm brewing inside me feels like an impending storm seconds away from wreaking havoc.

It's exactly what I need.

"That's it, pretty girl." The pressure on my clit becomes insistent. "Just a little bit more to push you over the edge."

The low scrape of his words and the feel of his fingers playing with both parts are what make me shatter. My pussy spasms as he continues to pump his finger in my ass. I arch as a tidal wave of sensation crashes over me, nearly dragging me to the bottom of the ocean. This release feels so different than the others I've experienced.

It's not just my pussy.

It's my ass as well.

The intensity is tenfold. Stars dance behind my eyelids as I groan out my pleasure. When the final spasm wracks my body, I collapse onto the mattress in a heap of limbs that feel as if they weigh a thousand pounds. My brain floats somewhere in the atmosphere.

It's utter bliss.

Ford carefully slips from my exhausted body. Almost distantly, I hear the door to my bedroom open and then close. I squeeze my eyelids tight and simply allow myself to be in this moment. When the door reopens minutes later, he pads back to the bed. A warm cloth is pressed against my flesh, the cottony material wiping away my arousal.

Only then does he cage me in with his strength. There's nothing in this world more comforting than his presence. It's been that way since the very beginning, and I don't think it'll ever change. No matter what happens between us.

He presses his lips against my spine before kissing my bare shoulder blade and then face.

"Is that what you needed, baby?"

"Yes." It doesn't make sense how he knew.

"Good. I'm glad I could give it to you."

There's the rustle of clothing before he scoops me up and drags back the covers before carefully setting me down. Then he slides in and gathers me up into his arms.

I tilt my head until my gaze can lock on his and search it in the darkness. "What about you?"

"What about me?" he echoes.

"I thought you came over to fuck."

"I came over because I can't sleep without you in my arms. It had nothing to do with fucking. I knew you were upset about dinner. It's the reason you ran away." He presses a kiss to my lips. "I'm not going to allow you to do that anymore. This is more than fucking."

A sliver of fear and uncertainty arrow through me. "It is?"

"You know damn well it is," he says harshly.

When I open my mouth to fire off more questions, he presses his lips to mine. "We'll talk more in the morning, all right? Go to bed. What you need right now is sleep."

His words swirl madly through my head. Instead of trying to figure out exactly what they mean, I take the easy way out. "Thank you for the book. You didn't have to do that."

"I knew it would make you happy."

My breath catches at the back of my throat.

Has anyone ever said that to me?

Such a small thing that means so much?

Instead of allowing the fear to take hold and strangle the contentment attempting to bloom to life inside me, I do as he said and drift off to sleep.

Held protectively in the warm circle of his arms.

Exactly where I want to be.

CHAPTER THIRTY

FORD

I rap my knuckles against the thick wood and glance at the plastic bag with the campus bookstore logo emblazed on it. I'm beginning to feel like a cat constantly scratching at the backdoor, begging to be let in. That image alone is enough to make me snort.

And yet...I can't say it's not accurate.

The more time I'm with Carina, the more I want to be around her. I could spend 24/7 with that girl and it still wouldn't be enough. Holding her in my arms every night, fucking her, has in no way dulled the ache that continues to grow inside me. If anything, it only feeds my addiction.

It's totally messed up and not at all what I expected when I threw out the suggestion that we should sleep together. I'd assumed we would screw a couple times and I'd lose interest the way I usually do. Then we'd part ways amicably.

Well, sort of. Whether our parents are married or not, she'll always be part of the fam. So, it's not like ghosting her was ever a possibility.

I glance at the bag in my hand for a second time and hazard a guess as to what her reaction will be. No matter how much I try to figure her out, she always does the unexpected. The way she keeps me on my toes is part of her charm.

Just as I'm about to knock for a second time, the thick wood swings open, and I find Juliette on the other side of the threshold.

"Well, well, well," she says, drawing out the words as she crosses her arms against her chest. "Look who it is."

I flash her a charming smile. One that's capable of melting female hearts. Not that I'm, um, trying to melt her heart or anything. Ryder would kill me if I even looked sideways at his girl.

Or, more accurately, he'd take me out on the ice.

I'd be nothing more than blood splatter.

And I can't blame him for it. My guess is that he's been secretly in love with her for years before he finally decided to nut up and do something about it.

It's more like I'm trying to distract her, so she doesn't ask any probing questions. Carina has been adamant that we keep our situationship on the downlow. I have no idea if she's mentioned it to her bestie.

Which kind of irritates me.

"Is Carina around?" I pat my backpack. "We're working on a project together."

From the way one brow slinks upward, it would appear that my smile has zero effect on her.

"She's in her room."

When Juliette doesn't budge from the doorway, I clear my throat. "Can I, um, come in?"

"Maybe."

I shift from one foot to the other and echo the response. "Maybe?"

I've never known Juliette to be anything less than cordial. Always pleasant to be around. Normally, her nose is buried in a thick tome of a science book. As a pre-med major, I can certainly understand why. Even though she's rocket science smart, she still studies her ass off.

So this attitude…

It's throwing me off my game.

"Before I let you in, I'd like to know what your intentions are with my girl."

"My intentions…"

"Yeah." She leans against the doorjamb as a fierce expression settles across her face. "I know you've been sneaking in every night and staying over." She drops her voice as dull color stains her cheeks. "FYI—you're loud as fuck."

It takes effort to fight back the smile that trembles around my lips. "Sorry about that. We'll try to keep it down from now on."

She glares, her face turning almost beet red. "I could hear you through my noise cancelling headphones."

"We'll, you know, try and play the quiet game while doing it."

She rolls her eyes. "Are you two together now? Is this *a thing?*"

All the humor bubbling up inside me vanishes with those two questions. "I'm not sure." There's a beat of uncomfortable silence before I blurt, "Has she mentioned anything to you?"

Damn.

I didn't mean for that to slip out.

There's a flicker in her dark eyes before it's quickly masked. "Just that you two had an understanding. Friends-with-benefits or something like that."

"Frenemies-with-benefits," I mutter reluctantly.

"Yeah, maybe that was it," she agrees with a nod.

All the emotion swelling inside me nosedives before exploding on impact and erupting into a fiery ball of flames. Without another word—which is almost worse—she steps aside, allowing me into the apartment. As I walk past, our brief convo circles through my head.

What the hell am I doing?

It's painfully obvious this girl doesn't want anything serious.
With me.

She's here for a good time, not a long time.

It's not like Carina hasn't been perfectly upfront about that.

More confusion spirals through me as I stutter to a stop and lift my fist to rap my knuckles against the bedroom door.

"Come in," she calls out, sounding far more cheery than usual. Probably because she hasn't figured out who it is.

I turn the handle and push open the door before stepping inside.

She glances at me from the middle of the queen-sized bed and does a double take.

"Hey," she says with surprise.

"Hi." When she continues to stare, I say with forced casualness, "I thought we could work on our project." I glance at the books spread out on the bed. "Although, if you're busy, we can do it another time."

At this point, I'm wishing that I hadn't stopped by. In fact, I'd go so far as to say that getting involved with her in the first place was a huge mistake. The intention had been to fuck her out of my system, not make her even more of an obsession.

Guess the joke's on me, huh?

"Yeah, that's fine. Give me a second to clean up and we can get to it."

When she jumps off the bed, my gaze slides over her. She's wearing leggings that hug every slender curve and an oversized pink Western dance sweatshirt that hangs off one shoulder. Her long blonde hair has been pulled up into a messy knot at the top of her head.

Her beauty is like a gut punch. It doesn't matter if she's dressed up or down. Or wearing nothing at all. She's the most gorgeous girl I've ever laid eyes on.

Shit. I really need to get the hell out of here before I do or say something that I end up regretting.

Everything inside me feels surprisingly scraped raw.

And on the verge of exposure.

Like someone's about to peel back my skin and take a peek inside.

I don't think I've ever felt so full of emotion. Any moment, it's going to bubble over, and I'll embarrass the fuck out of myself. I'll end up telling her how much I care.

How much I've always cared.

Even when I was poking and needling, pretending that I didn't.

I can almost imagine her reaction to just such a disclosure. It would start with her laughing her ass off before patting my cheek and flashing a sympathetic smile.

Poor Ford.

I take a quick step in retreat as she stacks the pile of books on her vanity. The paperback I bought for her is lying dog eared next to them.

"You know what?" I jerk a thumb over my shoulder. "I'm gonna take off. You look like you're knee deep in studying. Just text me when you want to work on this, and we'll meet up at the library."

She glances at me with a frown. "You're leaving? *Now*?"

"Yeah. I, ah, got a thing I just remembered." Maybe a little time alone will help me pull my shit together. It certainly can't hurt.

Her gaze drops to the plastic bag in my hand. "What's that? Something for the project?"

For a second, I stare in confusion, unsure what she's talking about until I follow her line of sight.

Fuck. There's no way I can give this to her now and make an even bigger ass out of myself.

What the hell had I been thinking?

All right, I might not know what I'd been thinking, but I can certainly tell you what I'd been thinking with.

The damn thing will get you into trouble every single time.

"Oh, this?" I give the plastic a little shake. "It's nothing."

She quickly swallows up the distance between us with a couple of long-legged strides. "Can I see?"

"No, I don't—"

Before I can pull an excuse out of my ass and flee the scene of the crime, she nips the bag from my hand and takes a peek inside.

I wince as dull heat creeps up my neck and then my cheeks.

Her hand dips inside the plastic, pulling out the thick material. There's a furrow in her brow as she holds it up and stares at it in stone cold silence. I can almost see her brain trying to play mental catchup.

Just kill me now.

I'm serious. This is nothing short of excruciating. My heart feels like it'll pound right out of my chest.

Unable to stand another second of this torture, I swipe at the orange and black material, only wanting to tear it from her hands and stuff it back inside the bag. Then I can get out of here before dumping it in the trash and wiping this horrific moment from my memory.

Just as my fingers brush the fabric, she jerks it away so that I end up clawing at the air.

Her gaze fastens onto mine. "Did you buy this for me?"

There's a beat of uncomfortable silence.

Fuck. Is she really going to make me say it?

Out loud.

So she can gloat.

By the steady look in her eyes—yes...yes, she is.

I plow an agitated hand through my short strands and jerk my shoulders. "I don't want you wearing anyone else's jersey," I mumble.

Like Maverick's.

If someone's name and number is going to be plastered across her back, it's going to be mine. Or I'll tear the damn thing off her body just like I did before. I steel myself, waiting for her to dissolve into laughter before tossing the garment in my face.

A second, then two, tick by and it doesn't happen.

Instead, she carefully sets the jersey on the desk before peeling off her sweatshirt. I didn't realize it before, but she's not wearing a bra. My mouth turns bone dry as I stare at her perky little breasts. It's so damn tempting to reach out and stroke her nipples. They're so damn sensitive.

I flex and tighten my fingers so I don't do exactly that.

Then she picks up the sweater and pulls it over her head, shoving her arms through the sleeves and tugging it down her torso.

It fits perfectly. Just like I knew it would.

Possessiveness crashes through me, suffusing every single cell.

"Turn around," I rasp.

She spins in a semi-circle until I can glimpse my name stamped across her back. Satisfaction floods through me until it feels like I'm an overinflated balloon on the verge of bursting.

With a sly look sent over her shoulder, she meets my eyes. "You like?"

"Yeah, I fucking like," I growl. "Although, I pictured you with it on and nothing else."

Without another word, she slips her hands beneath the orange and black material before sliding the leggings down her hips and thighs until it pools at her feet. She shimmies out of the panties as well before swiveling back around.

"More like you imagined?"

Fuck, yeah. I've been fantasizing about what she'd look like in my jersey ever since I picked it up at the campus bookstore. Did I just so happen to whack off to thoughts of her in it?

Guilty as charged.

"It's way better." I jerk my chin toward her messy bun. "Take it out."

Gaze pinned to mine, she reaches up and slowly pulls the tie from her hair. The long mass cascades around her shoulders and down her back like a bouncy golden curtain.

My cock stiffens at how fucking gorgeous she is in my jersey and nothing else.

I don't realize that I've stepped closer until she lifts her chin to hold my gaze. Just as her lips part, mine crash onto hers. As soon as she opens, my tongue sweeps into her mouth. I force her backward until her thighs hit the edge of the bed and she tumbles onto the mattress. We stay fused together as I quickly follow her down. She wraps her legs around my waist and grinds against me.

Fuck.

I need to slow my roll, or I'll go off like a damn shot.

Again.

If this behavior continues, I'll develop a complex. I've never been a one-pump chump. Even though I don't want to, I rip my lips away and force myself to take a deep, calming breath.

Confusion mars her expression as she props herself up on her elbows. "Is something wrong?"

"Just give me a minute," I mutter, feeling like a twenty-two-year-old virgin who's never touched a girl.

When that doesn't work, I roll away, rising unsteadily to my feet.

Before she can ask what's going on, I grip the hem of my T-shirt and yank it over my head. Then I shove the joggers and boxer-briefs down my legs until I'm fully naked. Heat ignites in her eyes as I stand perfectly still and allow her gaze to lick over every inch.

There's nothing more that I love than having her attention focused solely on me.

Although, it does nothing to stop my erection from pulsing with the insistent need to be buried deep inside her tight heat. If I'd been smart, I would have jacked off before coming over. But I'd been much too impatient for that.

A hiss of breath escapes from me as I wrap my hand around my dick and give it a few slow pumps.

Carina's pupils dilate as they stay fastened to me.

"Spread your legs, pretty girl. Show me the sweetness between your thighs."

She does exactly what I ask without question.

And I fucking love it.

Her pink lips are already slick with arousal. I just want to run my tongue over them and lap up every single drop.

Fuck. Those thoughts aren't helping matters.

I'm not even inside this girl and I'm ready to explode.

As I fist my shaft, need coils tight in my balls. Once they draw up against my body, I realize that release is imminent.

"Shove the jersey up. I want to see those pretty little titties."

Her fingers drift to the hem before yanking it up her body and bearing her breasts so that the material is bunched against her collarbone. Unable to help myself, I step closer. As soon as I tighten my fist, hot jets of cum spurt from the tip of my cock.

I grit my teeth as my movements quicken, sliding along the thick length.

My gaze stays locked on hers as I paint her belly with thick ropes of pearly white fluid. And just like always, my release seems to go on forever.

The sheer force of it shakes me to the very core of my being.

Carina widens her legs as cum lands on her bare pussy. There's something intensely satisfying about seeing it there. I just want to scoop it up and shove it inside her body.

My brain hitches at such a dark, primitive thought.

It's only when every last bit of jizz has been released that I relinquish the chokehold. Her chest rises and falls with each rapid breath.

Fuck, but she makes a gorgeous picture, lying there with my jersey shoved above her breasts, cum crisscrossing her torso, supple thighs spread wide as if she's making an offering of herself. I want to stand here and soak her in so that this mental snapshot will last forever.

"I love seeing you like this," I rasp, unable to keep the words trapped inside where they belong.

I drag my finger through the warm ejaculation until it's coated in thick white cream. Her body quakes as I push the digit inside her pussy, pumping it a few times before pulling it out and gathering up more. I stroke her lower lips with it until she's fully coated. That's all it takes for my cock to stiffen right up again. I give it a few leisure pumps to help it along.

"I really hope you plan on screwing me this time."

"Don't worry, pretty girl. You'll get the fucking you need."

When I press a kiss against her clit, flicking my tongue across it, a whimper of need escapes from her. My mouth slides lower, tonguing her entrance and tasting our combined arousal. There's something so sexy about that. I wouldn't have thought that would be the case.

But with her it is.

I lap at her until she's writhing beneath me, twisting and impatient for more. When she grows restless, I pull away just enough to give her clit a sharp little slap with the tips of my fingers.

"Be patient," I growl.

Her breath catches at the back of her throat as she grows even slicker.

"You like that, don't you?" It's not a question that needs to be answered. The evidence is there for both of us to see. What I want is to hear her admit that she likes having her pussy smacked.

By me.

Only me.

Color stains her cheeks as her eyes turn hazy, lowering to half-mast. When she remains silent, I bring my hand down again on her engorged clit.

This time a moan bursts free as she arches off the bed.

"Yes," she groans.

The sight of her squirming with need is almost enough to make me lose it. I don't think I've ever been so turned on in my life than I am at this very moment. Not only is she wearing my jersey, but she's covered in my cum. I've shoved it inside her. And before this night is over, I'll add more to it.

I want everyone to know, *especially her*, that Carina Hutchins belongs to me.

"See how easy that was? Now you get some cock." My hand tightens around my erection. This time, I have absolutely no intention of jacking myself off. When I come again, it'll be inside her sweet heat with her pussy spasming around me, greedily milking every last drop. "Is that what you want? What you need?"

"You know it is."

"You're right, I do. But I want to hear you say it. That's the only way you get to come."

"Please, Ford. Don't make me beg."

Her whimpered words are like a punch to the gut.

Did I ever think this girl would beg to have sex with me?

Nope. Not even in my wildest fantasies.

"That's exactly what I want, pretty girl. To hear you beg."

Her tongue darts out to moisten her lips. There's a slight waver to her voice when she whispers, "Please fuck me. I need to come on your cock. Do you hear me? I *need* it now."

I'd actually smile if I wasn't in so much pain.

"You're such a good girl. Now I want you to pull your pussy lips open so I can see exactly how much you want me. I want to see that pretty little hole gaping wide, sobbing for me to fill it."

Her breath catches as her pupils dilate.

Just when I think she might deny the request, her hands drift to her center and she grips the outer edges of her lips, stretching them open until I can see just how soft and pink she is inside.

A tortured groan escapes from me. "You're so fucking perfect." Even though I just came, moisture leaks from the tip of my erection.

"Tell me who that pussy belongs to."

This time, there's zero hesitation on her part.

"You," she murmurs. "It belongs to you. *I* belong to you."

Damn right she does.

"Lucky for you that good girls get a nice hard dick to come on."

"Thank fuck," she says with a relieved sigh.

When she releases the outer edges of her lips so they bounce back to their former shape, I shake my head. "Keep them open for me."

Not a sound of protest escapes from her as she pulls the glistening flesh apart for a second time.

So fucking perfect.

And mine.

This pussy belongs to me, and I plan on taking *very* good care of it. I'll stroke, lick, and kiss it as much as she needs. Until there's no one else she wants owning her sweet little cunt but me.

She might not realize it yet, but I do.

And that's all that matters.

With my hand wrapped around my erection, I carefully guide it to her soaked entrance.

"Keep it nice and wide for me, pretty girl. Every time I pull out, I want you to tempt me back inside again."

A whimper escapes from her as I press the tip into her body.

It's no more than an inch.

Only enough for the mushroom-shaped head to get swallowed up by her softness.

When she squirms beneath me, I slap her clit with the tips of my fingers. "Stay still. You get what I decide to give you."

"Ford," she whines. "Please. I need more."

"I know exactly what you need. I've always known."

She releases a shaky breath as I slide further inside her before withdrawing. Her eyes widen as she shakes her head.

"Are you really trying to tell me how to fuck you?"

Her teeth scrape across her lower lip. "No."

"I didn't think so," I say with a grunt before withdrawing and then rising to my full height so I can stare down at her.

She's so damn beautiful with her blonde hair fanned out on the comforter and the jersey bunched around her throat. Not only are her legs split open, but her lips are spread so wide that I can see the shiny wetness coating her insides. My gaze licks over the stunning picture she makes. It's so damn tempting to tie her to the bed and keep her like this forever.

My gaze zeroes in on her clit.

Just like the rest of her, it's so damn pretty.

I can practically see it pulsing with the need I've stoked to life.

Thank fuck Carina isn't as unaffected as she'd like me to believe.

Deep down, she wants me.

Needs me.

Needs what only I can give her.

"Entice me, pretty girl. Show me exactly how much you need my cock. Otherwise, I'll get dressed and walk right out the door. I'll leave you writhing on the bed all needy and horny."

"You wouldn't," she says with a sharp gasp.

She's right. I wouldn't.

There's no way I could walk away from her.

But she doesn't need to know that, does she?

This girl doesn't need to know that she holds all the cards in the palm of her hand.

"Please," she whines, voice rising on a sob. It's sweet music to my ears.

Her fingers stretch the delicate flesh, making her hole gape wider.

"That's so fucking gorgeous," I groan. "Show me more."

With her legs splayed completely open, she flexes her hips. The slender line of her back arches off the mattress as her eyelids feather closed. Her cheeks have pinkened as a throaty moan escapes from her. I don't think I've ever seen anything so fucking sexy in my life as Carina writhing away on the bed.

With my fist clenching my erection, I direct the tip back to her entrance.

Christ...I could watch her like this all damn night.

As soon as the head sinks inside her core, her eyelids crack open, locking on mine. Already the pupils look blown out.

"Thank you," she whispers.

"I could never resist you, pretty girl. You know that."

Another moan escapes from her as I sink inside, pressing deep until I'm buried to the hilt.

"Is that what your greedy little pussy needed? The full length of my cock?"

"God, yes."

The pulse of her tight heat feels so damn good. Even though I don't particularly want to, I pull all the way out and soak in the sight of her. Her pussy is swollen as it glistens with fresh arousal. Her fingers continue to hold her lips wide as she gyrates without me having to say a single word.

"You would die without my dick, wouldn't you?"

"Yes. Can't you see how much I need it?"

"I do, baby. I see it. Your sweet little cunt is dripping with need."

She presses her lips together before stretching them wide again. The sight of her gaping pink center turns me on more than anything.

This is it for me.

The only pussy I'll ever want.

Or need.

Unable to help myself, I lower my face to her core, needing to lap up some of her cream. Like the good girl that she is, she continues to hold her lips open. I lick the edges before thrusting my tongue deep inside.

Another tortured sob escapes from her as I fuck her with my tongue.

"Please, Ford. I need to come."

"Not yet, baby. I'm not done with you just yet."

A garbled response escapes from her.

Only when I've licked her clean do I suck her clit into my mouth. Her body quivers beneath mine.

I pull away just enough to growl, "Don't you dare come." Then I give her clit a sharp slap.

I stare at her spread pussy, loving that I'm the only one who gets to see her like this.

It's only when her jagged breathing returns to normal and she stops squirming that I ask, "Have you calmed down enough for me to continue fucking you?"

"Yes."

"Such a good girl." I spear the velvety softness of my tongue deep inside her again. "This sweet little pussy deserves so much love and I'm going to give it all to you."

I lift my head to meet her dazed eyes. She looks as if she's in the midst of a fever dream. Unable to hold off another moment, I straighten, needing to give both of us what we're so desperate for. With my hand wrapped around my thick length, I smack the engorged tip against her clit.

Once.

Twice.

Three times until her spine arches off the bed.

"Please, Ford," she sobs. "*Now*."

I'm so damn close to splintering apart, but I refuse to allow it to happen. This isn't going to be like all the other times when I've blown my load way too soon. I'm going to take this nice and slow so I can torture the hell out of her.

Out of myself as well.

I tip fuck her for a few more minutes, giving her no more than an inch or so. When I finally slide all the way inside, her greedy muscles contract around me. I can't help but pause and stare down at her. The sexy sight of her pinned to the mattress by my cock makes me want to slam into her tight heat and fuck her into oblivion.

I grit my teeth. It requires every ounce of self-restraint not to let my baser instincts take over. I'm almost out of my mind with the need to fuck.

As I force myself to pull out before sliding deep inside again, her pussy spasms. There's nothing more I can do other than follow her over the edge. Instead of covering her mouth to muffle her screams, the sweet sounds of her release fill the room.

And probably the apartment.

Maybe even the building.

But I don't give a damn.

It's.

The.

Best.

Fucking.

Sound.

In.

The.

World.

She sobs out my name, chanting it over and over like a mantra. And that's exactly what I want to be to her.

A mantra.

Her mantra.

The way she comes undone only makes my release even more intense. I'm almost dizzy with it as stars dance behind my eyelids. By the time I collapse on top of her, we're both breathing hard. Her arms entwine around my neck to hold me close.

There's no other place I'd rather be.

"You know," I say, when I'm finally able to catch my breath. "We should probably buy Juliette a better pair of noise cancelling headphones. Apparently, hers aren't cutting it. And let me tell you what, pretty girl," I say with a wide smile. "She's going to need them."

Carina groans before burying her face in her hands.

Yeah...it's a little too late for that.

CHAPTER THIRTY-ONE

CARINA

I slide into a parking spot at Taco Loco and cut the engine before checking my makeup in the visor mirror. My face is glowing and there's a sparkle in my eyes.

One that says I've been freshly fucked.

And the look isn't wrong.

After class this morning, Ford and I headed back to the apartment. I had a hard time keeping my hands off him. We had to stop ourselves from tearing off each other's clothes and doing it in the elevator.

It was tempting.

Oh, so tempting.

I don't know what it is about the man but whenever we're around each other, I find myself flat on my back. Or on all fours with my ass in the air.

Who would have suspected that Ford would turn out to be such a freak in the sheets?

And who would have guessed it'd turn me on so damn much?

The worst is when we're in class and he'll lean over and whisper all the dirty things he has in store for me. My panties will flood with heat and it's the only thing I can focus on for the rest of the hour.

And the big jerk knows it.

Does it on purpose.

Somehow, he's managed to find all my buttons and now that he has, he presses them every chance he gets. No one has ever figured me out so quickly and pieced it all together.

If he were so inclined, he could write a user manual for my body.

The man has uncovered things I had no idea existed.

It's official. I'm addicted.

When I squirm on the seat, already heating up, I shove those thoughts from my brain.

Know what will shut them down faster than anything?

Thinking about Pamela.

And our lunch date.

I need to do a little recon and figure out what her plans for the future are.

Just like I suspected, thoughts of my mother kill any lingering arousal pulsing through me.

After the morning spent with Ford, this is the last place I want to be. But I also can't sit around and fret about her intentions. I'd rather hear it straight from the horse's mouth. Then I can figure out a game plan. Maybe run interference if it becomes necessary.

I straighten my shoulders and force myself to exit the BMW before heading inside the restaurant. Once through the double glass doors, I stop in the entryway, recognizing the inky-haired girl who loiters at the hostess stand. We had a class together last year.

Lola.

As soon as I flash a smile, recognition dawns and her expression warms. "Hey, how are you?"

"Good. I haven't seen you around campus very much. Everything going well this semester?"

"I'm taking an eighteen credit course load and working here, so I pretty much have no life outside of that."

"Ugh. That sucks. But this is it, right? Then you graduate in the spring?"

Relief flickers across her face. "Yup. Can't wait. I'm more than ready to move on."

Most of the people I know aren't in any real hurry to leave college. They're too busy enjoying all the parties and being responsibility free. Well…as much as any twenty-one or two-year old can be. From the little that she's shared, it's not the same for Lola.

Upon closer inspection, she looks tired. There are faint circles under her eyes as if she's burning the candle at both ends. My heart goes out to her. I work at On Pointe studio a handful of hours each week because I genuinely like it and enjoy having my own pocket money. But there's no way I could afford to pay rent and tuition with my paycheck.

"Are you meeting someone for lunch?" she asks, drawing the conversation back to the reason I'm here.

My gaze reluctantly flickers to the dining area behind her. "Yeah, my mother."

"Oh, I think I just seated her." She tilts her head and studies me more carefully. "You two are carbon copies of each other."

I force a smile. "Yeah, we get that a lot."

When I was younger, I used to take it as a compliment. That's no longer the case. I don't want to be anything like Pamela.

She pulls a menu from the stack. "Follow me and I'll show you to your table."

Just as we step into the spacious room with colorful streamers strung across the wooden beams above us, someone shoves through the glass doors into the front entry. Lola throws a glance over her shoulder at the newcomer and her face contorts into a scowl. The irritation is like a crack of lightning.

Curious to see who's put that expression on her face, I glance behind me only to find Asher Stevens, one of the high-profile football players at Western. If the gossip that floats around campus is true, he'll enter the draft this spring. There are always a couple girls tucked beneath his brawny arms and this occasion isn't any different.

The females that cling to him look eerily similar to each other with long blonde hair, big boobs, and nipped-in waists.

Lola bares her teeth. It's almost a surprise when she doesn't snap them. Animosity pours off her in heavy, suffocating waves.

When he advances a step, she stabs a finger in his direction. "Stay right there. I'll be back to seat you in a minute."

A slow grin lights up his face as humor sparks to life in his bright blue eyes. "Whatever you say, sweetheart."

When her darker ones thin in response, his grin only widens.

She huffs out an aggravated breath before stalking into the dining area and muttering, "That guy is such an ass."

"I heard that," he calls after her.

"You were meant to," she snaps, raising her voice to be heard over the festive Tejano music that drifts through the sound system.

When we're a handful of feet away from the hostess stand, I clear my throat. "I take it you and Asher are good friends?"

She glances at me with narrowed eyes. When a smile quirks my lips, she snorts and the tension filling her muscles dissolves.

"Hell, no. He's just another conceited manwhore at Western who thinks he's God's gift to the female species."

"So…punched your ticket for that particular carnival ride, have you?"

She elbows me in the ribs as I pull up alongside her. "Ewww. You couldn't pay me enough money to sleep with that guy. He's a walking STI who's probably on a low dose of antibiotics at all times. I value my vagina way too much for that."

My shoulders shake with silent laughter. Nothing that's come out of her mouth is wrong, but girls—especially the jersey chasers—usually have the opposite reaction to the blond football player.

"Gee, Lola. You seem so conflicted. How about you stop being so wishy-washy in the stances you take."

A few chuckles tumble from her lips. "You're right, I should probably do a better job of keeping my opinions to myself. Especially when I'm at work." Our feet slow as she nods toward a woman sitting alone at a table for two. "I take it that's your mom?"

My gaze slices to the pretty blonde staring at her cell, tapping away at the screen which is difficult to do with her long nails. There's a different Birkin sitting on the table off to the side. This one is a vibrant orange color that screams money. She's wearing a silver, curve-hugging, long-sleeve top that bears just a bit of her midriff, shiny black pants that are skintight, and sky-high heels with red soles. Today, her blonde hair has been curled into soft waves that tumble down her back. My guess is that she's wearing extensions. Her makeup is flawless, and her forehead is smooth and unblemished.

"Yup."

From the corner of my eye, I watch the other patrons seated in the vicinity turn and stare before whispering to the people they're lunching with. The woman no longer understands what the word *understated* means. Instead of trying to blend in and call the least amount of attention to herself, she dresses like she's starring on a housewives' reality show.

A sigh escapes from me as my body deflates. Only now do I realize that asking her to meet here was a mistake. But it's not like I wanted to have lunch with her on campus.

Can you imagine the spectacle she'd make?

Just thinking about it is enough to make me cringe.

I haven't even greeted her yet and I'm already knee deep in regret.

Is it too late to turn around and hightail it out of here? I can text her from the parking lot that I wasn't feeling well.

Before I can take a hasty step in retreat, she glances up and catches my eye. Her hand rises in the air as she waves her acrylics. They're pink and encrusted with tiny gems that sparkle like diamonds in the sunlight that pours in through the windows.

My face heats when a few patrons turn and stare. We couldn't look more different if we tried. I'm inconspicuous and she's over the top. For this occasion, I chose a black Western ballcap that's pulled low over my eyes along with a sweatshirt and leggings that I threw on after dance class. There wasn't time to shower and change after Ford took off. So, I probably reek of sex.

Really hot sex.

And I have zero regrets about that.

"I'll give you two a couple minutes to look over the menu and then I'll be back to take your order."

"Thanks. Appreciate it."

"No problem." Her voice drops. "Now excuse me while I deal with that walking clap diagnosis."

With that, she swings away and disappears to the front of the restaurant. It takes effort to force my feet into movement. I'd much rather stand here and chitchat with Lola than deal with the situation at hand. My only consolation is that the quicker I get this over with, the sooner I can take off. It's always possible that I've blown everything out of proportion. Maybe I don't have anything to worry about and Pamela has changed.

Grown up.

Reprioritized what's important in life.

What? It could happen.

"Hey, baby," she says, rising to her feet and closing the distance between us. With her sky-high heels, she towers over me like some kind of glamazon who doesn't belong in such an ordinary environment.

From the corner of my eye, I catch the guy's reaction at the next table. His mouth is hanging open, and his eyes have widened as he continues to stare.

Ugh.

Our embrace lasts for a second or two before I untangle myself so we can settle in our respective chairs. I glance around, hating the attention she always seems to draw, and pull my cap a little lower over my eyes.

Unsure where to look, my gaze reluctantly settles on the leather bag. "Did you just buy that?"

"Crawford surprised me with it the other day." She beams like a new mother talking about her baby before trailing her fingers lovingly over the handstitched leather. "Isn't he the sweetest?"

"He's a genuinely nice guy," I say seriously.

"He certainly knows the way to my heart."

Yes. It's paved with Birkins.

Her obsession with over-the-top luxury items is borderline embarrassing.

Before I can say anything else, Lola stops by the table. Mom orders a skinny margarita and chicken fajitas. After I decide on the cheese enchiladas, the dark-haired waitress takes off again with the promise of two glasses of water.

"So, Mom—"

When her phone dings with an incoming message, she pounces on the slim device and glances at the screen. Her lips lift into a smile as she taps away on the miniature keyboard.

"Mom?" Annoyance floods my voice.

Her eyes flicker to me as she quickly sets down the cell. "Sorry. Just an old friend wanting to get together."

I suck in a deep breath and hold it captive in my lungs for a long moment before steadily forcing it out again. Instead of working my way up to this much-needed conversation, I decide to get straight to the point. It's only been five minutes and I'm already on the verge of snapping.

"It's fine." I clear my throat, prepared to delve in. "I wanted to know what your plans are now that you and Crawford are together. Are you moving back into the house?"

She shrugs before waving a hand. "I suppose at some point, but I'm not in any hurry."

"Have you two even talked about it?"

"Oh, he mentioned something about me selling the Florida property, but I'm not sure that's a good idea. I enjoy having my own place. Plus, all my friends are there." She gives me an *are you cray-cray* look. "How can I just abandon them?"

My brow furrows as all this circles through my brain. "I get that your friends are important, but how are you going to make a relationship work if you're not living in the same state?"

"Don't worry. We'll figure it out. Right now, we're just taking it day by day."

A pit grows at the bottom of my belly. She seems a lot more blasé about their relationship than he is.

"Mom, if you're not one hundred percent committed, then you need to be honest with Crawford so he doesn't end up blindsided."

Like before.

For the first time since I sat down, annoyance flickers across her normally smooth features. It's the first real hint of emotion I've seen from her in a while. Her tone turns snippy. "You'll excuse me if I don't take relationship advice from a twenty-one-year-old, thank you very much."

I open my mouth to snap back with a pithy retort when Lola stops by our table to drop off drinks.

"Your entrees will be out momentarily," she says, sounding harried.

I glance around and realize just how packed the place has become before forcing a smile. "No worries. We're all good."

Mom stares after Lola as she takes off, beelining for another table. Gone is the insipid socialite she pretends to be. In her place is the thirty-something-year-old woman who had a hard life and spent her late teens and twenties working her fingers to the bone.

"I remember what it was like to be her." Fear flickers in her eyes before it's quickly smothered. "And it will never be my life again."

I shake my head, surprised by the deviation in conversation. "I don't understand why you're bringing that up when we're discussing Crawford."

"Perhaps you don't realize it, but they're one and the same." She drums her nails impatiently on the table before shifting on the chair.

"How so?"

"As long as he's part of my life, I won't have to worry about money. He'll be there to take care of me."

Jeez.

What this woman is looking for is a sugar daddy who'll give her everything she wants without any kind of expectation in return.

I lean closer and drop my voice, not wanting to be overheard. "But...he thinks you're together again. He's under the impression you'll stay by his side and help take care of things at the house, like hosting dinner parties and events." I pause for a heartbeat before forcing out the rest. "All the things you didn't want to do the first time around."

The vulnerability filling her expression disappears as she rolls her eyes.

Can you believe that?

The woman actually has the audacity to roll her eyes like a surly teen being called out for bad behavior.

"In case you haven't noticed, the man is a workaholic. He's never around. He has no interest in taking off and going on vacation or spending quality time together." She thumps her chest. "I need a man who will focus on me. *My* wants. No one's ever done that before!"

I can only stare. What Pamela really wants is a man who has nothing else going on in his life so he can cater to her every whim and spoil her rotten with attention.

How is this woman an actual grown up?

It's like she's a selfish seventeen-year-old trapped in the body of a thirty-eight-year-old woman.

Even though I'm only twenty-one, I feel lightyears more mature.

It's sad.

Worse, I don't think there's anything I can do or say that will make a difference.

It's like screaming into the wind. And I'm smart enough to recognize that and save my breath.

Lola drops off our entrees before asking if either of us need anything else. I paste a smile on my face and shake my head. This lunch is going about as well as I imagined. Everything I was concerned about has now come to fruition.

"Let's not forget about all the benefits you've reaped with this marriage," she rebukes mildly. "Your education has been paid for and you drive an expensive car most kids your age could only dream about." Her blue gray eyes turn stormy. "You have no idea what it's like to hustle for a couple bucks."

Those comments are like a punch to the gut because she's not wrong.

"The love I have for Crawford has nothing to do with the monetary things he provides for me," I whisper, needing her to understand that we're not the same. I would never stick around for someone's money. "He's been a wonderful father. The only one I've ever known. He's kindhearted and dependable."

"Yeah, and his bank account certainly doesn't hurt either," she says before downing her margarita in one thirsty gulp.

"I don't love him because of his money," I grit between clenched teeth.

"Oh, Carina," she says with a weary sigh before her expression turns sympathetic. "You really need to stop deluding yourself. Everything has to do with money. *Everything.* Money is what makes the world go around and Crawford has more than Midas." She angles herself closer as her voice sobers and she drops the pampered princess act. "If you had any brains whatsoever, you'd sleep with Ford and get pregnant. Then he'd have no other choice but to marry you. Or, at the very least, support you in a comfortable manner for the next two decades. One day in the not-too-distant future, he'll inherit a multi-million-dollar company. It would be a mistake to let that slip through your fingers."

Her calculated plans curdle the contents of my stomach.

Is that what she did?

Got knocked up in an attempt to force someone to take care of her?

Except...it didn't work out that way. My father took off before I was even born.

The little bit of enchilada I've managed to choke down threatens to make an unexpected appearance.

Heat floods my cheeks. "How can you say that? Ford is like a brother to me." I wince as the lie slips easily from my lips.

She blinks as if she doesn't understand why I'm getting so upset. "What? You know damn well that someone will snap him right up. Might as well be you. It probably wouldn't even be that hard. He's always had a soft spot for you."

"No, he hasn't," I mumble, only wanting to put an end to this disturbing conversation.

"You need to be smart, Carina. Think about your future. That's exactly what I'm doing."

I've always suspected that this was how Pamela operated, but to hear the words fall so bluntly from her lips disgusts me.

When I remain silent, she picks up the fajita and takes a dainty bite. "Eat up, darling. It's really quite delicious."

CHAPTER THIRTY-TWO

CARINA

"Are you sure we can't cancel dinner tonight?" I ask as Ford pulls the Corvette into the long stretch of weathered brick drive.

He flicks a confused glance my way before throwing the car into park and cutting the engine. A sprinkle of rain hits the windshield. In one swift movement, he swivels in his seat so we're facing each other before reaching out and stroking gentle fingers along the curve of my cheek. In a matter of weeks, sinking into his touch has become second nature.

My gaze reluctantly settles on Pamela's shiny new Audi parked near the garage. The knowledge that she's just using him for expensive gifts makes me sick to my stomach. It's mortifying to realize that all of the people who whispered about her being a gold digger behind her back were correct.

That's *exactly* what she is.

And she makes no bones about it.

One of these days, Crawford will wake up and see Pamela for the conniving woman she really is. He'll realize that she never cared about him.

Then what will happen?

Fresh nerves explode inside me as the question circles viciously through my brain.

Will he kick me out of his life?

I'm not concerned about the money.

What terrifies me most is that I'll lose the one person who has always been there for me. I'll lose that stability.

And I'll end up losing Ford.

"Carina?"

It's only when his soft voice penetrates the thick haze clouding my brain that my attention snaps back to him. He searches my eyes for a long moment as if he's capable of picking through my private thoughts.

I force my lips into a smile. "Sorry. Guess I spaced out for a second."

"It seems like something's bothering you. Why won't you tell me what it is?"

"There's nothing." Even though I hate lying to him, the fib slips easily off my tongue. There's no way I can admit that my mother is just using his father. "I'm just thinking about the test I need to study for. It'll probably take me a couple of hours."

"Does that mean I can't crash at your place tonight?"

The growled-out question makes my panties dampen with need.

My gaze flickers toward the sprawling mansion through the light rain. "As long as we don't end up staying for long."

A slow grin spreads across his face. "Deal."

He seals the promise with a kiss. The moment his lips slide across mine, I sink into the caress, desperate to lose myself in it. A few heartbeats later, he draws away.

When my brow furrows and I tilt my face upward for more, his eyes ignite with heat.

"Later, pretty girl. I'll take care of all your needs later."

I groan as he turns away and climbs out of the sleek sports car before doing the same. Our steps quicken as rain sprinkles down on us from gunmetal gray clouds that fill the sky. I was hoping it would hold off until after dinner. Once we reach the porch, Ford throws open the heavy door before sauntering in.

"Hello?" His greeting echoes throughout the cavernous first floor.

"We're in the family room," Crawford hollers back.

As soon as we arrive in the double story room, I spot Crawford and Pamela cozied up on the couch. She's pressed against his side as her fingers trail up and down his thigh. Much like the other day when we met for lunch, she's all glammed up. There's not an extension or fake eyelash out of place.

I glance at Crawford and find him grinning widely. Every few seconds, his eyes flicker toward my mother. It's like he can't bear to look away for even a second. Reluctantly, I admit that I haven't seen him this happy in years.

It hurts my heart that she'll only end up breaking his.

It's tempting to pull him aside and talk some sense into him. If I thought there was even a snowball's chance in hell he'd listen, I'd do it.

I'd warn him against my own mother.

Unfortunately, the besotted expression on his face tells me that it would fall on deaf ears. He'd probably share my concerns with her and then I'd have a pissed-off Pamela on my hands.

"You guys are early," he says. "Dinner won't be ready for another hour."

Great.

That's definitely not what I wanted to hear. I was hoping our meal would be served immediately and then we could take off within the hour.

What really sucks is that Wednesday nights with Crawford were always a treat I looked forward to each week. I love dropping by the house and spending time together.

Now...I can't get away fast enough.

When Pamela strokes his chest before leaning in to nip at his clean-shaven jaw, my belly revolts.

Ford points toward the staircase that leads to the walkout basement. "Carina wanted to practice her solo, so we'll head down there until dinner."

I shoot him a grateful look for his quick thinking and saving us from an hour of watching them play kissy face with each other.

"Sure, sure. Sounds good," Crawford says, not bothering to glance our way.

Ford rolls his eyes before locking his fingers around my wrist and towing me from the room. Under normal circumstances, I'd yank my hand away, not wanting his father to suspect that we've become involved in a full-blown relationship, but it's doubtful he's aware that we're still in the room. His attention is solely focused on Pamela.

I don't understand it.

I really don't.

She treats him more like an afterthought, and he trails after her like a lovesick puppy.

I want to smack the man upside the head and tell him to open his damn eyes. He needs to see her for the person she is behind the pretty, Botox-injected mask. It makes me feel like shit to think this way about my own flesh and blood. Life would be so much easier if she'd just jet back to wherever the hell she came from and stopped messing with Crawford. But that won't happen as long as he insists on lavishing her with gifts and footing the bill for her luxurious lifestyle.

"I'm pretty sure I just threw up in my mouth," Ford grumbles as we turn the corner and head to the staircase that leads to the finished basement.

"Sorry," I mutter in embarrassment.

"What do you have to be sorry for? It's not your fault that our parents act like horny teenagers when they're around one another."

My teeth scrape across my lower lip as I consider how best to respond to that comment. Because that's exactly what it is.

An act.

Mom isn't head over heels in love with him. She's securing his affection and making sure she can still lead him around by the nose.

Once we reach the spacious studio, Ford closes the door behind him. There's an ocean of polished hardwood. Because of the shock absorbing subflooring Crawford had installed, our footsteps are silent. He spared no expense when adding all the little details like mirrored walls and a bar to stretch and practice positioning that makes it seem more like a professional studio.

This is my happy place.

Under normal circumstances, when I step inside the bright space, everything that weighs me down vanishes into thin air and I'm able to focus on the piece of choreography I'm working on. That doesn't happen this time. Thick tension continues to gather in my shoulder blades.

For just a second or two, I contemplate coming clean with him.

But how can I do that?

Instead, I beeline to the small room to change into booty shorts and an athletic top. I'm hoping that an hour of intense physical activity will help burn off the heaviness that continues to weigh me down, pinning me to the earth, making it impossible to suck in full breaths.

At least enough to make it through the remainder of the evening without losing it and calling Pamela out for the conniving gold digger that she is.

When I return to the studio, Ford is sitting against one of the mirrored walls. His gaze immediately fastens onto me as I pick out a playlist.

Just as the music floats through the space and I take my position in the middle of the floor, he says, "Truth or dare."

Holding the pose, I glance at him. "Dare."

"Dance naked for me."

CHAPTER THIRTY-THREE

FORD

*E*motion flickers in her eyes and for a moment, I wonder if she'll turn me down. But then her fingers drift to the thick band of her athletic bra, and she stretches the Lycra up her body and over her head before dropping the bright blue material to the floor. She shoves the stretchy shorts and panties down long lean legs until she's completely naked.

Fuck.

My gaze slides down her length, greedily taking in every dip and curve.

Carina is so damn sexy.

She's the one I dream about and now that I have her, I don't want to let go. Maybe this started out as a way to work her out of my system, but it backfired spectacularly.

Now I just need to convince her to make this the real deal. It doesn't escape me that every time I lay my hands on her, she melts into a puddle of goo. I'll just have to broach the subject when I'm buried deep inside the heat of her body. Once I've secured her agreement, we can move forward and stop hiding this relationship. Because that's exactly what it is.

A relationship.

My gaze stays locked on her as she takes her position. Music continues to play through the sound system. She rises onto her toes, the muscles in her calves and thighs bunching before she leaps gracefully across the floor. Her body bends like a willow branch as her movements turn sweeping. She uses every bit of space available to her and is poetry in motion.

I'm mesmerized by the sight.

When she lifts one leg, grabbing her toes with her fingers in a move that resembles the splits, I just about come all over myself.

My dick is so damn hard as it throbs painfully in my joggers.

The way she leaps, soaring through the air, looks effortless.

It's not. I've watched her perfect the movement over the years through grueling hours of practice. Until every line of her body is positioned the way she wants it.

Her head tips back as she arches her spine. Each limb is elongated, reaching outward. If I could take a mental snapshot to keep with me forever, it would be the way she looks right now in this moment. Not a stitch of clothing to hide her beauty as she pushes herself to the physical limit.

She's absolutely stunning.

The way she contorts her body, forcing it into positions that are in no way natural is impressive. She's so damn flexible. The faraway look in her eyes tells me that her mind is already floating. She's lost in the movement, absorbing the musical notes, using them to create something beautiful. Emotion flashes across her face as if she's in the middle of telling a deeply personal story.

Everything inside me pulses with need. It's like being ripped apart only to be put back together again.

As the last notes reverberate throughout the air, she folds over, the graceful length of her spine on display as she holds the position. Even from here, I see the way her ribcage contracts and expands with each labored breath.

"Come here," I growl. My voice sounds as if it's been roughed up by sandpaper.

A second or two ticks by before she breaks the pose and lifts her head just enough for her blue-gray eyes to fasten onto mine. Something sizzles in the charged air between us, and I'm slammed with a fierceness of emotion I've never experienced before.

Actually, that's a lie. These feelings have been brewing between us for a long time.

Years.

Only now am I willing to slap a label on them.

She pads quietly across the space that separates us. When she's within striking distance, my fingers lock around hers, and I tug her onto my lap. My hands stroke up the bare flesh of her slender back before sliding down again to the rounded curve of her ass, squeezing the taut muscle as my lips crash onto hers. She immediately opens so our tongues can tangle. And just like always, it's frenzied.

Explosive.

As if I've been deprived of oxygen and she's the air I need to sustain life.

I'll never get used to this feeling.

The need I have to possess her.

I can only liken it to a beast that I've kept tightly leashed for years and I can't do it any longer. More than that, I don't want to.

I rip my mouth away just enough to growl, "I need to fuck you."

Her fingers settle over my hard length before giving it a squeeze. A hiss of breath escapes from me.

"What's stopping you?"

Abso-fucking-lutely nothing.

My brain clicks off and instinct takes over. I shift her around so that I can yank down the material of my joggers until my erection can spring free. Her hands settle on my shoulders as I maneuver her over my boner. The moment she slides down the thick length, my eyelids feather shut.

There's nothing better in this world than being buried deep inside her tight heat.

When a whimper escapes from her, my hand snakes around the nape of her neck, dragging her closer until my mouth can settle over hers for a second time. As soon as she opens, our tongues mingle.

Bliss.

That's exactly what this is.

Carina flexes her hips, slowly sliding up and down my shaft.

I'm so turned on that it won't take much for me to lose it.

This girl unravels me in the best way possible.

Just as my balls draw up and it feels like I'll explode with the next upstroke, the door to the studio creeks open.

"Hey, guys…" Dad's voice trails off.

Carina freezes, her muscles stiffening. My arms tighten, trying to shield as much of her nudity as possible. She breaks the kiss and stares at me in muted horror, her face turning ashen before dull color slams into her cheeks.

I twist my head and look past the slope of her shoulder to meet Dad's eyes. His lips are compressed into a tight line. Even from here, I can see the stiffness of his muscles.

For a second or two, awkward silence hangs in the studio. It's the suffocating kind that chokes the air from your very lungs.

He clears his throat. "Dinner will be ready shortly. We'll see you upstairs once you're," there's a stilted pause, "dressed."

The door closes softly, leaving us once again alone.

A tortured groan escapes from Carina as she buries her face against my shoulder. "Please tell me that didn't happen."

"I wish I could."

"Crawford's angry."

"Nah. He sounded…surprised. That's all." And yeah, angry. There's no way I won't get an earful. "I'll talk to him, and everything will be fine." I run my hands up and down her bare back, only wanting to offer comfort. I hate that he saw her like this. And I hate that she's embarrassed about it.

Even though my father doesn't normally make appearances in the studio, I should have locked the door. It was careless.

When she remains silent, I say in an overly cheery voice, "If you want to look on the bright side, at least everything's out in the open now."

CHAPTER THIRTY-FOUR

FORD

Since that interruption was definitely boner deflating, Carina scampers off my lap to redress before we head upstairs to face the firing squad otherwise known as our parents.

Even though I assured her that everything would be fine, and that I'd smooth over the situation with my father, I'm secretly wondering if that'll be so easily accomplished. He's always been adamant that I keep my relationship with Carina strictly platonic.

Sisterly in nature.

Except...I've never felt that way about her.

From the first moment I caught sight of the girl, I was a goner. And not a damn thing in all these years has changed that.

My fingers wrap loosely around hers as we trudge up the staircase to the first floor. I'm not happy about how this went down, but it's a huge relief that we no longer have to hide our relationship.

I throw a quick glance over my shoulder to meet her gaze. "Are you all right?"

She jerks her shoulders as embarrassment stains her cheeks.

All too soon, we end up in the family room where Pamela and Crawford are waiting. Unlike earlier, they're no longer making googly eyes at each other. I suppose that's another positive regarding the situation. I didn't think there was anything capable of wiping away his sappy expression.

Guess I was wrong.

Their heads are bent together as they talk in low tones. My father's gaze slices to us as soon as we step into the space. His attention dips to our clasped hands and his jaw tightens.

"So…dinner's ready?" I ask with forced lightness, hoping we don't actually have to discuss what he walked in on.

It's not like we're children, for fuck's sake. If Carina and I want to engage in a sexual relationship, that's our business and no one else's.

Dad slowly rises to his feet. His icy gaze stays locked on mine. "Dinner can wait. I'd like to speak with you alone in the office."

My arm slips around Carina's waist as I tug her closer. It would be impossible not to notice just how stiff she's become.

I straighten to my full height, my tone turning clipped. "Is that really necessary?"

Dad grimaces. "Unfortunately, it is."

I huff out an aggravated sigh and glance at Carina from the corner of my eye. The color staining her cheeks has leeched away, leaving her normally vibrant complexion ashen.

"Fine," I say through tightly gritted teeth. "Lead the way."

After my father stalks from the room, I glance at Carina. "I'll be right back."

The only response I get is the tight jerking of her head. Misery fills her eyes as she lowers them to the floor as if she can't bear the sight of me.

"Oh, don't you worry about Carina." Pamela taps the couch next to her. "We'll have ourselves a nice, little mother daughter chat."

I glance at my former stepmother, trying to figure out what her thoughts are on the matter. She doesn't look nearly as upset as Dad. Instead of responding, my gaze fastens onto Carina. In this moment, she's the only one I care about. I don't want her hurt in the fallout. And I sure as shit don't want it to affect our relationship.

She'll see—this is nothing more than a hiccup. In the grand scheme of things, it doesn't matter.

Even though Pamela continues to look on, I slip my fingers beneath Carina's chin and angle her face toward mine until she has no other choice but to meet my steady gaze.

"Everything will be fine," I murmur just loud enough for her to hear.

"We'll see."

I hate the doubt that floods her eyes.

Only wanting to banish it, I brush my lips across hers. Then I pull back just enough to search her gaze before swinging away and following my father to his office. Or command central, as I like to call it.

By the time I reach the spacious room, he's already settled behind the massive mahogany desk. He stabs a finger at the handcrafted antique leather armchair on the other side. I drop down, just wanting to get this convo over with and put it behind us.

"What the hell were you doing in the studio with Carina?" my father growls as soon as my ass hits the seat.

"I would have thought that was obvious." The words shoot out of my mouth before I can think better of it.

He glares as his expression turns stony. "Don't get cute with me. We've talked about this. Frankly, I'm a little surprised that we have to do it again. I don't want you toying with that girl."

The accusation pisses me off. "Is that what you think I'm doing? Toying with her?"

He rolls his eyes. "Come on, Ford. You have to know there isn't a future for the two of you."

"And why is that?"

"Because you're about to be stepsiblings again," he says deliberately as if I'm slow on the uptake. "Pamela and I have just set the date for the wedding. We're going to have a quiet ceremony this spring at the house."

There's a beat of silence as I digest this information. "Don't you think this is moving a bit fast? You two just got back together a couple weeks ago. Shouldn't you make sure that she's actually going to stick around this time?"

Dull color crawls up his neck and cheeks.

Fuck. That was probably the wrong thing to say, even though it's a hundred percent true. And we both know it. This isn't the first time his ex-wife has come back to bewitch him. For whatever reason, he has a real weakness for the woman. She can waltz in and out of his life whenever she wants and he's grateful for whatever scraps of attention she tosses him.

Everyone around my father is able to see what's going on.

Except him.

It's frustrating.

I've kept my mouth shut because I never wanted to do anything that would hurt Carina.

"Watch yourself," he snaps.

We stare at each other before I slump onto the chair. "Sorry. It's just that she shows up and then disappears before popping up again months later. She never sticks around for long."

His shoulders stiffen as a muscle ticks in his cheek. "It's different this time."

Laughter rises in my throat. It takes every ounce of willpower to bite it back.

How is he this naïve?

The man wheels and deals in Congress for a living, negotiating with both sides of the aisle, making it possible for legislation to get passed. Political adversaries have attempted to pull the wool over his eyes, but they can't.

He's sharp as a tack and savvy.

But when it comes to Pamela?

The opposite is true.

And nothing I say will change his mind. It would be a pointless exercise and a complete waste of breath to even try.

"If you say so," I mutter.

"I do." He leans forward and folds his hands against the polished surface. "And we're not here to discuss my relationship with Pamela. We're here to talk about your lapse in judgment regarding her daughter." There's a pause and his voice dips. *"My stepdaughter."*

"Carina isn't your stepdaughter. Not at the moment."

"Ever since that girl came into this family, she's been like a daughter to me. It doesn't matter if we're related by blood or not." He stabs a finger in my direction. "And you know that."

"You're right," I concede. "I do." My father is a good man. He's treated Carina in the same manner that he's always treated me. There was never any *you're just a stepchild* with him.

"Then what the hell are you doing?"

My shoulders collapse under the heaviness of the question and the confusion that mars his expression.

"I care about her," I blurt. "I've always cared. I want to be with her."

He pushes away from the desk and sits back against the leather chair as he silently studies me like I'm a bug smeared across his windshield.

Just as I begin to squirm beneath the relentless stare, he says, "You know what I think?" He doesn't give me a chance to respond. "That you want Carina simply because she's off-limits. If I were to give you my blessing, you'd lose interest in the blink of an eye, and it would be over with. And you'd fuck up this family as a result."

His accusation catches me off guard.

Is that seriously what my father thinks?

Of me?

That I'm an immature asshole who only wants what I can't have?

"That's not true," I growl.

"How do you know? When have you ever been involved in a relationship that lasted more than a few nights spent between the sheets?"

Heat slams into my face. "Did you ever think that I haven't bothered getting involved with another girl because I couldn't have the one I actually wanted? The one I've always had feelings for."

His expression remains inscrutable. If I thought baring a little bit of my soul would soften his stance, I couldn't have been more wrong.

"End it now, Ford. Before it destroys this family."

Is he fucking nuts?

"I did that before, and it was the worst mistake I've ever made. I won't do it again."

He slams his fist on the desk as his voice escalates, echoing off the walls. "Stop being so damn selfish. Think about someone other than yourself for a change."

I rise to my feet. "This conversation is over."

As I glare, I realize that my hands are shaking.

Have I ever been this angry?

With my father?

No.

On both accounts.

As I stalk toward the office door, he says, "You realize my political opponents will have a field day with this, right? My son dating his stepsister?"

My feet ground to a halt as I grapple with a response. But there's nothing.

Nothing I can say.

Shoulders hunched, I slip from the room, only wanting to get the hell out of this house.

CHAPTER THIRTY-FIVE

CARINA

With one last reluctant look over his shoulder, Ford follows his father, leaving me alone with Pamela. A handful of seconds later, the office door closes, shuttering both Hamilton men inside the room.

I glance longingly toward the front entrance of the house. I'd give just about anything to slip through the front door rather than sit here with my mother.

There's a moment of silence before she says, "Oh my, Carina. He really has it bad for you. Well done." Her throaty laughter leaves me wincing. "And here you were at lunch, trying to act like you're so superior."

My head whips toward her, unable to believe she actually thinks that I could ever be as calculating as she is. That I would use someone for money and security.

"It's not like that," I say stiffly.

She tilts her head as her gaze bores into mine. "That's not judgment. I told you the other day that you should be working this situation to your advantage. I'm glad you've finally taken my advice." She glances toward the office. "It was always obvious that Ford had feelings for you. You were smart to hold him off and make him work for it. He's had time to sleep around and get it out of his system. Now, he's ready to settle down."

My chest constricts until sucking in breath becomes painful. "No."

A slow smile spreads across her face. "You and I are more similar than you'd like to admit."

"Please stop," I whisper. Hearing her say that makes me sick to my stomach.

I'm nothing like Pamela.

Nothing.

Needing a moment to think, I gravitate to the floor-to-ceiling windows that overlook the rolling hills of the back lawn. The skies have darkened even more as the rain picks up, plinking against the glass.

"Make sure you hold onto him, Carina. And all this will be yours one day. I couldn't be prouder."

Her words are like the blunt edge of a knife hacking its way through my heart. She's never said that about any of my dance or academic achievements, but she's practically dabbing her eyes and gloating that I've managed to sink my claws into Crawford Hamilton the second.

Nausea churns in the pit of my belly as the acidic taste of bile rises in my throat. Any minute I'll vomit all over the cream-colored couch.

Rubber-soled shoes squeak against the hardwood announcing someone's presence. "Ma'am, dinner is served."

"Thank you. We'll be along in a minute or so."

Just as the older house manager turns to leave, Mom says, "Dolly, would you be an absolute dear and make me another martini? Extra dry this time."

"Of course."

"Carina?" Mom prompts when I remain silent. "Would you like a drink to enjoy with dinner? We have so much to celebrate tonight."

I force a slight smile before shaking my head. I'm dying inside, praying that she didn't overhear our conversation.

Dolly's eyes soften just a bit as our gazes cling before she slips from the room as quietly as she appeared.

She's barely out of earshot when Mom says with a sigh, "After years of waiting on customers hand and foot, it's nice to experience the other side of things."

I shoot a quick look toward the kitchen. *"Mom…"*

"What?" Irritation bleeds into her voice. "I'm just being truthful. What's wrong with that?"

I drag a hand over my face, unsure what to say to this woman.

"You know, Carina, there are times when I get the distinct impression that you don't appreciate all the sacrifices I've made in order to get us where we are today. Do you think you'd have your own dance studio or all the luxuries you've grown accustomed to if it weren't for me? Your life has been very cushy, and you want for nothing." Her eyes narrow. "Maybe you should think about *that* instead of judging me as if you're so much better. Like me, you weren't born into this lifestyle."

As tempting as it is to stare out the window and mentally escape this conversation, that's not possible. My gaze carefully combs over her. With the blonde extensions, cosmetic surgery, injections, designer clothes and handbags, she's almost unrecognizable from the woman who gave birth to me.

Once upon a time, we were close.

We were like two survivors clinging to one another during a storm, just hoping to make it through intact. Now that we have, her personality has done a one eighty. She's become one of the customers she'd come home after a long shift at the restaurant and complain about.

It's not like I haven't changed.

Of course I have. It's only natural. But I don't feel I'm owed this life. I'm grateful to Crawford for everything he's provided. I'm also well aware that in the not-so-distant future, I'll need to stand on my own two feet and take care of myself.

My mother has no intention of doing that.

Ever.

"You're wrong. I'm appreciative of everything you've done. All the sacrifices you've made throughout the years. I remember the long nights and the double shifts you took just to make ends meet."

She sniffs. "Well, you certainly don't act like it. It's no secret that Crawford's friends and staff think I'm trash. I don't need to hear it from you as well."

My shoulders wilt as I force my feet into movement and settle on the navy chair. "I'm sorry. I never meant to come across that way. I just..." My voice trails off as I try to figure out a way to express myself without rousing her anger. "You know how much I care about Crawford. He's been so good to us. I would never want him or Ford to think that I'm using them for their money."

"You do realize that they have a ton of it, right? More than they could possibly need?"

"It doesn't matter," I snap in frustration.

She presses her lips into a thin line.

When she doesn't say anything more, I force out the rest, knowing I need to get it off my chest once and for all. It might not change anything, but I'll feel better for it.

"I love you, Mom. I really do. But I don't want to see you hurt Crawford. If you're not going to stick around and be the partner he needs, then you should end it now. Don't put him through the wringer again."

Her brows pinch together. "The last thing I need is a lecture from you, Carina."

"That's not what this is. I just want you to think about how your decisions affect him."

Instead of responding, she rises to her feet in one smooth motion. "The food is getting cold."

With that, she stalks from the family room, leaving me alone with only the tangle of my thoughts for company.

CHAPTER THIRTY-SIX

FORD

My father's ugly words churn through my head as we drive back to campus. It hurts that he would think the only reason I'm interested in Carina is because he made her off limits. My feelings have absolutely nothing to do with that.

Much like this car ride, dinner had been a quiet, uncomfortable affair. Carina mostly shoved food around her plate and Pamela sulked, barely murmuring a sound. My father sat at the head of the table and stewed. All that could be heard was the scrape of utensils against fine bone china.

In hindsight, I should have listened to Carina when she asked if we could skip out on dinner. It would have saved us a shit ton of grief.

When we arrived earlier, it had been twilight and just starting to sprinkle. As we make our way back to the apartment building, rain pours down on us. It's like the heavens have opened up. Instead of the soft strains of music to lighten the atmosphere, a stifling silence fills the space. It intensifies with every mile until it feels as if it could snap in two.

I flick a glance in Carina's direction. Her shoulders are hunched, and she's angled away as she stares out the passenger side window.

Not more than two words have passed through her lips since we got the hell out of Dodge. I have no idea what's going through her brain.

Normally, all I have to do is look at her and I know what she's thinking. There'd been a brief flash of relief across her features when I'd told them that we couldn't stick around for dessert. That's the only emotion I've been able to pull from her.

It's so damn tempting to reach out and touch her, but I have no idea if it would be welcome. We've come so far in the past couple of weeks. And now it's all been wiped away. Kind of like we're playing a game of Chutes and Ladders and we're right back to square one without any warning.

It fucking sucks.

When I can't stand another moment, I blurt, "Are we going to talk about this or are you going to keep ignoring me?"

The pathetic whine filling my voice almost is enough to make me wince.

Could I sound like more of a needy bitch?

Her shoulders stiffen as she straightens on the butter soft leather before slowly swiveling toward me. "That's not what I'm doing."

My fingers tighten around the steering wheel until the knuckles turn bone white. "Isn't it?"

"I'm sorry. I'm just trying to process everything that happened."

"What's there to process? We got caught having sex. It's not that big of a deal." Nerves explode within me as a sick knot twists in the pit of my belly.

She releases a shaky breath as her voice dips. "Crawford's really angry with us."

"I told you earlier, he'll get over it. Don't make more of an issue out of the situation than it is." There's a bite to my voice that I wish weren't filling it. But I don't like the direction this convo is headed. Already I can tell it won't be good. It feels as if there's an ocean of distance sitting between us.

And I hate it.

If only it were possible to rewind time to what we were before walking through that door tonight.

"The last thing I want is to cause a problem between you and your father." There's a pause before she tacks on softly, "It's not worth it."

Not worth it?

What the fuck does that mean?

I flick a quick glance in her direction, trying to get a read on her thoughts. Unfortunately, a second or two glimpse in the darkness isn't enough time to figure that out.

Instead, I stare at the black ribbon of road stretched out ahead of us, searching for a place to pull over. The sick knot at the bottom of my belly has swelled in size.

When the headlights fall on a convenience store up the road, I swerve into the parking lot and cut the engine before swiveling toward her. Rain continues to batter the roof of the vehicle, filling the silence.

Carina's eyes widen. "What are you doing?"

"Pulling over so we can hash this out."

Her tongue darts out to moisten her lips as her gaze flits away. "It couldn't have waited until we got back to the apartment?"

"No. Plus, I'm not altogether certain you wouldn't take off before we could actually do that."

The guilt that flickers in her eyes tells me everything I need to know, and it pisses me the fuck off.

We're more than that.

I deserve more than that.

Her voice dips. "Ford—"

"Tell me what you meant when you said this wasn't worth it."

Misery crashes over her features as she glances away. "This was just supposed to be sex. It's what we agreed to in the beginning."

My fingers slide beneath her chin before turning her face until she has no other choice but to meet my gaze. "I think we both know it was never *just* sex. You can try and fool yourself all you want, but I'm not buying it."

"Don't make this harder than it has to be."

My eyes widen and my mouth crashes open. "Is that what I'm doing? *Making this harder?*"

"Yeah." There's a beat of agonizing silence. And then another. I feel every second of it thundering through my veins. "I think this arrangement has run its course."

Those eight words tear my insides to shreds.

And there's no way to patch them up.

I suck in a deep breath and try to reel it all back in. I need to keep it fucking together. Obviously, I need to come at this from a different angle.

"If you're worried about our parents, they'll get over it." The effort it takes to keep my voice level is a challenge. It's so damn tempting to shake some sense into her before dragging her into my arms for safekeeping. I want to kiss her into submission until she finally agrees that whatever has been brewing between us for years is worth fighting for.

That I'm worth fighting for.

Does she really think otherwise?

How can she sit there and tell me that this relationship doesn't mean a damn thing?

For fuck's sake, what we have is different.

It's...*special.*

To look me in the eyes and tell me otherwise would be a lie.

"No, I don't think they will," she admits softly. "It would probably be best for everyone involved if we ended this and moved on."

Moved on?

How the fuck am I supposed to do that?

Wait a minute...

I sit up a little straighter, my entire body straining toward her.

"Is that what Pamela told you? That we shouldn't be together? That it's wrong? Or that people will talk?" I bite out each question, rapid firing them before she has a chance to answer a single one. I'm just trying to get to the bottom of what's changed. Why is she so willing to let this go?

Color drains from her face. "Crawford's been so good to me, I'd never want to do anything that would hurt him."

"Us being together won't hurt him."

"What if it causes problems for his re-election campaign? He loves politics so much. Could you really forgive yourself if you take that away from him? I'm not sure if I can."

I press my lips tightly together as frustration explodes inside me. "Would you still be looking to end this if his career wasn't a factor?"

She rips her eyes away only to stare out the windshield. The more time that ticks by, the harder my heart thrashes against my chest until it feels like there's a good possibility it'll bust loose.

"You have to know that we were never meant for the long haul. It was just supposed to be a bit of—"

"*Fun?*"

I can't believe we're seriously sitting here having this conversation.

I never expected it. Even after we got caught.

I thought she'd be embarrassed, and, after a few days, we'd laugh about the entire thing. Instead, it feels like she's trying to—

"Yeah."

It's so damn tempting to continue arguing but in the end, what good will it do?

Maybe she's being straightforward about her feelings, and it was never serious. She was in it for the sex.

I slump against the seat as those thoughts circle viciously through my head. I feel like a real dumbass for thinking it could have been more. That this was a relationship. The start of something that could stand the test of time.

It sucks to realize that it was all one sided.

With nothing else left to talk about, I twist around and restart the engine before pulling out of the parking lot and onto the road.

And just like before, neither of us say a word.

CHAPTER THIRTY-SEVEN

CARINA

Air leaks from my lungs as I stare sightlessly at the ceiling. When the alarm on my phone rings like an obnoxious bell, I roll over, swipe my cell from the nightstand, and tap the screen before returning to my back.

I should get out of bed. Dance starts in forty minutes, but I have zero motivation to get dressed or leave my room. It's been that way since I pulled the plug on my relationship with Ford.

For more than a week, we've been going to great lengths to avoid each other. Not even when he pushed me away in high school did it feel like this. There's a giant gaping hole where my heart should be. I don't understand how it's possible to miss him this much. It's like I severed a limb and will now have to live the remainder of my life with phantom pain.

Everything reminds me of him.

His scent on my pillows.

Dancing.

The book he left for me on the bed to find.

The jersey he bought me that's draped over my chair.

It's ridiculous.

I've slept with guys before and I've had a handful of relationships. Most didn't last that long, or I was never very invested to bother sticking around. When they came to an inevitable end, it was more of a relief than anything else. The guys in question were never important.

They didn't mean anything.

Not really.

But…

That's not how I feel about Ford.

And here I'd thought I was guarding my heart so carefully.

Turns out that nothing could be further from the truth.

I grab a fluffy pillow and drag it over my face before screaming at the top of my lungs until there's nothing left inside.

The door to the bedroom bursts open and a deep voice says, "Are you all right?"

I rip the pillow away only to stare at Ryder.

His brows are raised, and concern is etched across his face. His gaze darts around the room as if looking for the cause of my anguish. When he doesn't find a culprit, his eyes resettle on me, and his frown deepens.

Great. He probably thinks I'm losing it.

And maybe I am.

"Yeah, I'm fine. Sorry," I mutter, feeling like an idiot. "I didn't mean to wake you."

He shifts his big body in the doorway, looking distinctly uncomfortable as if only now realizing I'm in emotional distress. "You didn't." He jerks a thumb over his shoulder. "Juliette's taking a shower. Otherwise, she'd be here."

In an attempt to lighten the atmosphere, I arch a brow. "And you're not in there with her?"

That question is all it takes for a slow smile to spread across his face. "I was."

"From the sounds of it, you kept her up all night," I grumble.

He shrugs. "Guilty as charged."

"Kind of seems like I'm the one who should invest in noise cancelling headphones, don't you think?"

"I can loan you a pair if you need them."

I roll my eyes. "All I have to say is that you two are disgustingly happy together."

"Thanks."

My expression softens as I add, "It's nice to see. That girl is finally coming out of her shell and enjoying herself instead of spending every waking moment with her nose buried in a book. I'm surprised she made it to senior year without a total mental breakdown."

He sobers before leaning against the doorjamb and crossing his brawny arms against his chest. "Juliette has always been driven. Even before Natalie was diagnosed with cancer."

My voice softens at that reminder. "I've been trying for three years to get her to loosen her grip and she didn't want to hear it. You're the one who helped her do that." My lips lift into a smile. "You've been good for her."

Mirth dances in his blue eyes. "Thanks, Carina. That just might be the nicest thing you've ever said to me."

He's probably right about that.

"Don't get used to it."

"I wouldn't even think about it." There's a moment of silence. "So…is screaming into your pillow a normal thing for you? Are you releasing toxins from your body or something like that?"

"Yeah, something like that."

He shifts before glancing away and clearing his throat. "Is there, um, anything you want to talk about?" His voice turns hesitant. Halting.

I blink and stare until his gaze finally returns to mine. "Are we really doing this right now?"

One side of his mouth hitches. "Sure. Why not? I assume this has to do with Ford."

"Why would you think that?" I shoot back instead of pulling up my big girl panties and admitting the truth.

He pops a brow. "Because I have eyes, and I tend to use them. For as long as I've known you guys, something's been going on between you two. It was only a matter of time before it came to a head. Hell, I'm surprised it took this long."

Air leaks from my lungs as his comments circle through my brain. "The situation is…complicated."

"Maybe you haven't noticed but life is complicated."

True enough.

When I remain silent, unsure if I want to delve into this with him, he says, "Have you talked to Ford about it like the mature adult you are?"

Ouch.

"Kind of." I gnaw my lower lip before forcing out the rest. "We decided it would be best to stop seeing each other."

"Really? That's a surprise. Is Ford the one who came to that decision?" There's a meaningful pause. "Or did you?"

It doesn't take long before I'm squirming beneath the intensity of his stare. "It was me."

He searches my face for a long moment, almost as if trying to pick through my private thoughts. I don't like it. "I don't know what to tell you, Carina. Most people who are happy with their life choices don't shove pillows over their faces and scream."

Sheesh. The guy just got into a relationship and suddenly he's a world-renowned authority doling out advice?

"Like I said, it's complicated. Did Ford mention that our parents are getting remarried? Or that us being together could be an issue with Crawford's bid for re-election?"

Even though those are two solid reasons for pulling the plug, I don't mention the other one.

The one that bothers me most.

He shakes his head. "No, he hasn't said much of anything lately. The guy is moping around the apartment and being a real downer. And he's total shit on the ice. If he doesn't get his head out of his ass, he'll be riding the pine for the foreseeable future."

My heart clenches.

I hate that he's been hurt in all this.

More than that, I hate that I'm the one who inflicted the pain.

I never imagined that we'd get so deep so fast when I agreed to sleep with him.

After what happened in high school, maybe I should have.

Unfortunately, Ford isn't the only one I'm avoiding. I haven't spoken to Crawford either. Usually, we text every day. And he's checked in, but my responses have been one worded. I'm embarrassed that he walked in on us. Even the memory is enough to heat my cheeks.

I have no idea how to get our relationship back on track. I've been toying with the idea of stopping by so we can talk but I'm being a total chickenshit about it. I keep coming up with excuses and then another day slips by.

"I'm sorry to hear that about Ford. I'm sure he'll bounce back. It probably doesn't have anything to do with me, anyway."

His brows rise as he cocks his head, disbelief filling his eyes. "Do you really think that?"

I don't know. I don't know anything anymore.

The need to shut down this conversation thrums through me and I say quickly, "I really appreciate you checking up on me, but I should probably get my ass moving or I'll be late," I mutter, refusing to delve into the shitshow that has become my life with my bestie's new boyfriend.

With a pop of his shoulders, he shoves away from the door. "All right. I'm sure Jules will be around if you want to talk later." His gaze stays pinned to mine as his voice dips. "She's worried about you."

Juliette's a good friend. The absolute best one any girl could ask for. I'm going to miss her when we part ways next year. I shut down those thoughts before I turn any more maudlin.

I force a small smile. "There's no reason for her to be concerned. It's all good."

"If you say so."

Just as he disappears into the hallway, I call out, "Thanks again."

He throws a glance over his shoulder. "It's not a problem. You've always been there for Jules. If you ever need a male perspective on matters, I'm here."

It's a surprise when I have to blink back the emotion that stings my eyes. "I'll keep that in mind."

With that, he swings away before slipping inside my bestie's bedroom.

Even though my heart feels raw, I couldn't be happier for Ryder and Juliette. I'm over the moon that they found their happily ever after. Being able to watch their love story unfold has been more satisfying than any romance novel I've ever read. Even the spicy ones that have me pulling out my vibe.

Now that my decision has been made, I toss off the covers and roll from the bed. Fifteen minutes later, I'm dressed for dance class. I've thrown my hair up into a bun and have guzzled down six ounces of piping hot coffee before nibbling at a protein bar.

Juliette gives me a quick hug as I'm getting ready to leave and tells me that we'll talk tonight. Maybe that's exactly what I need. To unload and get her perspective on matters. As I close the door, I glance up and find the one guy who's been front and center in my mind this entire time.

Everything inside me freezes.

Even the air in my lungs.

He grounds to a halt as well.

For a long moment that hangs in suspension, we simply stare. I can't help but greedily drink him in. The urge to reach out and run my fingers over the sharp lines of his face pounds through me like a steady drumbeat. It wouldn't take much to close the distance that separates us.

And yet, the gulf feels like an ocean. Too expansive to cross with mere words or a single touch.

Only then do I realize that neither of us have uttered a word.

It's dead silent in the hallway.

That's all it takes for awkwardness to descend.

Was it really just a week ago that we were spending every spare second together and he was slipping into my bed each night?

I miss the way he'd hold me in his arms.

I miss him sliding deep inside my body, filling me to the brim.

I miss the way he'd grit his teeth, trying to hold back.

Or the way he'd stare into my eyes the entire time he was buried inside me. In those moments of intense connection, the world would shrink down until it felt like we were the only two people in the universe. I've never experienced that kind of intimacy with another human being.

It shouldn't surprise me that this happened with Ford.

That it's been him this entire time.

I shove those thoughts from my head before they can do further damage. I'm already precariously close to losing it.

I'm hanging by a single thread.

His gaze stays locked on mine. "Are you heading to class?"

"Um, yeah." I shift and tug the silver jacket a little closer to my body as if it has the power to protect me.

"Do you want a ride?"

Absolutely not.

Spending time alone with him—even ten minutes—would be the epitome of stupid. And while I'm a lot of things, that's not one of them.

"Sure. Thanks."

I almost wince.

He jerks his shoulders into a tight shrug. "It's not a problem."

My gaze drops to the broad set of them. It wasn't long ago that I'd trace my fingertips across every sinewy line before my mouth followed the path, needing to taste every inch.

When my tongue darts out to moisten my lips, his gaze dips to the movement. That's all it takes for his pupils to dilate, swallowing up the golden hue before he swings away without warning and stalks down the hallway. I release a shaky breath as a swarm of angry butterflies burst to life in my belly. It takes effort to force my feet into movement as I reluctantly trail after him.

This was a mistake.

One of many that I've made where Ford is concerned.

I'm mentally kicking myself for not turning down the offer. I should have pretended to forget something and slipped back inside the safety of the apartment before waiting for him to disappear down the hallway.

Even if it meant I was late for class. Now I'm stuck until we part ways on campus. The next ten minutes are going to be excruciating.

Well…more excruciating than life has already become.

Just as I reach the elevator, the bell dings, signaling the arrival of the car.

Thank fuck.

He glances at me before holding the metal door so that it won't close.

I hop on and wedge myself as deep into the corner as I can get so that there's as much physical distance between us as possible. Ford follows me on before stabbing the button designated with an L for the lobby. The doors slide shut, locking us inside the confining space together.

It doesn't take long for the atmosphere to turn claustrophobic.

His gaze slices to mine where it stays fastened. When he refuses to look away, my body begins to tremble under the intense scrutiny, and my palms turn sweaty. Just as the car lurches into movement, he slams his hand against the red stop button and a loud bell trills, filling the space.

My eyes widen as I plaster myself against the wall. "What are you doing?"

"Truth or dare?"

I blink, surprised by the question. "What?"

He tilts his head and narrows his eyes. Even from the distance that separates us, I feel the heavy waves of anger wafting off him. It's almost enough to choke on.

"You heard me. Truth or dare."

I drag my gaze away before sucking my lower lip into my mouth and chewing it.

There's no way I can pick truth.

I'm deathly afraid of what he'll ask.

Because I can't lie. I refuse to hurt him more than I already have.

And dare…

The possibility almost scares me more. I'm desperate for the feel of his hands sliding over me. It's only been a week, but it feels more like an eternity.

"Dare," I whisper before I can think better of it. I just need to remain strong. I can hold out against him for a couple of minutes.

Can't I?

He swallows up the distance that separates us until I have to tilt my chin in order to hold his steely gaze. "I dare you to kiss me."

Oh, god.

"Do you really think that's a good idea?"

"Fuck, no." He tilts his head. "But if you don't have feelings for me, then it shouldn't matter, right? It's just a kiss."

Is that what he believes?

That I feel nothing where he's concerned?

It would be so much easier if that were the case.

"You know that I care about you," I admit, unable to keep the words contained.

The corners of his lips curl into a mocking smile. "Do I?"

"Of course. I'll always care." Somehow, I need to dig myself out of the hole I've become mired in.

He steps closer before lowering his face until it hovers inches above my own. Intensity burns in his eyes. It would be all too easy to drown within their vibrant, honeyed depths and all the emotion that swims around within them. It's so tempting to reach up and stroke my fingers along the curve of his shadowed jaw. To trace the sharp angles. Instead of giving into the urge, I squeeze my hands into tight balls that hang limply at my sides.

"Because we're family?" There's an edge to his voice that feels as lethal as a razorblade. Sharp and agonizing. Little does he know that I'm powerless to protect myself against him.

"Yes."

"That's not what I want from you, Carina."

"It's all I can afford to give."

"Maybe." His expression turns as flippant as the word that just fell from his lips. "Then again, maybe not."

One hand snakes out, wrapping around the nape of my neck before drawing me close enough to feel the warmth of his breath drift across my parted lips. It stirs the air around us, turning it electric. The tiny hairs on my arms stand to attention as a shiver scampers down the length of my spine.

In that moment, I know that I need to get out of here. I won't be able to withstand much more of this onslaught.

"The clock is ticking," he growls, voice sounding as if it's been dredged from the very bottom of the ocean. "We're running out of time."

The alarm continues to ring as my gaze stays locked on his. I'm incapable of looking away. Before I realize it, my fingers tangle in the fabric of his hoody, dragging him even closer until there's not a whisper of air between us. The heat that emanates from him is nothing short of intoxicating. As soon as I stretch onto the tips of my toes, my mouth collides with his. In a surprising twist, he keeps his lips firmly pressed together. My tongue sweeps tentatively across the seam.

Have I ever had to work for Ford's attention?

Renewed fire sparks to life inside me as I double down on my efforts.

Once.

Twice.

Three times my tongue sweeps across his, demanding entry.

When his mouth remains firmly locked, I pull away enough to glare before sinking my teeth into his lower lip and tugging it. A sharp hiss of breath escapes from him as his mouth opens. A low growl vibrates in his chest as my tongue plunges inside to tangle with his own. The minty freshness of his breath invades my senses along with a taste that is uniquely Ford.

I've missed it so much.

I've missed *him* so much.

My palms flatten against his pectorals before sliding upward and tangling around his thickly corded neck. His hands settle on my ass, squeezing the muscle as he hauls me close enough to feel the thick jut of his erection against my lower abdomen.

That's all it takes for my core to dampen in response. I'm like one of Pavlov's well-trained dogs when it comes to Ford's cock. Just the feel of his hard length is enough to arouse me.

His mouth roves over mine. Teeth scraping, tongues licking, lips devouring. The sharp ache of hunger reverberates throughout my entire being. It's one that feels as if it will never be satisfied again.

Just when it feels like he'll swallow me whole, or maybe it's the other way around, his hands disappear from my backside and he breaks free from the tangle of my arms, taking a quick step in retreat.

My breath comes out in short, gasping pants as I press myself against the wall in order to remain vertical. Any moment, I'll slump to the floor in a gooey mess of raging hormones and lust.

His eyes turn stormy as he uses his thumb and forefinger to wipe the corners of his mouth. Without looking away, he reaches across the space and hits the button, sending the car into jolting motion once again. The bell stops trilling as the elevator descends to the lobby in silence. My heart thumps a painful tattoo against my chest.

As the taste of him floods my senses, my brain spins.

I need to say something.

Something that will change the trajectory of our relationship.

But I'm at a loss.

In the end, not a single sound escapes from me.

Disappointment crashes over his expression before it's hidden behind a mask of indifference. He drags his eyes away, only to stare straight ahead as if I'm no longer there.

I didn't think it was possible for my heart to break any more than it already has but I was wrong. It shatters into a million jagged pieces that will never be put back together again.

I wrap my arms around my middle, attempting to keep all the pain locked deep inside so it doesn't have a chance to leak out. So he doesn't see just how much this encounter, and the finality of it, has destroyed me.

All I know is that I will never be the same again.
My life can now be marked by two very distinct periods of time.
Before Ford.
And *after*.
I'm just not sure how to survive the *after* part.

CHAPTER THIRTY-EIGHT

CARINA

The sun sits high in the sky as I pull the BMW up the long stretch of driveway and park near the front door. Relief leaks from my lungs as I scan the weather brick drive and find my mother's Audi absent. Although, three other cars are parked off to the side.

Since it's the middle of the week, I imagine aides are working on Crawford's political strategy. He's usually surrounded by five or six at all times.

Unless Pamela is around.

I cut the engine, grab the takeout bag I picked up and slide from the vehicle before walking up the front stairs to the door. For the first six months I lived here, I couldn't stop myself from pressing the doorbell. Finally, Crawford sat me down and told me that it wasn't necessary. That this house was as much mine as his. He never failed to make me feel welcome.

My belly churns with nerves as I turn the silver handle and step inside the grand foyer. Even though the place was professionally decorated years ago, there's a warmth to the interior that makes me feel instantly at home.

This is the first time we've seen each other since *the incident*. That's what I've dubbed it in my head.

I'm fully expecting this convo to be awkward.

How could it not be?

But I can't allow this situation to linger between us. This issue needs to be hashed out and resolved. Not talking to Crawford has left a huge hole in my life just as it has with his son. If I can't fix my relationship with Ford, the least I can do is smooth over the one with his father.

I can also make sure they're back on track. I can take the brunt of the responsibility for what happened. Whatever I have to do to make everything right between them, I'll do it.

Conversation from Crawford's home office spills out to the entryway. Voices talk over one another, jockeying for top position. I should have expected that he'd be busy.

Maybe this impromptu visit wasn't such a great idea after all. The last thing I want to do is interrupt. I'll drop the food off in the kitchen, and he can dig in when he has time.

Just as I swivel toward the back of the house, a deep voice halts me in my tracks.

"Carina?"

I glance over my shoulder and find Crawford standing in the office doorway.

"What are you doing here?" Before I can respond, concern floods his expression. "Is everything all right? You never pop home during the middle of the day."

I force a smile. "Sorry about that. I probably should have called first to see if you were busy."

His gaze falls to the large paper bag in my hand. "You brought lunch?"

"Yup. But I can leave it on the counter for later." I glance toward the room behind him that continues to burst with voices. "There's more than enough to feed at least five people. You can have a working lunch if you'd like."

"That was very thoughtful." He glances at the chunky silver Rolex wrapped around his left wrist. "We've been at it for a couple of hours already. Now seems like the perfect time to take a much-needed break. They can run out and grab something and we'll enjoy the," he pauses to sniff the air, "Chinese, if I'm not mistaken."

A smile lifts the corners of my lips. "Yup. Spring rolls, pork dumplings, chicken fried rice, and kung pao chicken. There's plenty. I really don't mind sharing with your staff."

He waves a hand. "Nah. They can fend for themselves this afternoon."

Ten minutes later, we've set up our food on the glass table in the kitchen that overlooks the backyard. The pretty view never fails to soothe my soul when something's bothering me.

Or maybe that's just this place.

It's become a safe haven.

That wasn't a feeling I knew until after meeting Crawford.

We take a little bit of everything before digging in. Although, much like the night we were here for dinner, my appetite pulls a disappearing act. I thought for sure the amazing scent of my favorite takeout would pique my interest.

After a grueling, two-hour dance class, I should be famished.

Instead, there's nothing.

Nothing but a vague sense of unease.

With his fork, he points to my plate. "You brought over all this food, and I don't think you've taken a bite. Is there something you want to talk about?"

I huff out a breath and shove the dish away before staring down at my hands. The reason I decided to drop by in the first place was to clear the air. He needs to know that whatever was going on with Ford is now over.

The thought brings a pang to my heart.

But I'm doing what's best for the family, right?

That's what's important.

At some point, Ford and I can smooth over our relationship and forget that we were ever together. It's not like it lasted very long. It'll be a momentary blip of insanity that we can laugh about in the distant future.

The *very* distant future.

And we can continue to be a family.

When I remain silent, trying to figure out how best to get it all out in the open, he says, "Have you spoken with your mother?" He doesn't give me a chance to respond before his voice dips. "Is that what this is about?"

The question throws me for a loop.

"Mom?" I haven't talked to her since our conversation in the family room. It didn't seem like there was anything else to say after that. "No. Did something happen?"

His gaze flickers away as his normally strong shoulders wilt. "Pamela decided that she didn't want to get remarried after all."

My eyes widen as my mouth falls open. "Are you kidding?" Although, it's doubtful he'd joke about something like this.

"No." He lays his fork down and straightens on the chair as if putting on a brave face. "I was hoping she'd change her mind, but she booked a last-minute cruise to the Bahamas and left this morning."

The bomb he just dropped explodes in my brain, blowing everything to bits.

I can't believe Pamela did this.

Well…that's not true. I can totally believe it.

I can't help but wonder if I had anything to do with her decision to call off the wedding. Guilt pricks at me as I stare across the table at Crawford.

Then again, this is exactly what Mom does. I might be secretly relieved by the turn of events, but it's obvious that he's in pain. Crawford has never failed to see the best in her.

Even when he shouldn't.

"I'm sorry."

It takes every ounce of self-control not to admit that he's better off without her.

He forces a smile that doesn't quite reach his eyes before shrugging. "I should have seen it coming. The one thing your mother doesn't like is to be tied down. She wants to take off whenever the urge strikes, and that's not something I can do right now."

"That doesn't excuse her behavior," I grumble, unable to help myself.

"I know," he says with a heavy sigh. "We can't help who we love, can we?"

My greatest fear lurks like a monster in the darkness at the back of my brain. The question is out of my mouth before I can stop it.

"I'm not like her, am I?"

He blinks as if trying to play mental catchup. "Like Pamela?"

I nod, almost afraid to hear his answer. For Crawford to think that I'm a carbon copy of her would be devastating.

When he remains silent, searching my eyes, I admit softly, "I don't want to be."

Understanding dawns as he reaches across the table and covers my hand with his larger one. "Only in the very best ways, Carina. Your mother has a sparkling personality and so do you. That woman is the life of the party." He gives me a wink. "Just like you. For a lot of years, she busted her ass, so you had a safe place to live. Often working overtime to make sure you had whatever you needed."

Guilt suffuses me because he's right. There were times when she went without comfortable shoes for work so I could sign up for a dance class or afford the newest recital costume.

"It's one of the reasons I fell in love with her to begin with. I'm well aware that in this day and age, a woman doesn't need to be taken care of, but I wanted to make her life easier. Better. And for a while, we were really happy." A faraway look enters his eyes. "I didn't think that was possible after Sandra died. What I've learned throughout the years is that sometimes relationships or people are only in your life for a short period of time and don't last forever. You have to make the most of them while you can. Nothing is ever guaranteed." He refocuses his attention on me before leaning forward and ensnaring my gaze. "But you, my dear, are in it for much longer. No matter what happens with Pamela, I'll always be your father."

I don't realize that tears have gathered in my eyes until one spills down my cheek. I jump from the chair and fly around the circular table, burying my face against his broad chest as more wetness leaks from me.

Once the floodgates open, there doesn't seem to be a way to stop it. I don't remember the last time I cried like this. As emotion continues to pour from me, his arms tighten as if he'll never let go.

"I'm sorry, Carina," he murmurs. "Maybe I should have said all this to you a long time ago. I just assumed you understood my feelings."

"Do you promise to always feel that way no matter what happens with her?"

I need him to say the words.

Just once.

Out loud.

"I do. You're my daughter in every way possible and nothing will ever change that. *Nothing*."

I swipe at the tears as I pull away enough to settle on the chair next to him. "I was afraid that after you found me with Ford, you'd feel differently."

He shakes his head. "Never. Maybe I was shocked by what I walked in on, but that's all it was. Surprise." He releases a steady breath. "I never wanted Ford to take advantage of you or make you feel pressured to do something you weren't ready for."

"It was never like that between us," I tell him.

"After I found out that you were sneaking into his room and spending the night, I made sure it came to an end. I was so disappointed in him."

"Wait a minute…what?" I blink away the wetness as my head spins with this revelation. "You mean senior year?"

"Yes. I walked in one morning and found you curled up next to him. I pulled Ford aside after that and told him in no uncertain terms there wasn't to be a sexual relationship between you two." He sifts through the emotions in my gaze as doubt creeps into his whiskey-colored eyes. "You were too young. Too impressionable. Even then, I could see how enamored you were." He falls silent before asking in a softer tone, "I made the right decision, didn't I?"

My mind tumbles back to senior year and how close we'd grown. And then how my heart broke when he pushed me away. In that one moment of clarity, the entirety of our history shifts and changes, morphing into something different. He didn't freeze me out because he'd grown bored.

He kept his distance because his father insisted upon it.

"I love him," I admit.

"Yeah, I thought you might," he says with a slow nod. "And I don't think Ford ever stopped. He insisted that he loved you back then and I told him that he was too young to be making that kind of declaration. Especially when your mother and I were married, and we were a family."

My heart constricts with the realization that Ford has always cared.

Even when he was giving me shit and aggravating the hell out of me.

Not to mention, chasing other guys away.

"He arranged for your apartments to be next to one another so he could keep an eye on you and make sure you were safe."

And here I'd thought it was just another stroke of bad luck. I feel like such an idiot for not seeing everything that was right in front of my eyes this entire time.

"I hurt him," I whisper, more to myself than Crawford. "I pushed him away. I don't know if he'll forgive me after how I ended our relationship."

His expression turns sympathetic. "There's only one way to find out, isn't there?"

I nod, knowing exactly what I have to do as I shoot to my feet.

His gaze stays pinned to mine as he reaches out and takes my hand. "I wanted to protect you as if you were my own because in my heart, you were." He quickly corrects himself. *"Are."*

"I never knew my biological father. He took off as soon as Mom found out she was pregnant. As far as I'm concerned, it's you, Crawford. You're the one who's always been there for me. No matter what."

"That's the way it should be with family. Not only there through the good times, but the bad ones as well. And that's what we are, Carina. Family. We'll always be family."

"Yes." The tight fist wrapped around my heart loosens just enough for me to suck in a full breath. Maybe for the first time in years. When he releases my hand, I take a quick step toward the entryway before grounding to a halt. "I don't want to do anything that could damage your career."

His lips quirk at the corners. "What's important to me is that you and Ford are happy. If that happens to be together as a couple, then we'll deal with the ramifications and stand united as a family."

That's all it takes for the last of my reservations and doubts to fall away. I rush toward him, throwing my arms around his neck and hugging him tight as if I'll never let go.

"I love you, Crawford."

"I love you, too."

He pats my back before setting me free. "Now, go fix things with my son."

CHAPTER THIRTY-NINE

FORD

"Hamilton," Coach bellows. "Get your damn head out of your ass and pay attention to the play or you'll find yourself benched."

Just as I glance toward the coaching staff, someone slams into me, and I fall on my ass. As soon as I hit the ice, the air gets knocked from my lungs. My eyes water as I attempt to suck in breath. But it's agonizing. From my prone position, I stare up into the grinning face of Garret Akeman.

Fucker.

"Should have been watching where you're going, Hamilton. Didn't you learn that in mites?"

It takes a moment to scramble to my skates. "You're a real dick," I wheeze.

He laughs as if I'm joking around.

I'm not. The guy is a major dickhead.

King of the dickheads, as far as I'm concerned.

He'll take any opportunity to make a teammate look bad if he looks better in front of Coach Philips.

I skate closer, more than ready to get into it with him. What the hell do I have to lose at this point?

Not much. My life has imploded.

Just as I'm about to get in his face, Hayes and Colby skid to a quick stop, spraying ice as they shove my shoulders and force me back.

"Get the fuck out of here, Akeman," Colby snaps, spitting out his mouth guard. He's normally the chillest guy on the team. But not when it comes to Garret. After almost four years playing together, we've all had more than enough of his bullshit.

"Asshole," Hayes mutters.

With a wave, Garret skates to his side of the ice to take his defensive position.

Colby watches him before shaking his head. "Just when you think that guy can't turn into more of an asshat, he jackhammers to an all new low."

"Yup," I agree, continuing to glare.

Hayes studies me. "What the hell is going on? It's not like you to get knocked on your ass." He jerks his head toward Akeman. "Especially by him."

"Nothing," I mutter, not wanting to admit that there's an issue. My game has been shit ever since Carina cut me loose. It's like I can't focus. On anything.

That's never happened to me.

And now that we're over, I feel like a dumbass for thinking that it was anything more than fucking.

Because clearly, for her, that's all it was.

Some D between boyfriends.

Colby arches a brow as Hayes rolls his eyes behind the cage.

"Sure," Colby says.

"My guess is that this has something to do with Carina," Hayes tosses out, watching me closely.

I glower before grumbling, "It doesn't have anything to do with her. I've got a lot going on."

"Yeah, right," Colby says with a snort. "I think it has everything to do with her."

"It's pretty obvious that something's been going on with you two," Hayes adds.

I press my lips into a tight line, refusing to respond. I already feel like a loser. No reason for my teammates to know exactly how big of one I am.

Colby jerks his head toward the stands. "Is that why she's here?"

Ha! Does he really think I'm going to fall for such a lame trap?

Hayes glances toward the bleachers before grinning and waving.

It takes every bit of self-restraint not to snap my head around and scour the arena. But I know exactly what I'll find.

And that's another kick in the ass.

As difficult as it's been, I've kept my distance even though all I want to do is bang on her door and force my way inside. I want to take her mouth and kiss her until she finally admits that what we had was more than physical.

Just a bit of fun...

Even thinking about that casually-thrown-out comment pisses me the fuck off. We were *never* just a bit of fun.

From the very beginning, it was more.

She was my everything.

Sliding deep inside the welcoming heat of her body was like coming home.

To think that I'll never feel that again rips my heart to shreds.

"You boys interested in playing a little hockey or you just gonna keep jaw jacking over there?" Coach yells from where he loiters near the bench with three of his assistant coaches.

Rather than respond, we splinter apart, moving into position. The last thing any of us want is to skate suicides.

No fucking way.

As I wait for the scrimmage to resume, a splash of silver catches the corner of my eye, and my head whips in that direction. The moment I spot her sitting in the bleachers, every muscle goes whipcord tight.

Our gazes lock and hold for a heartbeat.

Then another.

I'm jarred from the trance as Hayes and Madden fight for possession. Madden quickly passes the puck to Colby who races toward the goal. I dig my blades into the ice a second or two too late and swear under my breath as I focus on the play unfolding around me instead of the girl who's been filling my every waking thought.

And the not so waking ones as well.

It's like there's no escaping her.

No matter how much I try.

Ryder and Bridger sweep their sticks out in front of them, waiting to see what he'll do next. Colby passes off the black disc to Hayes who drives it up the middle before getting swarmed and passing it back to me. Ryder picks up speed as I race toward the net, faking a pass to Hayes before aiming for the five hole and sending the puck flying.

Wolf falls to his knees and catches it with a gloved hand before flashing a lazy grin. "Nice try, asswipe. Better luck next time."

I circle the net and head back to my side of the ice. That's exactly how the next thirty minutes of practice go. As much as I try not to get distracted by Carina, every cell in my body is intensely aware of her.

But then again, that's how it's always been.

Even when I tried to distance myself and move on in high school.

I couldn't do it.

By the time practice ends, I'm a sweaty mess. I head to the locker room and take my sweet damn time showering. As I stand under the hot spray, it occurs to me that she could be here to see another guy. Every muscle tightens as that thought circles savagely through my head. If that turns out to be the case, I swear to fucking god, I'll wring the asshole's neck.

From day one freshman year, I made it crystal clear that she wasn't to be touched. Hell, I don't even want these dipshits looking sideways at her. If she realized that I made her off-limits, she never said a word about it.

I finish up in the shower and quickly dress, throwing on some deodorant before shoving my feet into slides. Now that practice is over and the pressure's off, there's a lot of laughter and shit talking going on around me. But I can't focus on any of that when Carina's out there.

Doubt continues to creep into my brain.

After the way she ended things, what's there left to talk about?

Abso-fucking-lutely nothing.

I'm almost *afraid* to hear what she has to say.

Whatever it is, it can't be good.

A humorless laugh bubbles up in my throat.

Exactly how many ways can this girl kick me in the balls?

That's what I'd like to know.

Riggs, Wolf, and Maverick haul their bags over their shoulders before heading to the door.

Mav glances back at me. "You coming or what?"

"Yeah, I'll be out in a minute."

Wolf shrugs. "Suit yourself. Don't worry about Carina. I'll keep her company until you grow a pair."

When I give him a one-fingered salute, he grins and pushes through the metal door into the arena. Maverick trails behind him with a shake of his head as if I'm too pathetic for words.

And that hurts, considering he's a junior.

When I can't stall any longer and the locker room has emptied, I pick up my bag and head for the door. As soon as I step into the arena, my gaze scans the bleachers only to find them vacant.

My heart hitches a painful beat.

Guess she really was here for someone else.

I drag a hand through my damp strands, trying to figure out if I'm relieved or disappointed that she couldn't be bothered to wait around.

Or worse—she took off with another dude.

"Hey."

I swing around only to find Carina standing a couple feet away. My gaze licks over her body, absorbing every detail. That's all it takes for need to crash over me. She looks so fucking good wearing a silver puffy jacket that hits her waist and a white knit hat with a pompom. Black leggings hug every lethal curve.

It feels like forever since we've stood this close.

Close enough to inhale her delectable floral scent.

My mind tumbles back to the elevator when I offered her a ride to school. I'd foolishly thought I could convince her with a kiss that she wanted me half as much as I needed her.

Unfortunately, that backfired in my face.

My tongue darts out to lick at my lower lip as if I can still taste her sweetness there.

Fuck.

All I want to do is reach out and haul her into my arms. I want to hold her close for safekeeping. Even more than that, I want this girl to belong to me forever.

I take a quick step in retreat, knowing that isn't going to happen. She kicked me loose and isn't interested.

Whatever she came here to say needs to be spit out so I can move the fuck on with my life. Even though my father won't be happy about the decision, we'll need to put an end to the weekly dinners for the time being. I can't do it anymore. I can't be around her until the need that pumps viciously through my veins is under control.

Fun fact—that might never happen.

There's an awfully good chance that the ache filling me will never go away. Not completely. It's like someone reached into my chest with their bare hand and ripped out my heart before dropping it to the floor at my feet.

Then they stomped on it for good measure.

The shittiest part of all this is that the organ might never belong to me again. I gave it away to someone who didn't want it and there's no way to get it back.

Instead of returning the greeting and attempting to be chill about the situation, I act like a little bitch.

"What are you doing here?" I wince at the icy snap that fills my voice.

She shifts from one foot to the other before drawing in an unsteady breath and then forcing it out again. "I was hoping we could talk."

Has this girl completely lost her marbles?

My eyes narrow as my upper lip curls. "What's left to say?"

A rush of color blooms in her cheeks as she worries her lower lip with sharp white teeth. "A lot."

I cross my arms against my chest. "Oh, yeah? Like what?"

"I have a question for you."

A question?

What the hell is this girl playing at?

"All right. Shoot."

"Truth or dare?"

I blink, wondering if I heard her correctly because that's always been my line.

A way of steering her into doing what I wanted.

Like kissing me.

Or touching me.

Or dancing naked for me.

All the things I was too chickenshit to ask for. So, I used the game as a guise.

When I remain silent, she repeats softly, "Truth or dare?"

"Dare."

She straightens her shoulders and lifts her chin. "I dare you to kiss me."

My muscles freeze as her words explode in my brain.

A heartbeat passes.

Then another.

"Don't make me double dog dare you," she whispers.

That's when I realize I'm scared to death. Scared I won't be able to stop once my lips brush across hers. Because when it comes down to it, she was always meant to be mine.

"Ford?" My name comes out sounding as if it's been roughed up and scraped raw. As if she's just as terrified as I am.

That's all the encouragement I need to swallow up the distance between us before reaching out and slipping my fingers beneath her chin. "Here's the thing—once I start, there's no stopping."

"I don't want you to stop." Her eyes search mine. "Not ever."

Her words crash over me like a tidal wave, threatening to drag me to the very bottom of the ocean. My voice drops, turning into more of a rasp as my fingers tighten around her chin, biting into the soft flesh. "Do you understand what I'm saying, Carina? If I lay my lips on you, then you belong to me. *You're mine.*"

The need to possess her rushes through me.

"I wouldn't have it any other way. I love you. And I'm sorry for pushing you away. I never—"

Unable to resist for another second, my lips collide with hers, swallowing up whatever she was about to say. Nothing else matters other than her saying I love you.

The first taste is a straight shot to my dick.

Just like it always is.

With my mouth roving over hers, I lose all sense of time and space. When I finally pull away, we're both breathing hard. The need to lay my hands on her thrums through me and I rest my forehead against hers, staring into her gorgeous blue-gray eyes. They're ones I could happily drown in.

"Do you mean it? You really love me?"

"I do. If I'm being completely honest, I have for a while." There's a pause as she sifts through the emotion in my eyes. "I spoke with Crawford earlier. He admitted to finding us in bed together senior year and then having a conversation with you."

My shoulders loosen now that the truth is finally out in the open. "I'm sorry about that. Maybe I should have talked to you about it, but he made me feel so damn guilty. Like I was taking advantage of you or the situation."

Sadness flickers in her eyes. "You didn't. At the time, our connection was more emotional than physical. We never did anything. Not really."

No, we didn't. Just some kissing and light petting.

But I wanted to.

God, did I want to.

I wanted to make her mine in the worst way possible. Had my father not interfered, I would have.

Eventually.

"I tried to tell him that but at the time, he didn't believe me," I murmur. "And I'm sure he didn't want to do anything that would upset Pamela."

The need to hold her close rushes through me and I tug her back into my arms until I can rest my chin against the top of her head. I'm almost afraid to disrupt the peace we've only just found.

"We'll have to tell them, you know. I can't keep any more secrets. If we're going to give this a real shot, then it needs to be out in the open. I won't hide." There's a pause before I add, "I won't be your dirty little secret."

She untangles herself enough to meet my gaze. "I'm sorry I ever made you feel like that."

I jerk my head into a nod. "Neither of us did things the right way and we both made mistakes. But this is our chance to rectify them."

"You're right, it is. Did Crawford tell you that Pamela took off?"

My eyes widen at this new development. "Are you serious?"

"Yup."

I search her gaze, trying to sift through everything swimming around within it. "Are you relieved about that?"

Guilt flashes across her face. "As terrible as it sounds—yeah, I am. Crawford deserves someone who's going to be a true partner to him in every sense of the word and that's not my mother."

I sweep my lips over hers for a second time, only wanting the taste of her to flood my senses. "I missed you so damn much."

"I missed you, too. More than I ever thought possible. I'm so sorry for pushing you away and hurting you."

"It's all right, pretty girl. As long as you realize that right here in my arms is where you belong, then whatever we had to go through was worth it in the end."

"There's no doubt in my mind or heart that I was always meant to be here with you."

I nip at her lower lip. "Good. Let's get out of here. The way I see it, you owe me a whole hell of a lot of make-up sex."

A throaty chuckle escapes from her. "Oh, you think so?"

"Yup."

"And what exactly did you have in mind?"

I flash a grin as all the possibilities run amuck through my brain. Even though we're alone, I tug her close and whisper the answer in her ear. She pulls away just enough to search my eyes as her pupils dilate, the black swallowing up the blue gray.

"I'm pretty sure I can make that happen."

With that, I lock my hand around hers and hightail it back to the apartment.

For the first time in a week, everything in my life feels like it's fallen into place, and that has everything to do with the girl at my side.

The one I'll never allow to get away again.

CHAPTER FORTY

CARINA

Ford's arms are wrapped around me, holding me securely against him as if he'll never let go. And I wouldn't have it any other way. It's been a few weeks since we cleared the air and already, it feels like we've been together forever. If I thought we'd get weird looks or comments since we used to be related, that hasn't been the case. It's almost as if everyone realized what would happen before we did.

He presses his lips against my neck as I bring the lime seltzer to my mouth and take a swig, draining the can. The Wildcats won another game tonight and the entire campus turned up to celebrate.

Slap Shotz is packed to the gills. It's standing room only. Which means that karaoke is well under way. People are on stage belting their little hearts out. Some are terrible. And they know it. They make a joke out of it. But a few are seriously impressive. When they sing, the bar falls so silent that you could hear a pin drop.

Juliette catches my attention from the other side of the table, mouthing the word 'bathroom.' I give her a nod before turning to Ford.

"I'm going to the restroom and then I'll stop at the bar and pick up another round."

His grip tightens. "Don't be gone long or I'll be forced to come find you."

A shiver dances down my spine as a smile twitches around the corners of my lips. "Are you actually trying to threaten me with a good time?"

He snorts. "Always, pretty girl."

When I rise to my feet, he tugs on my fingers. The movement sends me tumbling back down to his lap. His lips collide with mine, his tongue licking along the seam of my lips before invading my mouth. Just as I lose myself in the caress, there's a tap on my shoulder.

I tear myself away, only to find Juliette standing next to us with a smirk.

"Are you ready?"

I nod as my tongue darts out to taste Ford on my lips. His gaze drops to the movement and his honey-colored eyes darken with intensity. Already I know what will happen once we reach my apartment.

And I'm totally down for it.

Juliette's gaze slides to my newly minted boyfriend who continues to lounge on the chair, eyes pinned to mine. "Maybe you two could spend the night at your place every once in a while. I'd actually like to enjoy a little sleep for a change. You two are still loud AF."

I smack her arm as a wide grin spreads across his face. It's as if the man takes pride in being able to make me scream my head off.

What am I saying?

Of course he does.

Especially now that he's been able to last longer than a dozen or so strokes. Sometimes he'll make me come twice before finally losing control and tumbling over the edge with me.

Juliette loops her arm through mine as we navigate the thick crowd to the bathroom. There's a little bit of a line. We chat, talking about what the next month or so will bring along with exams and Christmas, which is right around the corner.

This year is flying by.

Before we know it, graduation will be looming on the horizon.

Once we finish up in the bathroom, we make our way to the bar and order another round of drinks. As I pay the bartender, someone squeezes my arm. I turn and find Fallyn along with her friend, Britt. It's been a while since I've seen them. The four of us exchange hugs and chat as we catch up.

"Last song of the evening," Sully says from the other side of the bar.

I'm about to turn back to the conversation when Wolf rises from his chair and saunters up to the stage.

I glance at Juliette and raise my brows. "Have you ever seen him get up there?"

She shakes her head, looking just as surprised by the turn of events. The other two girls are equally quiet as the four of us watch him choose a song before picking up the microphone. His gaze slowly combs over the sea of people as if searching for someone specific.

But who?

To my knowledge, he's never had a girlfriend. Not that the puck bunnies aren't constantly throwing themselves at him. It's like the more he holds them at a distance, the more they clamor for his attention.

As soon as the upbeat tempo starts, I recognize the song.

'Mr. Brightside' by the Killers.

Wolf brings the microphone close to his mouth as his gaze locks on someone.

I glance around and realize that he's staring at Fallyn.

Even in the darkness of the bar, it would be impossible not to notice the way her face turns ashen. Her gaze stays locked on him. It's like she's powerless to look away.

His voice is deep and raspy.

It sends a chill skating down my spine.

I asked Fallyn weeks earlier if she knew Wolf and she claimed not to. The way his attention stays locked on her says otherwise.

"I don't know what's going on here, but it's seriously hot," Juliette says.

I rip my gaze away from Wolf and glance at her before nodding in agreement. It feels like I need to be hosed off.

Or better yet, find my man to take care of business.

Actually, that's exactly what I'm going to do.

Once the final notes fade, I turn to Fallyn, prepared to demand answers only to find that she's disappeared. Wolf stares at the exit at the back of the bar as applause and whistles for an encore ring throughout the space.

A frown mars his expression as he leaps gracefully from the stage and cuts his way through the mass of bodies. He doesn't bother to acknowledge the girls who shout his name, attempting to wave him down.

Juliette and I say goodbye to Britt, who goes in search of Fallyn before grabbing our drinks and heading to the table. As soon as I set the beverages down, Ford pulls me back onto his lap.

"You about ready to head out?" he asks, his warm breath tickling the sensitive flesh near my ear.

I nod before snuggling closer and pressing my lips to his. "Yup."

With his arms banded around me, he rises from the chair. "Good, because I'm done sharing you for the evening. I need you all to myself."

A sigh of contentment escapes from me because I feel the same.

I want Ford all to myself.

And if I have my way, it'll be for the rest of my life.

EPILOGUE

FORD

Two years later...

I KICK the apartment door closed as I loosen the tie from around my neck. On a normal working day, I'm visiting job sites, looking over plans, and checking on the crews to make sure headway is being made. This afternoon, I met with a prospective client. So, it was necessary to dress the part.

Suit.

Crisp button-down.

Tie.

Added bonus—Carina loves when I get all dressed up.

She thinks I look like a model.

That thought is almost enough to make me snort.

More than that, she likes when I take off the gleaming leather belt, loop it around her wrists and fasten it to the headboard before stretching her out naked. The expensive silk tie gets wrapped around her eyes so she can't see all the delicious things I'm doing to her.

She can only feel them.

It only takes the thought of her all tied up and at my mercy to make me hard as steel.

"Where are you at, pretty girl?" I call from the small entryway. I need my woman and I need her now.

"In the kitchen," she says, raising her voice.

I beeline for the spacious room and find her bent over as she slides something into the oven. My gaze falls to her heart-shaped ass.

Carina has the best damn ass in the world.

It's the perfect handful.

And she's just as muscular as she was in college. She's putting in twelve-hour days at the studio she opened last year. It's the perfect blend of her passion and major.

On the nights when I'm not coaching at the local high school, I find myself stopping by at the end of the day to sit on the floor and watch her dance. I probably shouldn't mention that we've christened every room in the place.

Multiple times.

As she spins around to greet me, a smile lights up her face. "Hey, babe."

"Hey, yourself." My fingers wrap around the molding that frames the entryway as I lean forward.

Her eyes slide over me. "Have I mentioned how much it turns me on when you wear a suit?"

I smirk. "Nope, I don't believe you have."

"Liar." She tilts her head. "Sometimes I think you wear it on purpose just so I can rip it off your body."

Guilty. I fucking love when she has her wicked way with me.

I push away from the doorframe and saunter into the kitchen, stalking her around the marble island. "I think you like it better when I tie you up on the bed."

"I do." Her voice turns breathy as she retreats a few steps so that I'm forced to give chase. There's nothing I love more than catching her.

"I know. I love tying you up. Every time my fingers brushed

against the leather of the belt or tie, an image of you naked popped into my head. I've had a boner all damn day."

She forces out her bottom lip. "Aww, poor baby. That sounds terrible."

One side of my mouth hitches. "I'm sure it's swollen and in need of your special brand of TLC."

"You might be able to convince me to take care of that for you."

"Oh, yeah? It's just a possibility, huh?"

When her lower back hits the counter and there's nowhere else to run, a slow grin spreads across my face as I press my body against her slender curves. She tips her chin upward as if offering her mouth to me. I lick her lips before nipping at the plump lower one. I like them best when they're swollen from my kisses.

Or maybe it's from sucking my cock.

My girl gives the best blowjobs. I love tunneling my fingers through her long blonde hair and watching my thick length disappear between her lips. Especially when she keeps her gaze pinned to mine.

My hands wrap around her waist before hoisting her onto the gleaming counter. I push between her spread thighs before dragging the sweatshirt up her body and tossing it to the tile floor at my feet. The bra is the next garment to go. Once removed, my gaze dips to her bare breasts.

They're so fucking perfect.

I palm the softness before toying with her nipples, tweaking them until they're nice and hard. A whimper escapes from her as her eyes dilate with pleasure. Once I've played with them enough, I slide the leggings down her hips and thighs, making sure the thong gets removed so that she's completely bare.

I straighten to my full height and take a step back in order to get a good look at her.

She's so damn gorgeous.

Already my dick is throbbing in my boxer-briefs. I probably should have jacked off before I left the jobsite.

We've been together for two years now and, more often than not, this is exactly the way it is between us. She excites me like no one else ever has.

Or could.

"You're so damn beautiful, pretty girl."

"You're not so bad yourself," she murmurs in response.

"Now spread those legs so I can see exactly what belongs to me."

Without hesitation, she scoots back so that the soles of her feet are flat against the counter before allowing each leg to fall open until she's spread impossibly wide. In this position, I'm able to see every delicate inch.

A tortured groan rumbles up from deep within my chest.

Someone needs to tell me how the hell I got so lucky.

It's a question I ask myself on the daily.

Unable to resist a second longer, I eat up the distance between us before reaching out and trailing a finger from the top of her slit to the bottom and then back up again. In response, she arches, attempting to get closer.

Carina has always been sexual in nature and that hasn't changed.

Thank fuck.

She's not afraid to tell me exactly what she wants or needs.

It's just another thing I love about her.

I continue stroking her softness until she's squirming. Only then do I dip my finger inside her tight heat. My gaze stays pinned to her pussy. I love the way her body responds to me. The slickness that coats her lips. The way she moves her hips, silently pleading for more.

When I've tormented her enough, I hunker down until I'm eyelevel with her core. With my finger slowly pumping in and out, I lick her clit with soft strokes exactly the way she likes it.

It doesn't take long before she falls apart. Her pussy convulses around my finger as I lap up every drop of sweetness. It's only when her muscles loosen, and her cries fade that I press a kiss against her core and straighten to my full height.

A dazed expression fills her eyes.

And I love it.

Love that I'm the one who put it there.

That I'm the only man who'll ever put it there.

"You ready to be fucked, pretty girl?"

"That depends. Are you going to tie me up?"

A smile curves my lips. "Damn right I am."

When I push between her spread thighs, she wraps them around my waist. My hands settle on her ass, dragging her to the edge of the counter and lifting her against me. Then I swing us around and head for the bedroom. She whimpers as my hard cock rubs against her splayed open pussy.

As I cross the threshold, she groans, "I love when you have meetings."

Even though I'm on the verge of coming in my pants, a rough chuckle escapes from me. "I just love you."

Her arms tighten around my neck as she presses a kiss against my lips. "I love you too."

It's carefully that I set her down in the middle of the king-sized bed. She props herself up on her elbows and watches as my fingers slide over the brown leather belt. Her pupils dilate and her breath catches at the back of her throat as I unfasten the silver buckle, tugging it so that it slides easily from the fabric loops. Her legs fall open in silent invitation, giving me a tantalizing view of heaven. My face might have only been buried there minutes ago, but it doesn't matter.

It's doubtful I'll ever get enough of her.

All I have to say is thank fuck I don't have to.

Carina is mine.

She'll always be mine.

Just like she has been since the first moment I saw her.

Now, if you'll excuse us, I'm going to make hot love to my fiancée.

And yeah, I'll probably make her scream a few more times before I finally get mine.

That's just the way it is.

And there's no other way I'd rather have it.

* * *

Thank you so much for reading Love You Never! Want more of Carina & Ford? Subscribe to my newsletter for a free bonus epilogue!

The Western Wildcats Hockey series continues with Never Mine to Hold.

Looking to delve into another sports romance? Check out Sydney & Brayden from Campus Heartthrob now!

He Can Have Any Girl. Except the One He Wants.

Brayden Kendricks might be God's gift to the female species at Western University, but I want nothing to do with the dark-haired football player. The guy is an attention seeking you-know-what who soaks up fan adoration like it's his due in life for being hot and talented.

Damn. Did I just say that?

All right, fine...I'll grudgingly admit that Brayden is decent looking. I suppose if you're into guys who resemble Greek gods with abs of steel and chiseled pecs, then sure, one could consider him attractive.

Am I guilty of having a tiny, practically non-existent crush on him freshman year?

I'd prefer not to answer that question.

Thankfully, I quickly came to my senses and have made a concerted effort to steer clear of Brayden ever since. It hasn't been easy, considering that my bestie is now dating his roommate and we've been thrown together for an accounting project. You'd think after years of baring my teeth at him like a rabid dog, the guy would have gotten the memo that I'm not interested.

Apparently not, since he's spreading word around campus that we're going out.

I mean, can you even imagine?

Me?

Dating Brayden Kendricks?

I have four words for him...

No.

Way.

In.

Hell.

One-click Campus Heartthrob now!

"I absolutely loved both Brayden and Sydney, they both are so snarky and fun and their chemistry is through the roof" -Jenn, Amazon

"You feel like you know them as you read their story. And you will also feel their
emotions along with them; the attraction they feel but the heartbreak, as well" -Christi, Amazon

"I loved how their relationship progressed - they were hot and heavy, but also connected on a deeper level of understanding" - Kindle Konvert, Amazon

Turn the page for an excerpt from Campus Heartthrob…

CAMPUS HEARTTHROB

BRAYDEN

"Yo, Kendricks, grab me a cold one when you come back," Asher Stevens yells as I walk into the kitchen.

I give him a one-fingered salute to let him know that I heard him loud and clear. That guy drinks like it's his sole mission in life. By the time he graduates college in the spring, he'll be in desperate need of a liver transplant. My hat off to him though, he's at the top of his football game. I have no idea how he does it. It's one of the great mysteries in life that I've stopped trying to solve.

With a yank, I open the refrigerator door and peek inside. Other than a shit ton of beer and Gatorade, it looks more like a barren wasteland.

Fuckers.

Can't these guys keep up with the grocery shopping? We're all supposed to be pitching in with the domestic chores. Although, one look around this place will tell you that ain't happening.

With a sigh of resignation, I pull out one of the last bottles of water and twist off the top before guzzling down a quarter of it. Then I grab a Miller Lite for Stevens. I've tried broaching the subject of his alcohol consumption, but I'm not his damn mom. The dude is twenty-one years old, he can do what he wants.

Just as I slam the refrigerator door closed and spin around, Carson saunters in.

Carson Walker and I go way back. We're talking elementary school. He's practically part of the family. He was there for me when I needed a friend the most and got me through one of the toughest periods of my life. Even at twenty-one, I know that friends like that aren't easy to come by. We've been playing football together since second grade. First flag football before moving on to our middle school team and then high school. Luckily, we ended up at the same college and roomed together freshman and sophomore year before finding a house with a couple of teammates junior and senior year. Like me, he'll enter the draft in the spring. He's one of the best tight ends in the conference and was an All-American last year.

Before I can even open my mouth in greeting, he says, "Heads up, Kira just walked through the door."

Well, fuck me.

A groan slides off my lips.

Why?

Why can't she take a hint?

That girl takes crazy, psycho stalker to the next other level. It's almost as impressive as it is frightening. Scratch that, it's just plain frightening. There have been times when I was afraid I'd come home and find our pet bunny boiling away on the stove. Just kidding, we don't have a pet rabbit.

But still...

You get where I'm going with this.

It's fucking scary.

And she won't leave me alone. I've tried to gently tell her that it's never going to happen between us.

Are you kidding me?

Of course, it's not going to happen!

Like ever!

I've never even locked lips with this chick and she stalks me around campus, turns up in my classes, and shadows my every waking movement. I'm this close to taking out a restraining order. The girl needs to move on. Or move away.

Preferably the latter.

I've thoroughly enjoyed my time at Western University, but I'll be glad to get out of here after graduation and away from her. There's not much more I can take of this.

Carson's shoulders shake with silent laughter. "That's what you get for being so pretty."

"Fuck off," I mutter. Just because he's a good friend doesn't mean that he doesn't like to give me shit.

With a shrug he says, "Maybe you should just fuck her brains out and show her that you're really not all that special."

Again...

"Fuck off."

Not offended in the least, a smile breaks out across his face. "You know what you need?"

I'm almost afraid to ask.

"A girlfriend," he continues when I remain silent.

"No, thanks," I snort.

"I'm serious," he says, warming to the topic.

Sadly, I can tell he is.

I shake my head.

There have been a couple of girlfriends throughout the years. What I've found is that they're more hassle than their worth. My schedule is packed tight with football and school. Division I football is more like a job than an intermural sport. My life revolves around practice, lifting, film review, travel, and games. Most of the chicks I've dated get bent out of shape when they aren't at the top of your priority list and ultimately force you to choose.

Guess what gets downsized?

I'll give you a hint.

It isn't football.

After the first couple of times it happened, I decided girlfriends weren't worth the price of admission. Sure, it would be nice to find someone to spend time with but that's just not in the cards at the moment. And quite frankly, I'm not sure it will be in the near future. Not with wrapping up my last year of school and hopefully getting picked up by the pros. It's just easier to screw around with the jersey chasers. For the most part, they understand that sex is nothing more than an hour or so of mindless pleasure.

"Maybe then Kira would get the hint that there's no chance of anything happening between the two of you," he continues as if I haven't already nixed the idea.

I don't need to get myself entangled in one bad situation just to get out of another. What the hell would be the point of that?

"She should have gotten the hint when I flat-out told her that nothing was ever going to happen between us," I tell him.

"Again, if you weren't so damn pretty, girls wouldn't lose their damn minds over you." His lips curl around the edges before he tacks on, "Mr. Campus Heartthrob."

I wince at the title I've won three years in a row.

Christ.

Talk about embarrassing.

At first, I was flattered by it. I got a ton of pussy by winning that stupid title. My teammates were jealous, and I didn't mind rubbing that in their faces. But it gets old. Imagine that if you can.

Now the damn thing is just a nuisance.

Last year, I didn't even enter the contest and I won.

My lips flatten. "I prefer to think of it as ruggedly handsome. No dude wants to be called pretty."

"Please," he snorts, "your face could be plastered on a billboard. I'm surprised there aren't more crazies coming out of the woodwork."

"Bite your tongue," I grunt. I can't even imagine that.

"I don't know, man. I think the girlfriend idea is a valid one and you should consider it. Could be the solution to all your problems."

I shift my weight and take another drink from my bottle. "There's only one problem with your plan—there aren't any chicks that I'm even remotely interested in dating."

"Who said anything about this being a real situation? I'm talking about finding a friend who could pretend to like your ass for a couple of weeks. Someone who wouldn't mind doing you a solid."

I don't have any girls who are strictly friends. Even the ones who pretend to be platonic end up trying to parley it into something else.

"Nope." I shake my head. "Any other brainiac ideas?"

He jerks his head toward the backdoor. "Guess you could always try and make a run for it. Lay low at Rowan's girl's place for a couple of hours until Kira gets bored and leaves."

Yeah, the last time I did that, she waited around for five hours. Let that sink in.

Five.

Hours.

The woman is seriously tenacious. Must be in the stalker job description.

I turn the idea over in my head. It would give me a chance to see Sydney. And I rarely pass up an opportunity to do that. There's something about the blonde-haired, green-eyed, soccer played that has gotten under my skin.

Kind of like an itch that is impossible to scratch. And steroids haven't done the job either. If she's in the vicinity, my attention is locked on her. She's the only female capable of rousing my interest. I hate to admit it, but it's probably because she won't give me the time of day. there's definitely something to the saying that you always want what you can't have. And I can't have Sydney. That chick wants nothing to do with me, which is precisely why I like to mess with her.

Trust me, I realize that I'm not doing myself any favors, but I just can't seem to help myself. I get some kind of twisted satisfaction in provoking her ire. it's not hard to do. I pretty much just have to open my mouth and talk to her and she's going off the deep end. She's got a temper. I've seen it come out on more than one occasion. My guess is that she would be a real wildcat in bed. not that I'll be finding out anytime soon, but I would sure love to test out my hypothesis.

As tempted as I am to flee our off-campus house for the next couple of hours, I have a test to study for. I might have every intention of taking my game to the next level and playing in the NFL, but it's still important that I do well in school and earn my degree. Even the most talented players are one career ending injury away from being released from their contract. I'm taking every precaution I can to make sure that my future goes off without a hitch. Even if that means doing something instead of playing professional football.

Maybe some people around here don't realize it, but I'm more than just a pretty face. I've got the brains to back up all this brawn.

So, ducking out of here isn't going to work. I drag a hand through my hair and consider my options. "All right, I'm going to need you to cause a distraction so I can sneak upstairs without her noticing me."

His brows shoot up across his forehead. "How exactly am I supposed to do that? She's sitting in the living room. She's got one eye on the front door and the staircase."

Christ...this girl. She's going to drive me nuts.

This entire situation is ridiculous. I shouldn't have to sneak around in my own damn house. "I don't know," I snap with frustration, "think of something. I just need about thirty seconds to sneak up the staircase." I'm more than aware that I'm taking out my aggravation on someone who doesn't deserve it, which isn't like me, but I've had my fill of this situation. I want this girl to leave me alone. if I honestly thought that sitting down with her and having another conversation would end this, I'd do it in a heartbeat. But I've done that. Several times and she refuses to get it through her thick head. it's like it doesn't even matter that I'm not interested in her.

He shakes his head as if I'm the crazy one. "I'll do my best but I'm not making any promises."

As soon as Carson exits the kitchen, I realize that we didn't come up with a code word.

Fuck!

How am I supposed to know that the coast is clear?

I seriously can't believe that this is what my life has come to. I'm skulking around my own damn house to avoid some chick.

But what else am I supposed to do?

Deal with her craziness? Waste my time for the next hour or so fighting off her advances?

No. I don't have the time for that.

I tiptoe across the kitchen like it's a minefield before arriving at the wide entryway that leads to the dining room. Since there's nothing but a table and six chairs, no one is in there. Everyone is hanging out and chilling in the living room. Loud, rowdy voices fill my ears.

Well, here goes nothing.

Just as I'm about to peek around the corner to see if it's safe, Carson materializes on the other side. We both startle as my heart slams against my ribcage.

"Fuck, dude...you nearly gave me a heart attack." I point to the living room. If he's here, then no one is distracting Kira. Worse, he could be drawing attention in this direction. Exactly what I don't need. "What are you doing over here? You're supposed to be causing a distraction."

"She's gone."

My brows rise. "Really?" Well, hot damn! It looks like I've lucked out for the evening.

"Yeah. She's not in the living room and I checked both bathrooms. They're empty. Maybe she saw that you weren't here and took off."

That was easier than expected.

All of my muscles loosen. I hadn't realized just how tense I'd become. "Thanks, man. I owe you."

"No problem." He smirks. "Don't worry, I'll think of some way for you to repay me." Before I can answer, he swings around and heads back into the living room.

I grab my bottle of water along with Asher's beer before heading out of the kitchen. Once the beverage has been passed off, I do a cursory inspection of the immediate vicinity just to make sure that Carson isn't fucking with me. Not that I seriously think he would do that. We've been friends for too long for that. If there's one guy that I trust, it's him. Rowan Michaels would be a close second.

A quick glance around the room as I head to the staircase proves that Carson wasn't yanking my chain. Kira is nowhere to be seen.

As ridiculous as it is, I need to do something about this situation before it gets anymore out of hand. There's no way I can spend the rest of senior year looking over my shoulder and avoiding my own house. I need her to understand that we're never going to get together. Hell, at this point, there's no way I can even be friends with the chick.

Not with this crazy ass behavior.

"Kendricks, where you going?" Asher yells from his sprawled-out position in an armchair.

"Got a test to study for," I call back, trudging up the steps.

I've never been a slouch in the partying department, but three years later, it's getting old. Barely do I remember my freshman year. I spent most of it shitfaced, trying to drown the grief that had been my living breathing companion.

Not that it's a surprise, but it didn't work.

What did happen is that I nearly flunked out of college and got my ass kicked off the football team. Coach Richards pulled me aside after the season was over and told me that I had a choice to make. I either pull my shit together or get the hell off his team.

One or the other.

That conversation had been a rude awakening. And it was exactly what I needed to hear. The year before, I'd lost one of the most important people in my life. I couldn't lose football, too. I returned home and dried out over the summer. I focused my attention on working out and getting stronger so that I could show Coach that he hadn't made a mistake when he recruited me. When I returned to Western for my sophomore year, I swapped out the alcohol for pussy. I guess if you can't drown your sorrows in beer, girls are a close second. Except...it doesn't actually solve anything or make your problems disappear.

"Pussy," he shouts after me.

I let the taunt slide off my back, knowing that I don't have anything to prove. "Yup."

As I disappear onto the second floor, I swing right and pass by two closed doors before arriving at mine. Now that I don't have to worry about Kira, my mind gravitates to the exam I need to study for. I grab hold of the handle and push open the thick wood before stepping inside. I probably have three solid hours of work to put in. After doing my damnedest to flunk out freshman year, it's taken a lot of hard work to raise my GPA. The fact that, two years later, it's over a three point zero is a point of pride for me.

I'm jerked out of those thoughts by a noise as my gaze jerks to the queen-sized bed at the far end of the room.

And the naked girl lying on top of it.

"Hey, Brayden," Kira coos, shifting on the comforter as she spreads her legs wide, "I've been waiting for you."

One-click Campus Heartthrob now!

JUST FRIENDS

REED

With a sigh, I collapse onto the couch in the living room of the house I share with a couple of guys from the hockey team and pop open a can of cold beer, guzzling down half of it in one thirsty swig.

Goddamn, but that hits the spot.

Know what else would hit the spot?

Yeah, you do.

It's the second week of September, and Coach Richards has us skating two-a-days, lifting weights, and running five miles for extra cardio.

As if we need it.

Oh…and he added yoga to this year's regimen.

Fucking yoga.

Can you believe that shit?

Let me be perfectly clear—I'm not into contorting my body into a pretzel and breathing deeply from my diaphragm. Sure, I get it. He wants us to work on our flexibility. And I'll do it, but that doesn't mean I have to like it.

Coach R is a total masochist.

Or is it sadist?

I can never keep those two straight.

No matter. Whatever kind of *ist* he is, the man thoroughly enjoys working our asses over. The only amusement I get is from listening to all the incoming freshmen piss and moan about what a tough schedule we have.

Welcome to Division I hockey, boys. Buckle up, it's going to be a bumpy ride.

Pile on fifteen credit hours and I don't have time for much else.

"Reed, baby, I've been waiting all night for you to return."

A curvy female drops onto my lap like an angel falling from heaven before she twines her slender arms around my neck and pulls me close.

I stand corrected. There's always time for *that*.

Hell, half the time, *that's* what gets me through the grind. Sex is an amazing stress reliever, and don't let anyone tell you differently. I'm way more chill after I've blown my load. And if I'm fortunate enough to do it twice in one night, then it's like I've slipped into a damn coma.

Pure bliss, baby.

Luckily for us, the Red Devils hockey team has its fair share of puck bunnies on campus who are always willing to provide some much-needed stress relief on a regular basis. God bless every last one of those ladies. They have no idea how much their *team spirit* is appreciated.

That being said, there are always exceptions to the rule.

And the girl currently cozied up on my lap is exactly that.

Megan thrusts out her lower lip in a sexy pout. "How is it possible that we've never hooked up before?"

The answer is simple. I go to great lengths to avoid her like a particularly nasty case of crabs.

She flutters her mascara-laden lashes and tilts her head. Her voice becomes lispy and toddler-like as she twirls a dark curl around her finger. "Don't you think I'm pretty?"

Pretty?

No, Megan is flat-out gorgeous.

Her long, black hair is as shiny as a crow's wing as it floats around her shoulders in soft waves. She has dark eyes that are tipped at the corners. And her skin is sun-kissed all year round. And if that weren't enough to have any guy giving her a full-on salute, she's also got gravity-defying tits and a nice round ass.

Have I imagined fucking her from behind and smacking that bubble butt a few times before blowing my wad?

You bet Megan's perfectly round ass I have. The girl is a walking wet dream.

And from what the guys on the team tell me (because they're a bunch of loudmouth assholes who like to brag), she can suck a dick like nobody's business. That being said, I won't be finding that out firsthand anytime soon.

I've made it a point to steer clear of Megan because every time I look at her, I see Emerson.

And imagining that I'm nailing my best friend is a definite no-no.

When I don't immediately respond, Megan grinds her bubble butt against my junk—which is something I really don't need, because just the thought of Emerson alone is enough to have me popping wood.

It's a messed-up situation.

One that Em is blissfully unaware of. Which is exactly the way it needs to stay. She can't find out that I've got the hots for her. Emerson Shaw is one of the first friends I made when Mom and I moved to Lakefield the summer before freshman year of high school. And we've been tight ever since.

While I enjoy having a casual, friends-with-benefits relationship with a number of girls on campus, I've never considered sleeping with Em.

Okay, maybe I've *considered* having sex with her. It would be hard not to imagine stripping her naked and getting jiggy with a girl who looks like that, but I've never done anything about it.

I've screwed too many women not to know that getting naked changes a relationship. And I like Em way too much to risk sleeping with her. She's the one person who has always had my back. And let's face it, I can be a hell of a lot more honest with her than my teammates.

Can you imagine me baring my soul to those assholes?

Exactly. I'd never hear the end of it.

My friendship with Emerson also gives me all this insight into the female psyche that I wouldn't otherwise be privy to. It's like taking a peek behind the magic curtain. I'm not willing to throw that away when there are plenty of random chicks I can get my rocks off with.

Moral of the story? Friends are a lot harder to come by than hookups.

"Reed?" Megan nips my lower lip between her sharp teeth before giving it a gentle tug and releasing it.

I blink back to the girl wriggling around on my lap. "Yeah?"

Her hands flutter to my shoulders before settling on them. "You're so tense."

Damn right I am. All I can think about is Emerson, and that's all kinds of wrong.

"Let's go upstairs." Her tongue darts out to moisten her lips as she whispers, "I know *exactly* what will fix that."

If any other girl were making the offer, I'd already be dragging her up the staircase to my bedroom. But that's not going to happen with Megan.

I just can't do it. Maybe I'm not *technically* doing anything wrong, but it still feels like I'm breaking some kind of friendship rule. Emerson may not realize I'm thinking about her like that, but I do.

And that's all that matters.

Guess I'll have to find a different girl to get busy with. Preferably a flat-chested blonde with big blue eyes who doesn't resemble Em. Or maybe a redhead, just to mix things up a bit.

Megan's eyes light up when I set my beer down and wrap my hands around her waist, until I carefully remove her from my lap. "Sorry, sweetheart. I've got homework to finish up for tomorrow." I tack on the lie to soften the blow. "Maybe another time?"

Her face falls. "Sure, no problem."

Before she can pin me down on a time and place, I beat a hasty retreat from the living room and head upstairs. Once I've taken refuge in my room, I fire off a text to one of my go-to girls.

Fifteen minutes later, my booty-call for the evening strolls through the door.

Know what I like most about Candace?

The girl gets right down to business. There's no need for small talk, and that I can appreciate. I'm in the mood to fuck, not debate world politics or climate change.

The door hasn't even closed and Candace is already shedding her clothes. Since she hasn't bothered with a bra, her titties bounce free as soon as her shirt is discarded. Her nips stiffen right up when the cool air hits them.

It's a beautiful sight to behold.

Except...

Nothing stirs south of the border. Not like it did when I was thinking about a certain someone downstairs who shall remain nameless. But I'm not concerned. I just need to harness my mental capabilities and focus on the task at hand. Which is getting my dick to work properly.

I yank off my T-shirt and toss it to the floor as Candace flicks open the button of her teeny-tiny shorts before unzipping them. With her gaze locked on mine, she shimmies out of them.

And wouldn't you know it...

No panties in sight.

Just a gloriously bare pussy.

Works for me.

Well, that's what *normally* works for me.

At the moment, limp dick-itis has set in.

Once Candace has stripped down to her birthday suit, she struts her sexy stuff toward the bed where I've made myself comfortable. Her eyelids lower as a knowing smirk curves her red-slicked lips. I rake my gaze over her toned body.

The girl is absolutely perfect.

"I've missed you." She crawls across the mattress until her hands are resting against my bare chest. "I'm glad you texted."

She says that now, but it probably won't be the case when she gets her hands on my junk.

What the hell is wrong with me?

I thought this kind of thing only happened to older dudes. I'm way too young for Viagra. I've seen first-hand how that shit can mess you up.

As a joke last year, one of the jackasses on my team got his hands on a couple of those little blue pills and slipped them to one of the freshman players. The poor guy was sporting wood for days. Unfortunately, a trip to the emergency room became necessary. When Coach R was apprised of the situation, he reamed our asses good and threatened to bench the entire team for the season. We skated suicides until our legs practically fell off.

No, thank you.

Candy trails her purple-tipped fingernails down my chest before pushing me against the mattress and straddling my torso. Then she leans over and licks a wet trail down my body until reaching the waistband of my athletic shorts. This encounter is going to nosedive real quick if I can't get it up in record speed. Not knowing what else to do, I squeeze my eyes tight as an unwanted image of Emerson pops into my head.

Dark hair, lush curves, bright smile.

Candace chuckles as she pulls my hard length from my boxer briefs like it's a much-anticipated Christmas gift. "There's my big boy!"

I groan.

I am *so* screwed.

One-click Just Friends now!

MORE BOOKS BY JENNIFER SUCEVIC

The Campus Series (football)
Campus Player

Campus Heartthrob

Campus Flirt

Campus Hottie

Campus God

Campus Legend

Western Wildcats Hockey
Hate You Always

Love You Never

Never Mine to Hold

The Barnett Bulldogs (football)
King of Campus

Friend Zoned

One Night Stand

If You Were Mine

The Claremont Cougars (football)
Heartless Summer

Heartless

Shameless

Hawthorne Prep Series (bully/football)
King of Hawthorne Prep

Queen of Hawthorne Prep

Prince of Hawthorne Prep

Princess of Hawthorne Prep

The Next Door Duet (football)

The Girl Next Door

The Boy Next Door

What's Mine Duet (Suspense)

Protecting What's Mine

Claiming What's Mine

Stay Duet (hockey)

Stay

Don't Leave

Stand-alone

Confessions of a Heartbreaker (football)

Hate to Love You (Hockey)

Just Friends (hockey)

Love to Hate You (football)

The Breakup Plan (hockey)

Collections

The Barnett Bulldogs

The Football Hotties Collection

The Hockey Hotties Collection

The Next Door Duet

ABOUT THE AUTHOR

Jennifer Sucevic is a USA Today bestselling author who has published twenty-four new adult novels. Her work has been translated into German, Dutch, Italian, and French. She has a bachelor's degree in history and a master's in Educational Psychology from the University of Wisconsin-Milwaukee. Jen started her career as a high school counselor before relocating with her family and focusing on her passion for writing. When she's not tapping away at the keyboard and dreaming up swoonworthy heroes to fall in love with, you can find her bike riding or at the beach.
She lives in the Michigan with her family.
If you would like to receive regular updates regarding new releases, please subscribe to her newsletter here-
Jennifer Sucevic Newsletter
Or contact Jen through email, at her website, or on Facebook.
sucevicjennifer@gmail.com
Want to join her reader group? Do it here -)
J Sucevic's Book Boyfriends | Facebook
Social media links-
https://www.tiktok.com/@jennifersucevicauthor
www.jennifersucevic.com
https://www.instagram.com/jennifersucevicauthor
https://www.facebook.com/jennifer.sucevic
Amazon.com: Jennifer Sucevic: Books, Biography, Blog, Audiobooks, Kindle
Jennifer Sucevic Books - BookBub

Printed in Great Britain
by Amazon